ACCLAIM FOR

MARIO ESCOBAR

"Through meticulous research and with wisdom and care, Mario Escobar brings to life a heartbreaking story of love and extraordinary courage. I want everyone I know to read this book."

—Kelly Rimmer, *New York Times* bestselling author of *The Warsaw Orphan*

"A beautifully written, deeply emotional story of hope, love, and courage in the face of unspeakable horrors. That such self-sacrifice, dedication, and goodness existed restores faith in humankind. Escobar's heart-rending yet uplifting tale is made all the more poignant by its authenticity. Bravo!"

—Tea Cooper, *USA TODAY* bestselling and award-winning author of *The Cartographer's Secret*, on *The Teacher of Warsaw*

"This is a powerful portrait of a woman fighting to preserve knowledge in a crumbling world."

—*Publishers Weekly* on *The Librarian of Saint-Malo*

"In *The Librarian of Saint-Malo*, Escobar brings us another poignant tale of sacrifice, love, and loss amidst the pain of war. The seaside town of Saint-Malo comes to life in rich detail and complexity under German occupation, as do the books—full of great ideas and the best of humanity—the young librarian seeks to save. This sweeping story gives us a glimpse into the past with a firm eye towards hope in our future."

—Katherine Reay, bestselling author of *The London House*

"Escobar's latest (after *Auschwitz Lullaby*, 2018) is a meticulously researched story, recreating actual experiences of the 460 Spanish children who were sent to Morelia, Mexico, in 1937. Devastating, enlightening, and passionately told, Escobar's novel shines a light on the experiences of the victims of war, and makes a case against those who would use violence to gain power. Although painful events in the story make it hard to read at times, the book gives a voice to so many whose stories are often overlooked, while inspiring the reader to never give way to fear or let go of one's humanity."

—*BookList*, starred review, on *Remember Me*

"Luminous and beautifully researched, *Remember Me* is a study of displacement, belonging, compassion, and forged family amidst a heart-wrenching escape from the atrocities of the Spanish Civil War. A strong sense of place and the excavation of a little known part of history are reverently handled in a narrative both urgent and romantic. Fans of Arturo Pérez-Reverte, Chanel Cleeton, and Lisa Wingate will be mesmerized."

—Rachel McMillan, author of *The London Restoration*

"An exciting and moving novel."

—*People en Español* on *Recuérdame*

"Escobar highlights the tempestuous, uplifting story of two Jewish brothers who cross Nazi-occupied France in hope of reuniting with their parents in this excellent tale . . . Among the brutality and despair that follows in the wake of the Nazis' rampage through France, Escobar uncovers hope, heart, and faith in humanity."

—*Publishers Weekly* on *Children of the Stars*

"A poignant telling of the tragedies of war and the sacrificing kindness of others seen through the innocent eyes of children."

—J'nell Ciesielski, bestselling author of *Beauty Among Ruins* and *The Socialite*, on *Children of the Stars*

"*Auschwitz Lullaby* grabbed my heart and drew me in. A great choice for readers of historical fiction."

—Irma Joubert, author of *The Girl from the Train*

"Based on historical events, *Auschwitz Lullaby* is a deeply moving and harrowing story of love and commitment."

—*Historical Novels Review*

THE
TEACHER
OF
WARSAW

ALSO BY MARIO ESCOBAR

THE
TEACHER
OF
WARSAW

a novel

MARIO ESCOBAR

HARPER MUSE

Library of Congress Cataloging-in-Publication Data

Names: Escobar, Mario, 1971- author. | Abernathy, Gretchen, translator.
Title: The teacher of Warsaw : a novel / Mario Escobar ; [translated by
 Gretchen Abernathy].
Other titles: Maestro. English
Description: [Nashville] : Harper Muse, [2022] | Summary: "International
 bestselling author Mario Escobar captures the strength of the human
 spirit and the enduring power of kindness in this moving novel based on
 the true story of a brave Polish teacher who cared for hundreds of
 orphans in the Warsaw Ghetto"-- Provided by publisher.
Identifiers: LCCN 2021058269 (print) | LCCN 2021058270 (ebook) | ISBN
 9780785252177 (hardcover) | ISBN 9780785252184 (trade paper) | ISBN
 9780785252191 (epub) | ISBN 9780785252207 (downloadable audio) | ISBN
 9781400238323 (international edition)
Subjects: LCSH: Korczak, Janusz, 1878-1942--Fiction. | World War,
 1939-1945--Poland--Warsaw--Fiction. | Holocaust, Jewish
 (1939-1945)--Poland--Warsaw--Fiction. | LCGFT: Biographical fiction. |
 Historical fiction. | Novels.
Classification: LCC PQ6705.S618 M3413 2022 (print) | LCC PQ6705.S618
 (ebook) | DDC 863/.7--dc23/eng/20211210
LC record available at https://lccn.loc.gov/2021058269
LC ebook record available at https://lccn.loc.gov/2021058270

Printed in the United States of America

22 23 24 25 26 LSC 10 9 8 7 6 5 4 3 2 1

To all the teachers, good and bad, who had a hand in making us what we are today. To Janusz Korczak, who understood that dignity is the sacred treasure no one can ever steal.

I exist not to be loved and admired, but myself to act and love. It is not the duty of those around to help me but I am duty-bound to look after the world, after man.

Janusz Korczak, *Ghetto Diary*

Only that which wills to preserve itself has the right to be preserved for others. So choose and speak for me, ye memories, and at least give some reflection of my life before it sinks into the dark!

Stefan Zweig, *The World of Yesterday*

We wanted to be free and owe this freedom to nobody.

Jan Stanislaw Jankowski, Polish Resistance leader

CONTENTS

PART II: LIVING FOR AN IDEA

PART III: A PLACE NO MORE

CONTENTS

A NOTE FROM
THE AUTHOR

In July 2018, before the world became a more dangerous place, I went to Lima, Peru, to attend the country's largest bookfair. It was my first time in Lima, and I gave talks and signed books. I was not prepared for the surprise that HarperCollins Español had for me. One morning we went to one of Lima's biggest synagogues. After a short tour, I was introduced to a slow-moving and polite elderly gentleman. His impeccable Spanish had a Polish lilt. He was Hirsz Litmanowicz, a Holocaust survivor who had been at Auschwitz and then at Sachsenhausen. Together with a group of children, Hirsz had been subjected to all sorts of experiments by cruel SS doctors. He managed to survive and, after a harrowing journey through Germany and some difficult years in France, eventually immigrated to Peru. Part of his life had been portrayed through Spielberg's *Schindler's List*. After listening to his riveting story, I walked through an exhibit at the synagogue called *Janusz Korczak: A Life Dedicated to Children*. I took a flyer and put it in my pocket.

One year later, I was sitting in my office looking at the flyer about Janusz Korczak that was propped on a bookshelf. His narrow, chiseled face, graying beard, and sad eyes reminded me of Miguel de Cervantes's immortal Don Quixote de la Mancha. Korczak often said he was "the son of a madman." He always feared inheriting his father's mental illness, but instead he became a great defender of children. Right then and there, I decided to write his beautiful, sad story.

This pediatrician/teacher, whose real name was Henryk Goldszmit, revolutionized pedagogy in the first half of the twentieth century. He was an excellent writer, radio host, and columnist, though his greatest contribution was running a Jewish orphanage in Warsaw. His work was so widely recognized that his ideas influenced the 1924 and 1959 Declarations of the Rights of the Child and inspired the Convention on the Rights of the Child adopted by the United Nations in 1989.

In early 2020, nearly two years after my visit to Lima, I took a very different trip. This time I traveled to Warsaw as a nominee at the Empik 2019 Bestseller Gala. The morning of the awards ceremony, my family and I visited the building that had been Korczak's orphanage. That white facade with simple, straight lines had housed the pedagogue's dreams of creating happy, free childhoods for girls and boys who would grow up to make the world a better place.

That night in a nationally televised ceremony, I received the Empik Award for bestselling foreign novel. Ebullient, I made my way up the steps to the lectern and thought of the deep suffering the Polish people had faced under various empires, especially Nazi then Soviet authoritarian rule. I thought of the figure of Korczak bringing light to that darkness, and I recalled Stefan Zweig's words about turbulent times:

"But, after all, shadows themselves are born of light. And only he who has experienced dawn and dusk, war and peace, ascent and decline, only he has truly lived."

The Teacher of Warsaw is much more than a story about the life of Janusz Korczak and his orphanage. It is the memory of those who, at some of the world's darkest moments, when evil's grip on Europe seemed eternal, fought to turn the hellish Warsaw ghetto into a dignified, inhabitable place. Like the mourner's Kaddish, a traditional Jewish prayer for the dead, this book seeks to rescue names from oblivion, the names of so many who suffered and died for their love of freedom.

Madrid, June 22, 2020

PROLOGUE

WARSAW

JUNE 22, 1945

I have heard that when you say the names of the dead, you bring them back to life again. Reading the Teacher's hidden diary, I wonder if that is an editor's real job. Perhaps our mission is to resurrect the stories that time and misfortune have erased.

There through the window are the ruined buildings of my beloved city, forever sad and sieged by death. I wonder if this is the story that can shake us all free of despair. Summer promises peace, but the shackles still circle the wrists and arms of our people. How short-lived our reprieve! We are cursed with bad luck: occupied for generations by czarists, Austrians, and Teutons, then freed a few decades ago from the Soviet scourge that once again looms mercilessly over us.

Just a few days ago Agnieszka Ignaciuk told me the story of this diary. Books are born long before the editor delivers them to the printer and the bookstores to their hungry readers. Each story has its own soul that predates the ink-printed paper, the carefully bound spine, and the cover engraved in gold letters. Agnieszka had managed to escape the horror of the ghetto and to hide out for the rest of the war in a house on the outskirts of Cracow. She and her son were some of the few silent witnesses to survive a world that has disappeared completely.

Nearly impenetrable darkness has covered the earth for the past five years, as if several galaxies snuffed out their shining stars to make way for shadow. Then, at the midnight of humanity's terrible winter, that small, lovely woman with wise eagle eyes placed into my hands Janusz Korczak's typed manuscript. She acted like she was passing along a forbidden fruit that would eternally expel me from the semblance of paradise my life had recently become. I had survived the Nazis, side-stepped the shooting squad, and avoided getting massacred during the 1944 uprising. Now I was back at my profession and unwilling to grant that everything had changed irrevocably.

The manuscript was wrapped in rough, corrugated paper pocked by dried splotches of coffee and ashes and bound tightly by esparto twine. I clipped the twine and fingered the battered corners of the yellowed pages inside. Before diving into the reading, I remembered the Teacher. Everyone I know called him the Old Doctor. He was quite popular because of his radio programs, novels, and children's stories, but for me he was just *Teacher*. I met him at a summer camp long before the war, when I was still a dreamer and believed that life was a long climb toward glory.

As my eyes took in the first few lines, a thick lump formed in my throat. The letters disappeared, and I heard his voice that was as strong and secure as it was wise and kind. Everything around me melted away—the bad omens of that summer, the gutted buildings that were now little more than their once-beautiful facades, the sinkholes from the shells that made the streets nearly impassable, the rag-clad children, the women ravaged by hunger and by Soviet men. It was just he and I in the middle of a ruined world.

PART I
SUMMER'S END

CHAPTER 1

BIRDS OVER WARSAW

My students resisted the end of summer with the ferocity of a ship-wreck survivor clinging to his life jacket in the middle of a storm. Existence seemed eternal at their age. Nothing satisfies young minds determined to enjoy things 'til the very last second. They grasp time and squeeze all the juice out of it, like we did with those lovely oranges Stefania brought that afternoon of September 1, 1939.

Children and teachers alike all turned to look at her when she got to the river. Though I always found her pretty, she had surpassed the time when beauty is primarily external. We had met thirty years before, and without her my life would have amounted to nothing. When I saw her that day, her dark hair was streaked with gray, and her face reflected the constant effort of tending to the children.

A year ago she had been staying in Palestine. We were both thinking about going to live there, though the irony was not lost on us: two Polish Jews accustomed to the freezing northern winds returning to the hot lands of our ancestors. But the children had brought us back together, and now, with summer lazily dissipating and the rumors of war turning into confident declarations, Stefa seemed as peaceful and loving as always.

"Hello, boys and girls. I've brought more of the good ones," she said, lofting the oranges toward the group of older students.

Everyone caught them midair and started peeling them right away. Stefa came up to me and gave me a hand. She hefted me from the rock where I sat and waited for me to steady myself on my weary legs. Then we walked along the river to enjoy the cool breeze.

"Things are getting pretty bad in Warsaw. There are terrible rumors floating around," she said.

"Dear Stefa, you don't need to worry. Think about the past forty years. We've lived through a horrifying war, formed a free nation, and chased the Soviets out of Warsaw. We've survived all of it. The Polish people are quite accustomed to suffering. Each generation repeats the cycle in its own way. You and I happen to be at the end of one, and soon others will take our place for the next."

Stefa frowned. My tranquility was unsettling to her. She believed I thought too much about things and analyzed them to a fault, as if the human heart could be predicted. She glanced up. The sky was so shining and bright that it seemed nothing could ruin that calm.

I kept talking. "Each generation is like one of nature's seasons, repeating itself in endless cycles. It's an eternal rebirth starting with spring, when everything seems solid and unmovable and people think things will always be like that. Then with summer a new generation awakens and turns everything on its head. Their provocative creativity questions all established notions, and then their heyday gives way to autumn. The next generation rediscovers individualism and the human capacity to achieve personal goals, but they neglect the social fabric until the most dangerous and destructive generation shows up. The winter generation exists in a seemingly unprecedented social crisis; it's marked by mass confusion and the complete destruction of all that seemed solid. There's no point in resisting the inevitable."

Her pace slowed, and Stefa's eyes glanced from one silvery gleam to the next on the calm, constantly moving waters. "So what you're saying," she said with a sigh, "is that whatever's going to happen is going to happen, and there's nothing we can do to stop it."

The reflection of the water glinted off my glasses. I leaned over and studied my image in the river as my hand stroked my stubbly chin. I looked older than I recalled. Time had mercilessly plowed up my dry face and washed out the rosy cheeks of my youth.

"I've lived for six decades now. That's six times the lifespan of a child, and who knows if I'll reach a seventh. Sooner or later, we're all going to disappear, Stefa; it's just a matter of time. Memory is always cloudy and presages the decrepit coming of death. Think about the great men of our time. The emperors, the businessmen, the great revolutionary heroes— they all overcame hundreds of obstacles to reach the pinnacle, and what good did it do them? Maybe they had a decade of glory, perhaps two or three decades in the best of cases, and at the end all that was left was a deep fatigue. Old age means being tired: going to bed worn out and waking up out of breath."

At that, Stefa burst out with the laughter she reserved for my philosophical moods. She knew it would unsettle me and shake me out of restrictive reverie. "All conversation always ends up about you. I've never known anybody else who loved and hated himself as much as you do,

Janusz. You and I may be old, but what about them?" She cocked her head toward the children. "What are you going to tell them if the Nazis take over Poland? That it's just a generational cycle? That you fought in the Great War so now it's their turn to suffer?"

I tsked. "We should be getting back to them anyhow. Let the Nazis do what they've got to do. War seems inevitable, but the enthusiasm isn't there like it was in 1914—much less 1920. I don't foresee this lasting long, and I sure hope they get what's coming to them."

We walked slowly back toward the students. The older ones were debating politics while the younger ones were splashing and throwing themselves with carefree abandon into the water. It was contagious, and I wanted to do the same. Growing up has always meant worrying about all that might happen and everything wrong with the world, as if we were powerless to change it. The oranges had disappeared, and the peels were now being tossed around in a newly minted game.

Balbina came up with her husband, Feliks. They had only been with us a short while but had quickly adapted to the routines at Dom Sierot, the orphanage that had cost us so much to build and upkeep and that some conservative media called the palace of the poor.

"Dr. Korczak," she said, "have you heard the rumors? Before we left the city early this morning, on the radio they were saying—"

"Balbina, we've been hearing rumors for months now. Adolf Hitler seems hell-bent on retaking Danzig, but what he really wants is to take Poland, then all of Europe if Chamberlain lets him. It's best to just let things take their course. It will be as God wills."

A scuffle broke out among the children, as if my words sent their Polish blood boiling. Though there were several Communists among them who wanted the country to become a Soviet republic, and just as many Zionists who clamored for all Jews to return to the promised land,

Return Policy

With a sales receipt or Barnes & Noble.com packing slip, a full refund in the original form of payment will be issued from any Barnes & Noble Booksellers store for returns of new and unread books, and unopened and undamaged music CDs, DVDs, vinyl records, electronics, toys/games and audio books made within 30 days of purchase from a Barnes & Noble Booksellers store or Barnes & Noble.com with the below exceptions:

Undamaged NOOKs purchased from any Barnes & Noble Booksellers store or from Barnes & Noble.com may be returned within 14 days when accompanied with a sales receipt or with a Barnes & Noble.com packing slip or may be exchanged within 30 days with a gift receipt.

A store credit for the purchase price will be issued (i) when a gift receipt is presented within 30 days of purchase, (ii) for all textbooks returns and exchanges, or (iii) when the original tender is PayPal.

Items purchased as part of a Buy One Get One or Buy Two, Get Third Free offer are available for exchange only, unless all items purchased as part of the offer are returned, in which case such items are available for a refund (in 30 days). Exchanges of the items sold at no cost are available only for items of equal or lesser value than the original cost of such item.

Opened music CDs, DVDs, vinyl records, electronics, toys/games, and audio books may not be returned, and can be exchanged only for the same product and only if defective. NOOKs purchased from other retailers or sellers are returnable only to the retailer or seller from which they were purchased pursuant to such retailer's or seller's return policy. Magazines, newspapers, eBooks, digital downloads, and used books are not returnable or exchangeable. Defective NOOKs may be exchanged at the store in accordance with the applicable warranty.

Returns or exchanges will not be permitted (i) after 30 days or without receipt or (ii) for product not carried by Barnes & Noble.com. (iii) for purchases made with a check less than 7 they were universally united in their disdain for the those of the National Socialist variety.

"All right, all right!" I called with my hands raised. "This is exactly what the Fascists want on a beautiful day like today. It's Friday, the start of a wonderful weekend, and here we are talking about their dreams of wars and takeovers. We've been holding our breath for three years now. Whatever's got to happen will happen."

But my words only stoked their thirst for debate. I rolled my eyes, removed my glasses, and sat back down on my rock.

"The Soviets are the only ones who can stop the Nazis. Stalin will defend us," one of the older students said.

"Like he did with Spain in the civil war? He left them high and dry, and now the poor republic is in exile, and General Franco has the country in his dirty fist. We have to wait for help from the British and the French," another piped up.

While they kept this up, Ágata's son, Lukasz, came up and showed me a frog he had caught down by the water. He carefully transitioned the creature into my hands, and I studied it for some time. "Tell me, will it turn into a handsome prince if I kiss it, Lukasz?" I joked.

"No, Teacher, it's just a frog."

I pursed my lips at him and cocked an eyebrow. There went adulthood encroaching on him before my very eyes. I shook my head. "No, no, dear Lukasz, this right here is a prince. Igor is his name, and if he finds a beautiful princess, he'll get his human form back as well as his kingdom."

The boy studied me gravely, weighing just how terrible the crime of fantasy was and regretting my way of teasing him.

"Oh, come now," I coaxed. "You can't lose your imagination. The world should never be what reason, adults, and society force it to be. We've got to keep looking with their eyes," I said, nodding toward the youngest of the bunch who were now engrossed in an all-out battle. I jumped up and went over to them. They immediately ceased their warring, turned to smile at me, embraced me, and dragged me into their fray. As a boy, I had rarely played with other children, but I enjoyed them at all times now.

"Teacher, you're on our team," explained young Pawel. He had come to us just a few months before, after his drunken father had been run over by a trolley while crossing the street. As awful as it was to recognize, that tragedy was the best thing that could have happened to the child.

"Of course I'll be on your team."

Kacper tugged at my sleeve. "No, you're on our team! They have more people, and we're younger." Kacper always managed to melt my heart. He looked like a little cherub with his tight blond curls and dark eyes set just a bit too close together. He spoke with a lisp and kept us all busy with his mischief.

"Hmm," I said, taking a step back and looking back and forth between the teams with a serious, investigative air. "It seems the young cherub is correct. I really should help the weaker side." With that, I picked up a stick and charged into the battle. Swordplay ensued with pine cone grenades launched back and forth between bushy hideouts. War is an endlessly delightful pastime for children.

Suddenly something like thunder roared overhead, but the sky remained clear. I scanned the horizon. A formation of large silver birds was flying toward Warsaw.

The children stopped short. The teachers and helpers rose to their feet, and we were all silent. The only sound was the roar of the Junkers planes' diesel motors. My eyes blazed, and I clenched my teeth to stay the anger.

I thought of Nietzsche's false prophet Zarathustra, the madman who died hating the world. His prophecies of supermen seemed to be coming true, but the Junkers planes were not what belied his prophecies. It was seeing Kacper's face twisted in confusion and terror. He gripped my legs frantically, as if I could do something to stop the oncoming war. At that moment I decided I would indeed defeat those monsters who aimed to conquer my world. I murmured Franciszek Karpiński's morning song: "Man whom you created and saved, showered with your gifts. . . ."

Kacper heard my humming and looked up. Despite the threatening roar of the motors, he smiled once again. There it was. After all these years, now in old age, there was my place in the world. I clenched my weak, thin, knobby fists and felt like the most powerful man in the world. These little chicks made me strong. The star that my grandmother had always seen in my boyhood face would have to shine out now as the sky surrendered its lights to the all-embracing darkness.

CHAPTER 2

BURNING FLAMES

Boredom is the hunger of the soul. The noblest souls—resisting the discouraging slouch of time and destiny—have never been bored. I was awake while everyone else slept. The children breathed in chorus like an ocean melody, inhaling as the waves gathered and exhaling as they broke and returned to sea. There was never complete silence in the orphanage, and I loved that.

In the lovely villa where I grew up, silence reigned nearly all hours of the day. Silence to me had always felt like death. Yet once the bombing raids on Warsaw started, silence felt like life. The raging motors growling through the dark Polish skies were like the screeching flocks of crows that circled cathedrals in the winter. After the motors came the whistling, like question marks slicing down to announce death. Then the explosions shattered glass and eardrums and made our hearts jump. Fear replaced boredom with a different kind of soul hunger: desperation.

If the bombs were not terrifying, they would have been beautiful. They reminded me of the fireworks shows I enjoyed in my childhood, when firecrackers would light up the night. The loud pops would get me out of bed and over to the window, where I would stay with my nose glued to the cold, frosty glass that reflected my pupils.

Stefa and I took turns keeping watch during the bombings. In the working-class neighborhood on the outskirts of the city where our orphanage was, few bombs had fallen, but we could see fires in the distance. It was like an interminable night of the St. John's Day bonfires the Catholics would light every year. Yet over the past few days the effects of the war were spreading like ripples from a stone tossed into a lake.

Most figured that Poland would pull off another miracle, like in 1920 when Warsaw's citizens saved the young nation from the Soviet plague. I was not so sure about that, though I did not mention it to anyone. I did not want to become a grumpy, bad-luck prophet. To me, our beloved city was in sweet denial, like Vienna had been a few years before when it still whistled Anzengruber's refrain, *"Es kann Dir nix g'schehn"*: "Nothing can happen to you!" That is the curse of old empires and cities that have faced a thousand misfortunes. They rely on the fact that calm always returns after the storm. But the Nazis were not just a simple storm, not even a winter front that left old Europe wracked and exhausted. Hitler's Germans were an eternal winter that allowed no regrowth anywhere.

The floor seemed to be vibrating, and a hot breeze that smelled like struck matches and dust blew in, carrying leaves from an early autumn. Then I heard the squawk of the bomber planes approach like threatening birds flying south to escape winter's chill. I grabbed my blanket, and, before I could even wake her, Stefa was already running to my office in her nightgown. Side by side we stared through the round window at the flames that were inching closer. There was no need to talk. We knew what was about to happen.

The planes' murmur grew to an angry, hoarse roar above us before the whistling began. Those whishing sounds meant luck or death to more innocent lives.

The rooftops of nearby buildings were baptized by bomb fire. People ran through the streets. There were no shelters for Warsaw's poor, just the basement of the old church and one warehouse.

"Should we wake the children?" Stefa asked. I smiled at her ludicrous rhetorical question. The whole orphanage was awake except for Pawel. The world could have literally been burning up beside him and the child would have remained sweetly relaxed and resting.

Flashes fell above us like phoenix tail feathers, and we looked up to see fire spreading across our own roof. "Let's get them to the basement!" I said.

Stefa ran to instruct the teachers to take the pajama-clad children down to the basement while I crawled out the window and made my way across the shingles. Fire was spreading on my left. Over and over I tried to smother it with the blanket, but my attempts seemed to have the opposite effect.

A plane flew low over the building, so close I could see the swastikas and smell the diesel. The shingles had been cool from the night's chill, but now they were getting hot. I knelt over and over to put out the flames. Eventually more teachers came and joined the effort, along with Stefa, after she had seen the children to safety.

"It's not going out!" she hollered in desperation.

"We'll get it!" I hollered back, choked up with dread. For twenty-seven years we had been in that building that stood tall and proud in a

Christian neighborhood. We were there on purpose so that Jewish and Christian children could live together. Long ago I had learned that the only way to knock down the walls of prejudice and hatred toward difference was coexisting and building friendships that allowed the children to fight and then be reconciled again.

My joints were starting to complain. The body seems to make itself tyrannically present as we age, as if vocally renouncing its interest in life and documenting its tiredness so that its tenant is fully aware of how little time is left to enjoy physical existence.

I was burning my hands, the fire burned in my face, and the rebellious flames were jumping all around me. Finally, the planes flew off, and the winds died down as the infernal death sound of the motors faded. Then we did manage to put out the flames.

Returning inside exhausted, Feliks sighed. "Another sleepless night."

Balbina headed to the kitchen to fix coffee. We gathered around the table, and no one spoke for a while. We sipped slowly, the mug uncomfortable in my hands that still tingled with the heat from the flames.

"Should we send the children away from the city?" Zalewsky asked. He was our doorman, a Christian.

"The front is moving quickly. There really isn't a safe place to send them," I said with more indifference than I wanted. I knew I should be encouraging my staff and helping them stay hopeful.

"Our army will hold out," one of the younger teachers insisted. His enthusiasm was barely keeping his desperation from turning into sheer panic.

"The most important thing is for us to stay together. The Allies will get busy, and then things will get better." My words sounded believable, and everyone but Stefa nodded. She knew me too well.

We dispersed, still holding our mugs. We would have to wake the children in a few minutes, though most had only slept a few hours. But we had to keep to our schedules and rhythms or else everything would come crashing down. The only way to hold on to normalcy was to pretend it existed until we all believed it did.

"You know very well the Allies won't get here in time," Stefa said. But it was without reproach, just a warning. She wanted me to know I could trust her. I was a father to many children and to quite a number of adults, but not to her.

I hung my head. "Nope, they won't."

"So what will we do when the Nazis invade?"

I had been asking myself that for quite some time but still had no answer.

"The same thing we've always done. We're here to take care of the children and keep them safe. They must be protected until they can take care of themselves."

She raised an eyebrow, unconvinced but understanding. That was the day I started to write my diary. It was not an autobiography—there was nothing about me worth documenting—but the hands were circling the clock with increasing speed, and the sphinx was glaring at me in challenge. There was not much time left.

CHAPTER 3

THE POWER
OF WORDS

I had not been outside the orphanage in a few days. I wanted to remember Warsaw the way it was before war, under the calm light of midday—the radiant city that had begun to shine in the few short years its independence lasted. It is always much easier to live in memories than to be truly submerged in a toxic, strangling reality. Nonetheless, I grabbed my hat from the hook and my cane and was halfway out the door when Stefa's sweet voice called out. She wanted me to walk with her in the garden a bit before heading downtown. We did so, at first in silence and enjoying the crunching of autumn leaves underfoot. Then we sat on a chilly bench and looked at the cloudy sky. It was going to rain.

"Maybe we should leave," she hazarded.

"That ship has sailed, my friend. The British didn't grant me a visa. You should've stayed in Palestine. It won't be long before the Germans enter the city, and we all know what they do to Jews. We've heard from many friends what's been going on in Germany, but it's even worse in Czechoslovakia and Austria."

"Maybe they're exaggerating," she said, but her face denied her words. She knew as well as I did how the Nazis were humiliating the Jews and taking everything they had. It was nothing new. For centuries we Hebrews had been persecuted in Europe for all sorts of things: killing Christ, starting plagues, ruining harvests. The main difference between all previous waves of persecution and now was that most twentieth-century Hebrews had no idea why we were being persecuted.

Jews from the past lived and died proudly because they believed they were chosen, and suffering seemed insignificant to that truth. The law pulsed vividly in their famished bones, and they did not care if their bodies were thrown to the flames or their country was stolen: their souls were longing for a better country, their long-lost Jerusalem. But we were despised for obeying the laws and faith of our ancestors even though most modern Jews no longer believed we were a chosen people, and most did not even worship the God of Abraham and Jacob.

"Ah, you know very well they're not exaggerating. Friends have written me about the abuses of the Germans and the Austrians themselves against our brothers in Vienna. Last year on March 13, a frenzied mob set out on a witch hunt. They were cruelest with the most respected Jews. They dragged the rabbis by their beards into the synagogues and forced them to scream 'Heil Hitler!' at the Torah. Some of the wisest men in Vienna were forced to get on their knees and scrub the streets and the bathrooms of the SA's barracks. What did the rest of the world do then? Nothing. And they won't do anything now. Once the Nazis are in Warsaw, many who smile and greet us in the streets every day will be the first to join the mobs in publicly shaming us."

"So you agree with me. We need to get out of here. There's still a way out by sea. We can take a boat to England, and from there to Palestine, where they'll let us in as refugees."

I looked at the orphanage. It was a bit charred from the fires but still intact. My whole life was there. Plus, inside there were about two hundred reasons to stay. "We can't just leave the children."

"We'll get them out little by little," Stefa went on. "Surely the Nazis won't go that far—they're just harmless kids—but you're a public personage, and they love to humiliate and ruin anyone who might question them."

"Do you remember three years ago? The Polish authorities kept my children's program from going on air. They accused me of being a Zionist and of hiding my Jewish identity under my Polish name, Janusz Korczak. In our country there are already plenty of people who hate us, without even knowing who we are. But today they've asked me to return on air, not to do a program like last year on Pasteur but simply to raise morale in the city."

I stood, not wanting to be late. Stefa stood, too, and her face was clouded with sadness. I would have gone with her to the end of the world, but getting out and leaving the children behind was asking too much. I nodded, put on my hat, and walked down the gravel path toward the gate. I did not look back at my friend. Her sadness weighed heavily on me, but I needed to shake it off before going on the radio.

Yet my spirits grew darker as I walked the streets of our working-class neighborhood. The faces I passed were pale and thin, but the horror worsened the closer I got to downtown. I had seen the city in 1920 after the Soviet attack; even so, I could hardly believe my eyes now.

The bombing had been going on for several days. Most of the government and military high command, including Commander-in-Chief Edward Rydz-Śmigly, had fled to exile in Romania with the equipment and ammunition needed to defend the city. Our valiant mayor, Stefan Starzyński, had stepped up, distributed weapons to the people, and formed a citizens' defense network. The rumor was that the Germans were coming up from the southwest, near the district of Ochota.

The hour-long walk to the radio station tired me out. Some buildings were still smoking from the previous night's bombings. A dozen bodies were lined up, covered in white, bloodied sheets. My heart skipped a beat at how small some of those bodies were. I trudged up the stairs and pushed the door open without knocking.

"You're late, Doctor!"

I took off my hat and headed to the studio without answering. The images from the street were too present with me. The announcer glanced sideways at me and asked, "You all right?"

I sipped the water they had set out for me and wished it were vodka. "Yes, let's get started."

The announcer signaled with his hand to the technician to put us on air. I cleared my throat and saw the red light flash.

"Here, from Radio Warsaw 2, the Voice of Poland! A few days ago the vile Nazis destroyed our transmitter in Raszyn with their bombs, but we'll continue broadcasting from our humble studio. Today we have with us the famous doctor and director of the children's home, Janusz Korczak. Thank you for being with us in this dark hour, Doctor."

"Thank you. My dear citizens of Poland and beloved Varsovians, in recent years we have enjoyed the phrase, 'Peace for our time.' The workers stopped digging trenches, and construction of bomb shelters ceased. People were convinced that our generation would not have to see another war. Then Adolf Hitler rose up and demanded more and more territory in exchange for our peace that was so precarious yet so dear to us. In 1935, we cared little for the fate of the inhabitants of Saar. We were unruffled by what happened to Jews and Communists persecuted by the Nazis after the annexation of Austria. Even the Sudeten Germans and then more and more of Czechoslovakia succumbed to the voracious appetites of Hitler and the sons of the Third Reich while Europe looked on unperturbed, sighing in relief over the peace—peace for our time, no matter the cost, no matter who gets sacrificed to sustain it. Then the Nazi leader's greedy eyes turned toward Danzig to take another bite out of Europe. And we, the Poles, were his next sacrificial victims."

I paused for a deep breath. After adjusting the knot of my tie, I went on.

"Then the bitter taste of violence coated our throats. Fate had chosen us, and we could no longer look away. The German war machine started to tread on us, crushing our dreams of liberty. Today as I walked toward the radio studio, I saw my reflection in the broken glass windows of empty stores strewn with debris. In some of them, women waited in interminable lines hoping to find bread to take home. Surely they were thinking of the coming winter. I saw groups of crestfallen soldiers in tattered uniforms falling back. At the very doors of the radio station, lined up in a row, the bodies of the most recent bombing victims are resting peacefully, far removed now from the cares and fears of this life. That's what convinced me to change what I had prepared to say to you.

"I was going to ask you to resist, to hold out for the French and the British, to cling to the burning mast of the desperate. I had thought about reading some of the poets who pushed us to freedom from German, Austrian, and Russian occupation. But I'm not going to do that. Poland is a strong nation that will withstand the invasion of the Germans and the Third Reich. We will survive the ashes of our cities and raise a new patriotic army. But right now, it's best to lay down our arms. I'm not asking you to give up—don't hear me wrong. The hardest part is yet to come. I'm asking you to resist while loving life; to resist without letting poisonous Nazi ideas seep into our brains and our schools; resist when the oppressors want to turn us into accomplices to their abominations; resist, and you will overcome."

The announcer looked at me with bewilderment, unsure whether to applaud or to kick me out of the studio. There were tears in his eyes, and he was breathing hard. The sound of cold, hard truth after too long without it seemed to be too much for him. I was trembling. I did not want to believe my own words. Peace, as well as the war, had already succumbed to the vitriolic message of the great false prophet, Hitler.

CHAPTER 4

BARBARISM

The day I met her, Agnieszka Ignaciuk and I did not start off on the right foot. Sometimes I can be downright cruel. I do not think about my words or the effect they might have on someone. Agnieszka was very pretty, one of those rural beauties that only come out of Poland. Her eyes were as deep blue as a cat's, her face a perfect oval. Her tightly curled hair was pulled back in a ponytail. She came to the orphanage early one morning. They had been living in a town close to the German border, but when her husband died of typhoid fever, she sold the small farm that was not enough to sustain her and her son, Henryk, and they came to Warsaw to start a new life.

Like so many others just as gullible, Agnieszka had believed the capital city held opportunities that the rest of life denied her. Though she was a trained teacher, she was willing to do anything. She did not flinch at scrubbing floors or nursing the aged. But within weeks she and Henryk were alone, penniless, and desperate.

One day Maryna Falska came upon Agnieszka begging in the street with her young son. Agnieszka's once-lovely pink dress was tattered and torn, and the boy's clothes were just as bad. Maryna brought them to her orphanage, left Agnieszka to rest, and tended to the boy. When she learned they were Jews, she thought it would be best for them to transfer to our orphanage. She sent them with a letter of recommendation, and I think that is what made me start off suspicious.

Maryna Falska and I had had a falling-out a few years prior. She sacrificed ten years of friendship when a few donors complained about a Jew like me being in charge of the pedagogical aspects of the orphanage and boarding school we ran together. Instead of standing up to that kind of prejudice, she invited me to leave, and we had not spoken since. Yet the young widow Agnieszka knew nothing of this history when she showed up at Dom Sierot.

Sabina, the sewing tutor, brought her to my office on the top floor. I was lost in thought about how to obtain sufficient food for the children given recent scarcities, and two more mouths to feed were the last thing I wanted.

"Dr. Korczak, this woman has brought a letter for you."

I looked up and studied the woman above my glasses, which had slipped down on my nose. A child was peeking out from behind her dirty skirt. For a moment it felt like I was seeing myself as a boy, forever hiding behind my mother or grandmother.

"Good day," I said coolly. I was generally more polite, but our food supplies would only last a few more days, and many of our faithful donors had fled the city or were reticent to give, fearing for their own futures.

"Dr. Korczak, my name is Agnieszka Ignaciuk, and this is my son, Henryk."

I presumed she would ask me to take her son into our home, but I knew I could not feed another one. Besides, the children were no longer allowed to attend school, and my tutors were overwhelmed with the work.

"Pleasure to meet you, but I'm afraid we don't have room for young Henryk. The city is in a state of war."

Her trembling hand placed a letter on my desk. Her fingers were long and thin like a pianist's, and she carried herself elegantly despite her threadbare clothes. Her eyes held the awake look of people who have had the privilege of a good education.

I slit the top of the purple envelope with my letter cutter, not recalling at that moment that purple was my former friend Maryna Falska's favorite color.

Dear Janusz,

I hope you're well, given all that we're going through right now. I've heard that things are getting difficult at Dom Sierot. They certainly are for us over here.

The young woman bearing this letter is Mrs. Ignaciuk, and she is joined by her son, Henryk. I found them in a deplorable state on the streets downtown. They've been with me for a week, but when I learned they were Jews, I thought they would be more comfortable in your home.

I'm deeply grieved at what's happened between us and hope that one day you can forgive me.

Always yours,
Maryna Falska

The deepest cuts come from those we love the most. Maryna and I had been very close friends. I met her when she was still quite young and retained the elegant demeanor of her aristocratic upbringing. She had fought actively against Russian occupation and been exiled. In exile, she had married the wonderful doctor Leon Falska, an idealist and dreamer like Maryna. Leon died of typhus in Lithuania, and their young daughter followed soon after him. Alone, Maryna moved to Kiev and began running a home for adolescents. Kiev is where we met, both of us young and courageous. She returned to Warsaw, and we joined up with Maria Podwysocka to start an orphanage and boarding school called Nasz Dom, Our Home. Besides my faithful Stefa, Maryna was the closest friend I had.

"I'm sorry, Mrs. Ignaciuk, but I can't take charge of you."

Agnieszka looked at me with disappointment and frustration. "Why? Maryna assured me that you—"

"Another time, under different circumstances, yes; but you've got to understand we're in a war."

The sad eyes of Henryk from behind his mother's legs tugged at my heart, but I was still stormy about Maryna.

"I can work—I'll do anything. I'm trained as a teacher, and I speak German, but I'd be thrilled just to cook and clean. Please, Dr. Korczak!"

I shook my head firmly. She did not press but turned to walk out, her head hung low. The child followed me with his eyes, and again I thought of myself when I was younger: a solitary, sad boy who never fit in anywhere.

I stretched back in my chair, let my shoulders slump, and closed my eyes. Sometimes it felt like the weight of the world was on my back.

Then I got up as quickly as my sixty-plus years allowed and went to the door, but the woman was already gone. I went down the stairs too quickly and almost tripped, but there was no sign of her in the hall. I opened the front door. It was cold and raining. She was already walking toward the gate when I called out hoarsely, "Mrs. Ignaciuk, wait! Please come back for a moment!"

Agnieszka turned and gave me a pleading look. A desperate mother cannot afford any pride but must be willing to do anything for her child.

"Forgive my behavior. I know it was inexcusable, but I'm under a lot of pressure right now. I was just about to go speak to a donor. We're in a tight spot. We simply don't have enough food."

"I understand, Dr. Korczak. I don't want to be a burden. We will work and do anything."

"Don't worry about that at the moment. Where are your things?" She shook her head. "Well, never mind that; we'll find you some clothes. But I want to ask you a favor."

We walked back to the entryway and stood at the door. She looked at me expectantly. "Do you play piano?" I asked.

"It's been quite some time."

"But do you play?"

"My fingers aren't what they once were, but I think I could try."

We went back into Dom Sierot long enough for me to find her a coat and a hat, borrowed from Stefa, and to leave Henryk in Balbina's care. Then we were back outside and walking. "We're going to the home of a very wealthy Jew, Marta Goldstein. She doesn't live far from here. She adores the piano but has no one to play for her. I think that might warm up her frigid heart."

We walked briskly toward the grounds of Mrs. Goldstein's mansion. That old harpy had a heart harder than granite, but she was my last hope for filling the pantries that week. When we got to the wrought iron gate, I rang the bell, and the elderly housekeeper came out.

"Dr. Korczak, the mistress is not in the finest of spirits today. Her whole body is aching. I'm afraid she won't want to receive you, and even if she does, she won't give you a cent."

"No matter, today heaven has sent me an angel. This is Agnieszka."

"Pleased to meet you, ma'am." The housekeeper gave a slight bow before opening the gate to us. We walked behind her through the lawn that had fallen into disrepair after years of neglect. The housekeeper sighed and gestured around. "And to think of how the most famous parties in Warsaw used to be here some thirty-four years ago. All the nobles fought to get an invitation."

"Even though their owner was a Jew?"

"I'm sure you recall that her husband owned the factories that made machine guns for the Germans. He became unthinkably rich, especially after the Great War."

"What happened with their children?" Agnieszka asked, intrigued.

"A curse has always followed the Goldsteins. Some say it's because of the deaths their weapons have caused around the world. The oldest child died in the Great War, fighting at the front, the day before the war was over. The daughter's fate was worse. She and her young children drowned when their ship sank. They were on the way to America to be reunited with her husband."

We climbed the worn stairs and went inside. Though the house had certainly seen better days, it still exuded splendor and wealth.

"Who was it?" a voice from farther inside demanded.

"It's Dr. Korczak and a woman . . ."

"Surely you didn't tell them to come in. My head's about to explode any moment."

I went into the parlor without invitation or introduction. When seeking a donation, it is always better to act like a clown than to play on pity. People do not want to hear sad stories. They want me to make them feel good and to assure them that their actions will be rewarded either in this life or the next.

"My dear Mrs. Goldstein, it's been quite some time since I've visited. I wanted to see how you're holding up. I see that the bombs haven't fallen near your house."

"How flattering. You're a true gentleman, and there aren't many left, I can tell you that."

"Allow me to introduce Mrs. Ignaciuk. She's one of the teachers at Dom Sierot. In these difficult times, I thought it would be good for you to hear a bit of music."

The old woman blinked. Her white skin and gray hair were set off by the contrast of her intense black suit. I had figured out that she had not left her house for over twenty years.

"Please, would you do that for a poor old woman?" she asked politely and in the next second turned toward the housekeeper and snapped, "Bring them some tea and pastries!"

I was unfazed, already well acquainted with the two faces of the old millionaire. She was a witch dressed as a gentle old lady.

Agnieszka went up to piano but drew back a bit when she saw it was a Steinway & Sons, one of the most expensive models available. Surely she had never played on such a fine instrument. Then she sat down carefully. As her fingers hovered over the keys, she was transformed from the helpless widow I had met but an hour before into a nymph about to play a celestial instrument.

The parlor had felt suffocatingly closed up when I first barged in. But the music filled it, opened and lightened it. A glance at the wealthy old bat showed me that the music was taking her back to happier days. I felt sad for her. After two or three songs, when I sensed that she would be feeling more generous, I leaned over and said, "This wretched war is leaving many orphans in the streets. Most of our donors are fleeing to the coast, and my children are hungry."

She frowned at my interruption of the pleasant sounds, but I went on. "I don't know what you might be able to help us with. We have enough food for two days. The authorities in Warsaw are overwhelmed, and the Germans will take the city soon."

"The authorities in Warsaw have never been known for their competence, and it's only gotten worse since independence. We'd be better off under German rule, though everyone speaks poorly of that little man with the mustache."

"Adolf Hitler," I supplied.

"An Austrian corporal, they say, but it seems he's getting Germany what it actually deserves."

Her words were like daggers in my heart, but I made no sign of disagreement. "The electricity is out in the city, and many neighborhoods are without running water. There are refugees everywhere, and we're overwhelmed."

The old woman sat up a little and raised her right hand. "Dear girl, pause a moment for some tea before it gets cold. Where did you learn to play like that? Don't tell me it was here in Poland."

"No, ma'am, when I was young my parents sent me to boarding school in Germany until I was fourteen. When they passed away, an aunt and uncle took me in and saw to it that I studied education. I worked as a teacher, which is how I met my husband, and then we got married. His dream was to create a model farm and employ peasants."

The old harpy raised her eyebrows at that. It smacked of communist Marxism.

"Was your husband a follower of Lenin?"

"No, ma'am, he was a Lutheran Christian, though his parents, like mine, were Jews." Agnieszka's words did not have a calming effect.

"Well, I don't care for all that religion nonsense. The religious types are always after money. Dr. Korczak, you know as well as I do that money doesn't grow on trees, and since my husband died my reserves are only dwindling. But I feel sorry for your children. Don't worry, I'll give you a check. I don't want the empty bellies of those poor Jewish children on my conscience. Though I assure you that once the Germans are here things will go much better."

"Haven't you heard what they do to Jews?" Agnieszka asked, confused.

"Those are just rumors and war propaganda. As far as I know, there are still Jews in Germany. That's where my family is from." She signed a check and handed it to me. It was by no means a fortune, but it would supply food for a few weeks. She continued, "You can come whenever you want with your friend. Music is the only thing that soothes my old, tormented soul."

We bid farewell and walked out content. Things were getting worse in the city, but with this money I could get food from some farmers and butchers I knew. As we walked back to the orphanage, Agnieszka said, "I feel bad for the old woman."

"Who, the housekeeper?"

"No, Mrs. Goldstein. She's a Jew?"

"Yes, but she doesn't know it," I said. My stomach growled, letting me know it was time for lunch. At Dom Sierot we could certainly not be faulted for overeating. Hunger is one of the worst evils. It takes over your soul and distracts you from everything else all day long.

"What do you think will happen when the Nazis come? Please be frank with me, Dr. Korczak."

The news that had reached me from Austria and Germany was not good. I tended to hold back with most people, but for some reason I spoke plainly to Agnieszka. "Something terrible is about to happen. I fear the worst. The Nazis are beasts, and they'll spare no one in Poland. We Jews will be the first to go, but sooner or later their evil will spread all over our beloved country. I'm afraid, Agnieszka, that Poland will soon become one large unmarked grave."

CHAPTER 5

BELOVED WARSAW

The son of a madman. From an early age I presumed I would, in some way, inherit my father's madness. The fear of sharing his fated illness drove me away from love and from having children of my own. In my mind there was a connection between solving the world's problems and solving the problems of my childhood. Some described me as the sculptor of children's souls, though to me that sounded as pretentious as it was false. If I thought of myself as anything, it was as a tutor walking alongside his students for a short stretch of their journey.

After that awkward first introduction, Henryk and I hit it off very well. One morning I needed to go downtown to talk with the officials who were dealing with refugees coming into Warsaw. Henryk was by the door, looking rather bored, so I invited him to come along. He studied me with his big eyes and nodded his head.

He was quite a keen boy, especially for being only ten years old. He played the piano confidently, could paint with skill, could draw a very realistic human face, and spoke both German and Polish naturally. His parents had not taught him Yiddish.

"Where are we going, Teacher?"

It made me chuckle to hear him address me like that. Most of the children used my last name or just called me "Doctor" or even "Old Doctor," like my radio persona.

"Well, it's a bit far, but your mother tells me your legs are strong."

"Now they are. When we weren't eating, I was always tired and sleepy."

"That's normal. Your body was trying to conserve its energy. We have a nearly perfect machine, but we have to gas it up every now and then."

With the electricity being out, the trolleys were not working, and I did not allow myself the expense for a taxi. So we walked for nearly an hour before reaching our destination. It was not raining that day, but a cold wind was blowing in from the north.

"Do the bombs scare you? Last night was particularly bad. They hardly let us sleep at all."

Henryk looked up at the mostly clear sky where just a few bright clouds were painted across the azure backdrop. "Well, sometimes I think that death isn't so bad. I think of it like a beach in the summer, with a comfortable chair and a soda."

Smiling, I closed my eyes and pictured the scene.

He went on. "Every time I think about heaven, I think about my dad. He's waiting for me there with my grandparents. I know that as soon as he sees me, he'll buy me a big ice cream cone and introduce me to Jesus."

That comment surprised me. "Are you a Christian or a Jew?" I asked.

The boy stopped walking for a moment and stood, thinking. "What's the difference? I think Jesus was a Jew."

"He certainly was," I concurred. "I imagine that in heaven there won't be separate areas, that we'll all be there together—that is if the good God accepts me, which remains to be seen."

Henryk took my hand and, with disarming tenderness, said, "Don't worry. If I get there first, I'll make sure they open the gates for you. Besides, the stuff you do for us kids is really good. If anyone deserves heaven, it's you."

I had never felt deserving of anything. I made choices and took actions simply based on what my conscience dictated, but his words touched me.

"I don't know if God hears me, but when I was young, I asked him to give me an interesting life. I said I'd do whatever he wanted me to, but I just wanted my existence to matter. Does that make any sense?" I asked the child.

"No, but I'm guessing God heard you. Your life has certainly been interesting, hasn't it?"

I nodded thoughtfully. It certainly had. I had been able to study medicine, I had lived in Ukraine, Germany, and Switzerland, and I had traveled to Russia and China. I had served as a medical officer in the Great War. Unbelievably, I had become well known as an author and pedagogue. But what I was most proud of were my boys and girls.

The sound of approaching planes brought my musings up short. The Germans did not typically attack during the day, but they were bolder now since our air force no longer existed. I looked around for cover and spied a semicovered alleyway beside a church. "Over there!" I shouted, pointing. We ran to the alley and crouched down.

Two German planes were flying very low. They dropped a few bombs and then opened machine gun fire on the crowds running in terror. From where I crouched I saw a young, strawberry-blond Polish soldier fall. He was still moving. I darted out from my hiding spot and started dragging his body back toward us, but it was slow going. Henryk joined me, and between us we managed to get the body under a covered doorway. Bullets skimmed by us, but the attack was over within minutes, and the planes flew back to their base. I examined the young soldier. He had several bullet wounds and was bleeding heavily from his abdomen.

"Go ask the soldiers for help," I said, pointing to a group of soldiers passing by in a horse-drawn carriage.

Right then, the door of the house opened, and two women appeared. One was young and the other middle-aged. The older woman snapped, "What are you doing at our house? You're getting the doorway all bloody!"

Her comment perplexed me, and I was speechless.

"Get that body out of here right now!" she insisted. Anger shot up like fire in my head as I continued applying pressure to stop the hemorrhaging. "Are you deaf?" she said, giving the soldier's body a little kick.

"Madam, hold your tongue or I swear I'll show you the force of my fist!" I growled.

The two women balked and took a step back, huffing. "How rude! It's that Jewish doctor."

The soldiers came over, and three of them hoisted the wounded man into the carriage. When my hands were free, I turned back to the two women. The younger one demanded, "Now, dirty Jew, tell me who's going to clean this up?" and she spat in my face.

I clenched my fists and was about to grab the women by their collars when Henryk returned. He tugged at my coat and said in a serious tone, "Remember about turning the other cheek."

I grumbled but turned away from them and took Henryk's hand

while the women continued spitting and calling after us, "Get away, Jews! The Germans will give you what you deserve!"

When we got to the door of the administrative building, I washed the bloodstains off at a fountain, smoothed my hair over, and we went up to see the secretary. The man was a good-hearted government worker. A bomb had hit part of the building, and his office was a shambles.

"The fires have taken some of our files, but we're trying to get organized. War is a terrible thing, and there's no doubt that we're losing. All of Poland west of the Vistula has fallen. It won't be long before our beloved city does too. We don't have enough supplies to hold out for a long siege, and we haven't been able to get electricity and water back up. Plus, typhus is spreading."

"Take heart," I said, patting his back. "The Allies might just get here in time." We all knew that would not happen, but it did no good to lose all hope. That man needed to keep believing in the possibility of victory. He was one of the few members of government who had not fled to Romania.

"I can get you a few sacks of potatoes, some fruit and milk, eggs, and flour to make bread."

"That sounds wonderful, thank you so much," I said.

We left the office and started walking a different route back to the orphanage since the way we had come was covered in rubble. Going down a parallel street from one we had taken earlier, we saw two figures lying on the ground. We approached, and the scene took our breath away. I leaned down and spoke gently to a blond-haired girl who was clinging to the arm of the inert woman.

"Hello, sweetie, what's your name?" A knot was blocking my throat. Thick blood was oozing out of the mother's head. I took her pulse and confirmed she was still alive, but with her wounds she would not last long.

"Aleska," the girl croaked with a despondent look. She could not have been more than three years old, but she knew something bad was happening.

"Aleska, do you know that your name means 'defender of humanity'?"

She shook her head.

"Is this your mother?"

"Yes, sir . . ."

Her eyes showed her terror. Henryk piped up, "You don't have to be scared of him; he's a teacher."

"Your mom's not going to be able to move," I said slowly. "She's hurt. Do you understand that?"

"Yes, Mr. Teacher."

"Do you know where you live?"

She shook her head again. "We're not from here. We came from our town because of the war." She kept her tight grip on her mother's hand, which I noted was starting to grow cool.

"You need to let her go. She can't go with you anymore." I was fighting back the tears that filled my tired eyes.

"I can't leave her alone. My daddy is a soldier, and she won't know how to get back home when she wakes up."

Henryk knelt down and stroked the child's face. "Aleska," he said, "your mom's in a better place now. You don't need to worry about her." She scrunched up her eyebrows at him, not understanding. Henryk went on. "Your mom's in heaven, with God. He'll take care of her there. You can come with us."

"But my mom is right here," the child said, looking at the now cold body.

I could not hold back any longer. I knelt and took the child in my arms, but she refused to let her mother's hand go. I remembered the death of my own mother two decades before. She had been in a hospital, sick with typhus after having nursed me back to health from the same disease. Being an orphan is the saddest of human conditions. It breaks the umbilical cord that ties us to the past and reminds us of the happy childhood years.

"No, don't take me, please! I can't leave her alone! I'm scared!" Aleska was hysterical.

Henryk took off his jacket and covered the woman's face. That somehow helped the girl. She let go of her mother's hand and clung to me ferociously.

"Will she be all right?" She studied me through her tears.

I closed my eyes before that terrified gaze, before the meaninglessness of it all, before the horror of a mother's pointless death right in the middle of the street. "She will be, Aleska. She will be."

We left slowly, almost on tiptoe, as if we were the ones who had committed this vile atrocity. A mother is always a mother, even if she lies dead on the cold, dusty cobblestones of a bombed-out city.

I'm old, I groaned inwardly as we walked away. *No matter how hard I work for the future, death laughs at me once again. Each death witnessed brings us closer to our own. That pale mistress scoffs at our striving after life.*

The warmth of my chest gradually took the chill out of Aleska's trembling body. Henryk walked beside us without his jacket. I glanced and saw he was holding the girl's hand. This was a ray of hope in the midst of so much gloom, and it made me smile. There's nothing purer than a child's heart.

CHAPTER 6

THE MURMUR
OF THE DEAD

Sometimes it is best to let ourselves be carried along by fate. History always denies us the chance to recognize when we are at the beginning of an epoch-defining movement. Decades before, I would never have imagined the fall of the czarist empire. Despite its contradictions and all the inequity, it seemed unchangeable. While I was fighting in the Russo-Japanese War—which is only a manner of speaking, as I was a field doctor and never fired a single shot—the Russian army seemed untouchably powerful; yet it succumbed to the Red Army in the midst of the confusion of the Great War and the civil war. And that same period of history led to the previously unimaginable dismantling of the Austro-Hungarian Empire and the destruction of the Ottoman Empire.

I do not recall the first time I heard Adolf Hitler's name. Surely it was toward the beginning of his career, since I have always been faithful to follow German news. But I do recall the specific warning given by a distant cousin who came to visit at the end of the twenties. His family had lived in Munich for around forty years. He felt as German as I felt Polish, though to the rest of our respective countrymen we were nothing but foreign Jews. He was telling me about unrest in the city, how an anti-Jewish force was spreading across Munich and all of Bavaria after the failed Communist uprising. I did not find it important at the time. Anti-Semitic political parties have always abounded in Europe, whether in liberal France, aristocratic Austria, or Prussian Germany. That news did not worry me, similar to how I barely took note of Hitler's rise to power some six years before the German attack on Warsaw.

After a few weeks of war, Warsaw was lost, along with the rest of Poland. The Germans and Russians devoured it like wild dogs mercilessly tearing into fresh prey. It was just a matter of time now. I was almost wishing for the Nazis to enter the city so that the wanton deaths due to hunger and the infernal bombings could stop. I presumed that bad peace would be better than a good war.

One particular morning I was restless. I made up my mind to return to a practice I had undertaken rather assiduously at other times in my life: talking to the dead. Transcendence and hope are two of the things that modernity has tried its best to steal from us, but I still visited the tombs of my parents and grandparents in the Jewish cemetery.

It was a cold day that threatened to rain. We grabbed two rickety umbrellas and headed for the door. Henryk had become my sidekick and wanted to join me on all my outings. His mother approved, grateful that I could play the role of father and grandfather.

"And where are you off to today?" asked Zalewsky, our Christian doorman, seeing us on the threshold. "Don't stay too long; it's dangerous to be out walking."

"We're going to listen to the murmurs of the dead awhile," I said.

Zalewsky frowned briefly, then smiled. He was used to my hare-brained comments. He took off his hat and opened the doors for us.

"Don't Christians speak with their dead?" I asked on my way out.

"Yes, we talk with them, but they don't answer back."

His eminently reasonable answer, a la Sancho Panza, made me laugh. I knew I was a Quixote, but every time I spoke with Zalewsky, I realized how much we Poles, just like the Spaniards, could be mainly divided into Quixotes and Sanchos.

Henryk and I walked a long while, holding hands. My tired legs were starting to complain and let me know they could not go many more miles. My body was deteriorating, and my strength with it. Since I had turned sixty, the decline of my bones and muscles had sped up. I had never been a strong man but had at least always been tireless and done everything with vigor.

We got to the edge of the cemetery. It was neither ornate nor impoverished, just like the city's Jewish population. My grandfather had always said that class and religious differences chase us from birth to the grave, and he was right. Jews had one place, Christians another; and even Protestants and Orthodox believers had different final resting places.

"Who have we come to see?" Henryk asked. The walk seemed to have worn him out as well.

"Cemeteries are treasure boxes of memories, but most people don't want to remember. Do you see all these gravestones?" The boy nodded. All around, the trees had lost most of their leaves, and we could see their trunks turned green by the humidity. These trees fed off the bodies decomposing underground. "The gravestones are the calling cards of those who've gone before us. Doctors, lawyers, artists, housewives, prostitutes, rabbis, and teachers all lie down to rest together. In the same row you might find a ruthless banker and a philanthropist who tried his whole life to improve humanity. That's why people prefer not to come here. They'd rather not look their destiny straight in the face."

"We're all going to die?" the child asked.

"Of course, Henryk. But dying old men fail to grasp this truth that even a young boy can recognize."

Henryk looked all around at the forest of gravestones and trees. It spread for some miles and seemed to be endless.

"Some of the tombs are bigger and prettier than the others," he observed, pointing out the central drive with the mausoleums of our Hebrew community's rich and powerful.

"It's a final act of vanity, one last attempt to defeat death."

"What is death?"

The boy's thoughts plumbed deeper than what his small body would make one presume, and his question left me speechless for a moment. Finally, I said, "Death is when forgetting wins. As long as we remember the ones who lived, they are still among us."

Henryk's face contorted with the effort not to cry. "So my dad will die all the way when I stop remembering him. I can barely remember what he looks like anymore when I close my eyes. We used to play at home and cause a ruckus. Mom would get all riled up, and it was so funny. I really miss him."

I knelt and wiped his tears away. "You won't forget him, I promise." I took his hand and led him to my grandparents' grave. The chill was cutting through our clothes, and the cemetery, much of it in shadows, seemed more ominous that morning than on other occasions.

"This is Hersz Goldszmit. He was a doctor like I am. He committed his life to fighting the Russians and was part of the Jewish Enlightenment movement, Haskalah."

Henryk's face adopted the look children get when adults use words that are beyond them.

"Don't worry about what certain words mean. The important thing is trying to search out a person's heart. My grandfather was an important man in Warsaw, though his brother, Jakob, my great-uncle, was even more well known. He was a journalist and a writer. In a way, I'm like a combination of the two."

"I've read some of your stories, and I really like them. I've never known a writer before."

"Don't trust writers! They're liable to sell their souls to the devil in exchange for a good story." Henryk gave a little laugh. I led him on through the cemetery.

"And here are Józef and Cecylia," I said, leaning on the granite stone. I took a deep breath to calm my rising tears. I preferred for Henryk not to see me cry.

I recited a short prayer, arranged a few small stones near the grave, and put my hat back on. Not far off we could see a man sitting in a folding chair. He bent forward, and we heard music. Henryk and I looked at each other in surprise and spied on him through the trees.

"Dear Ebicka, I'm sorry I haven't been able to come lately. The bombing has been nonstop. I've brought you your music, and here's the port you love so much." At that, the man poured something over the gravestone without stopping his monologue. "Do you remember how we would while away the afternoons talking? Those hours flew by, and then it was night, and I would read you poetry while you cooked dinner. Candlelight dinners, and we were just grateful for another day together. You were my companion. And now I've got to walk alone. I'm too cowardly to come to you, but it won't be long now. What good is a sad old man in this world? Lovers should die together, get to the end at the same time. It's just cruel to be separated right when we need each other most."

The man was crying as he spoke. He was dressed oddly in a suit jacket, as if ready for a party. The scene stirred up such envy in me that I wanted to curse. He had the luxury of lamenting the loss of something I had never had.

The gentleman knelt and embraced the tombstone, which remained a cold rock instead of the warm arms of his wife. A tear did slip down my cheek then, and I took Henryk's hand and led him away.

"Why aren't you married?" he asked.

"I didn't want to have children," I said simply.

He cocked his head at me. "But you love children, don't you?"

"How do you know? I might be fattening you all up so I can eat you during the night. Haven't you read the story about Hansel and Gretel?"

He smiled big at that. I went on to tell him what I had told few others. "The truth is, my father went insane, and I've always been afraid that the same thing will happen to me. I thought that if I had children, they might inherit that disease. I'm the poor son of a madman."

I began gesturing wildly and dancing a ridiculous jig, and Henryk burst out laughing. That was enough to cast off the gloom of the cemetery as we walked away. We arrived back at Dom Sierot exhausted and very hungry. We did not realize that our long walk had been the last we would take in freedom. In a few days we would no longer be masters of our own destinies.

CHAPTER 7

WARSAW, THE GERMAN CITY

That day I felt the outrage that fills a child's heart when an adult has done something stupid. Warsaw was lost. Just two days prior the city had held out impressively. The Varsovians have always been proud of their heroism. It took the Nazis almost thirty days to bring us to our knees even with the ferocity of their attacks. Without food, running water, or electricity, our people resisted to the end, hoping against hope for help from France and Britain. Yet our allies made no effort to come to our aid.

Yesterday, General Walerian Czuma's troops were marched out of the city after Warsaw had officially surrendered the day before. It was the saddest parade I had ever seen: dirty, ripped-up uniforms; worn, muddy boots; many soldiers without a helmet; and weapons pointed to the ground. The sad looks on their faces asked us to forgive them for abandoning us to our fate, but it was not their fault. Evil sometimes spreads so far and so fast that no one can stop it. General Czuma was the only one who had not left us, who had fought bravely to the last moment, whereas so many of our leaders had fled in terror.

We Varsovians all watched that long column marching away. It was an abominably unfestive end to September. Everything was sad and dark. Part of me was relieved: finally that part of the nightmare was over for the Varsovians. Over eighteen thousand civilians had been killed in the bombings and the fighting, and half of the city's buildings were destroyed or unusable. *Now the Germans will be our masters*, I thought, *but even the cruelest tyrants know they must care for the slaves they seek to exploit.* Oh, how wrong I was.

Sunday came despite it all, but the bells did not ring out over the city. The day of resurrection had become the day of death.

The dining room was silent as a grave during breakfast. In Dom Sierot, there was no differentiation based on age or rank, and tutors and students all sat together. That day we were to hold an extraordinary assembly of parliament to analyze the situation in which we now found ourselves. Twenty children elected by their peers, as well as a few teachers, would lead this assembly.

Breakfast was sparse: dark bread with butter and milk for the younger children. Stefa leaned over and spoke into my ear. "We really must get the children to the coast and try to make it to Switzerland. I'm afraid of what the Nazis might do to them."

"Don't worry. We're okay for now. Let's think about it later. It would be very hard for another country to receive so many children and tutors. Besides, the ports are surely already under German control."

"But we can always bribe a fisherman. They go out to work at night, and no one's watching them."

"Shall we discuss it in the assembly?" I asked.

But she shook her head and whispered, "No, one of the children might say something when they visit their relatives, and it would reach the Nazis."

Agnieszka was sitting across from me. Worried, she asked, "Should we stay in Warsaw? Won't it just be more dangerous?"

With all these concerns floating about, I decided to call the parliament to order right after breakfast and before we all tended to our morning duties. We cleared the tables and arranged ourselves. All the children and caretakers were there, and those elected to the assembly were up front.

I spoke first. "My dear children and teachers!" The hustle and bustle died down, and all eyes turned to me. I cleared my throat and launched into my discourse.

"Well, the Germans have won the war here. This is sad news for us, but at least the fighting is over. We hope we'll have running water and electricity again soon as well as access to food. Things will get back to a kind of normal. For now, none of us can leave the building or the grounds except for the teachers on unavoidable business. As soon as we know what conditions our occupiers will place on us, we'll take the necessary measures and adapt to our new routines."

Next, Pawel stood and spoke. "Children's parliament, tutors, and Teacher: Our community has never gone through anything like this. Not even the oldest students here who're finishing high school have lived under the rule of a foreign power. We won our independence twenty years ago, and now we're getting split up again between the Soviets and the Germans. I, for one, don't know which is worse, Teacher."

Igor, a student with Communist leanings, stood and challenged Pawel. "The Soviet Union brings liberation. The problem is that the bourgeois society sees it as a threat, but they bring brotherhood and harmony between people groups."

Pawel frowned, unimpressed by Igor's pro-Soviet enthusiasm. "What kind of alliance can there be between communism and Nazism? They're just two sides of the same coin. I'm not defending the way the bourgeois oppress their workers, but democracy is the only fair system humankind has ever known."

I stepped in. We were not there to debate the merits of communism and democracy. The students and teachers needed to reflect on what it meant to be a defeated country. "Well, boys, we'll debate political systems another time. We still don't know what the Nazis will do, but I imagine that before long they'll apply their Nuremberg laws from Germany to our city now that we're under their control."

Many of the children did not understand what I meant, so I briefly explained the racial laws against the Jews and other ethnic groups considered to be impure.

Rahel stood and said, "Some Christians already treated us badly before the Nazis started bombing us. I don't know if they'll put those anti-Semitic laws in place, but in Poland Jewish and Christian children can't go to the same school. The tutors walked us to school for years because of the things racist kids would do to us on the way, and we all know we can't have the same life they have."

The girl was correct. Despite the improvements of the Republic of Poland, society continued to discriminate against our community. Even Roman Dmowski, one of the nation's primary ideologues, argued that the Jews hampered the formation of a new national identity. Retrograde ideas do more damage in the minds of elite thinkers than among the ignorant.

"My dear children, you're correct that discrimination is nothing new, but the yoke of the Nazis will undoubtedly oppress the Jews in ways we've not yet even imagined. Many Poles have asked us to get over our differences and assimilate. Many Jews have essentially stopped being Jewish, and yet even so, the Gentiles refuse to accept us. We remain in a no-man's-land, despised by all, both Jews and non-Jews. The only one who truly protected us in Poland was the late Marshal Józef Piłsudski. Let us remember that, from 1935 to 1937, anti-Semitic uprisings left many Jews dead or wounded.

"We've already suffered economic boycotts, like what happened to our Jewish brothers in Germany. Even before the German attacks, there were numerus clauses in place in the universities limiting how many Jewish students could attend and requiring them to sit in separate seats from Aryan students. Even today Jewish storekeepers are required to publicize their race so that clients know the owner is a Jew. Our ritual sacrifices are outlawed, and the college of medicine seeks to keep Jews out of the practice or to only allow them to treat other Jews. Nor are we allowed into journalist associations, and some politicians want to send all the Jews to Madagascar."

"So," Pawel interrupted, "it sounds like we won't notice much of a difference." This elicited laughter from the rest of the children. But what was coming for us was no joke.

"The Nazis hate all the Poles, but they hate us twice as much. I'm convinced that we'll be the first to feel the effects of their unleashed fury. We must be prepared. I think we need to propose and approve certain rules. First: no one goes out of the house alone, and no one leaves without a very good reason. Second: we don't respond to provocation from Germans or anti-Semitic Poles. Third: we strive to resist peacefully. This means we just keep going about our lives. That's what they can't take away from us. God helped his people defeat Pharaoh and brought them back from exile in Babylon. He saved them from the Persian Empire and the Romans. And now he'll save us from," here, I drew my proclamation out for dramatic effect, "these uncircumcised fiends!"

The room erupted in laughter. Then we voted and approved the new rules and closed the assembly.

Afterward, I went to my office. I had to go downtown for an important meeting. The director of education wanted to explain what we were to do as power was transferred to the Germans. I was gathering my papers into my briefcase when Agnieszka knocked at the door.

"Dr. Korczak, I heard you were going downtown. Can I join you?"

"It won't be a pleasant trip," I warned her. The city had suffered terrible attacks, and there were cadavers lying everywhere, not to mention the ruined buildings and people begging for food at every corner.

"That's fine. I need to see someone, and I don't want you to go alone, Doctor."

"Agnieszka, for the thousandth time, call me Janusz. I could be your father, but I still feel young and spry."

"I'm sorry, Janusz."

"These gray hairs are simply an effect of years passing. I assure you I'm no grander than yourself."

As we went downstairs, Agnieszka talked about how afraid she was. "And Henryk told me that the other day you took him to the cemetery."

"Did that bother you?"

"No, it just surprised me. People don't tend to take children to graveyards."

We bundled up and headed out. October had begun chillier and less pleasant than it typically was. "Well," I said, "I don't know much about what other people do. I think we can learn a lot in cemeteries, don't you?"

"Death is a great teacher," she conceded as we exited the gates and started walking down the street.

The area around Dom Sierot had not been terribly affected by the bombings, but downtown, the city had been ripped apart at the seams.

We did not come upon a single German soldier until we reached Market Place. The Germans were patrolling the area in small groups, sometimes only in pairs. People steered clear of them. Our path took us near two huge Germans. One had skin as pink as a pig's, and the other was ashen. Both of them had the ridiculous little mustache of their leader. The fatter one said something ugly to Agnieszka. I looked him in the eye and replied in German, "Shouldn't you be ashamed? This woman is a mother and a widow. Do you have a mother or a wife?"

The soldier was taken aback, surely surprised that I could speak his language. I hoped this made us more human in his eyes. At least he did not know we were Jews. He stepped back and let us pass. Agnieszka smiled at me, and we continued walking toward the cathedral. That exchange was the merest of anecdotes compared with what was happening in the rest of the city.

In front of the damaged church, an elderly Jew was walking with a boy, likely his grandson, of some four or five years. A group of soldiers stopped them and demanded to see identification. With no provocation, one of the youngest in the group, with an entirely angelic face, grabbed the old man's beard and started mocking him. Agnieszka held me back from going to them.

The old man begged the soldiers to leave them be. The blond-haired boy beside him was berserk with tears at what they were doing to his grandfather. One of the soldiers took out a pair of scissors and cut off the man's beard, then held it aloft like a trophy for all to admire. They punched the old man and left him lying on the ground as they walked away. The boy tried to raise him but was not strong enough. All around watched with either indifference or fear.

We went up, and I asked, "Are you all right?" I was indignant at what I had just witnessed.

The elderly gentleman looked up. He was praying in Yiddish, and his eyes were bleary with tears. He had wet himself. He was nearly paralyzed with fear and shame. We helped him get up, and I asked in Yiddish, "Do you live near?" The man was completely dazed and could not answer. The child pointed, and we were able to follow his lead and get the man to their house in a Jewish neighborhood not far away.

After that, Agnieszka wanted to go back home. She was shaking like a leaf every time we went anywhere near a group of soldiers.

"We can't be afraid of them. That's precisely what they want," I said.

"But I am afraid. They are devils, not people."

"They certainly seem that way, my dear, but the saddest part is that they are simple human beings like we are. That one," I pointed, "is probably a cobbler from Hamburg. And that one," I signaled another, "a butcher from Berlin. And that fat one is a cook from Frankfurt. They're just normal people who have been given absolute power."

We made our way behind St. John's Archcathedral and were greeted by the most jarring scenes yet on our walk. Professor Kirschenbaum was walking down the sidewalk balancing several books under his arm. He was one of the University of Warsaw's renowned history professors, just a few years my senior. Two German military police addressed him. He responded in perfect German and held out his papers.

The corporal hollered out, "You're a dirty Jew!" He grabbed a bucket and mop from a nearby store and dropped them on the ground.

"I'm not sure I understand," the distinguished professor said.

"Herr professor, now you're just a dirty Jew street cleaner."

Kirschenbaum remain composed and asked to see the officers' credentials while slowly backing away. The corporal grabbed him by the shoulders while the other officer threw the books into the mud. They forced him to his knees and made him start cleaning. The historian finally took up the rag, wet it in the bucket, and started scrubbing the mud-covered stones while the Germans laughed. Some of those passing by also stopped to laugh.

As I headed their way, one of the officers kicked the bucket over, drenching Kirschenbaum's clothes. Agnieszka could not hold me back this time.

"What are you doing?" I demanded in German. "For the love of God, it's a poor old man, just a professor." These two were not so easy to talk down.

The corporal put his hands on his hips and answered, "And who do you think you are? We're in charge now. This is our land, and you're all foreigners. Either accept the way things are or be prepared to suffer. Now go on about your business."

"My business? Helping the helpless is my business. Isn't that what your Luther taught you?"

The corporal grabbed me by the flap of my jacket. I was prepared for a blow, but a voice from behind me called out, "Corporal, let that civilian go immediately!"

He dropped me. I turned to thank my savior and came face-to-face with a German official. He continued, "Now pick that man up and give him his books!" The two underlings obeyed, and Kirschenbaum backed away with a thank-you. The two officers slunk off like startled dogs, and Agnieszka and I were left alone with the officer.

"I'm sorry about that, Herr," he said.

"Doctor Korczak," I supplied.

"Herr Doctor, I am Captain Neumann. I was just looking for a medic, in fact."

"Is the German army in short supply then?"

The captain smiled, which lightened the tension. "To be frank, two days from now we'll have the victory march, and all the soldiers are required to be in training. There's no campaign doctor in all of Warsaw, and my chauffeur has taken ill. He's just over there." He pointed to a Mercedes with its top down.

"It's been many years since I've been in practice, and my specialty is pediatrics, but I can take a look at him."

The chauffeur was slumped over in his seat, holding his right side.

"Tell me what's hurting."

"For two days it's been hurting right here a lot," he said.

A short examination told me it was very likely appendicitis. "You'd better get to the hospital immediately before the appendix bursts."

The captain raised an eyebrow. "And will they treat us at the hospital?"

Agnieszka and I joined them in the car, and I gave them directions. Within fifteen minutes we had arrived. We supported the man 'til an orderly met us and helped him into a bed. An old friend of mine from my medical days, Dr. Jakobski, came out to meet us.

"Korczak, what are you doing with these Germans?" he asked in Polish.

"The driver's appendix is about to burst. You'll have to operate immediately."

"They're the enemy. Let their Nazi doctors cure them."

I smiled and touched his shoulder. "Love our enemies, remember?"

The doctor, who was very religious, scowled and headed to the operating room behind the officer's chauffeur.

"Thank you," the captain said, removing his peaked cap. "How can I repay you?"

I studied him for a moment. They were too much like us. It was easier to hate them when I did not know them. "Do good, Captain. That will be enough repayment."

We were a mess of different emotions when we left the hospital. There was deep fear but also the satisfaction of having held out for one more day.

The meeting with the minister of education was bleak, but at least Agnieszka was able to take care of whatever she had to do in the meanwhile. On the way back to Dom Sierot, the streetlights turned on. So the electricity was back. I had a brief spark of hope that the Germans might not be the brutal murderers we all imagined them to be; that they might be content to simply rule over us like the Russians, Austrians, and Prussians had done in the past; that they would eventually let us live with an ounce of human dignity.

But the government of my beloved country would shortly be in the hands of the cruelest assassins to come to power in the last several centuries.

We were too tired to eat when we got back inside the orphanage. Agnieszka and I were the only two who really knew what was going on outside of Dom Sierot. We had to protect these children. They were all that kept me in this world, the sole reason for my existence.

CHAPTER 8

STEFANIA

Nothing we do alone lasts. I was always a solitary man, though I hardly had time for myself. There were precious few moments I spent resting or reading alone in my room. All my life I was a loner, starting from when I was a sad, melancholy little boy with no real playmates. Yet fate surrounded me with marvelous human beings. And Stefania Wilczyńska was my right hand for years.

We met in 1909 when we both served in an orphan aid association. I had been working with children for as long as I could remember, whether in summer camps with my friends or taking street orphans to city shelters. Later I specialized in pediatric medicine, intending to dedicate my full energy to children—though what really made up my mind was a trip I made to London in 1910. There I toured several hospitals and orphanages. The English were about a century ahead of us in terms of public and private institutions serving children. Perhaps that was because England was one of the first countries where the life of a commoner mattered as much as that of an aristocrat.

I still vividly recall that café meeting when Stefa and I talked about what would become of Dom Sierot. It was invigorating to see how an indescribable force drew our spirits together. She possessed what I was lacking. I had always been able to get people excited about my ideas, though I ran a bit short on patience with the children themselves. But for her, the children had always mattered most. I liked to play with them and write books on pedagogy, but Stefa had infinite patience with each and every child in the house. The orphans adored her. She was endlessly affectionate, attentive, tender, and kind as only a mother can be.

Her only other passion in life besides the children was Palestine. She was the one who got me to see myself actually as a Jew, something I had always shrugged at like a boring episode from the past. Though I would not dare tell her this, I had never felt so lost and alone as when Stefa was not here. She traveled to Palestine, and I felt helpless.

Back when the children could still go to school, every morning she would prepare them a snack to take for their break, and she knew exactly what each child preferred. She was the model of motherhood all the girls learned from, and she offered the boys the affection they missed or had never even had from their own families.

Now that things were bad in Warsaw, I wondered if we had done the right thing by staying. But the truth was we had never had any other option. For both Stefa and me, the children keep us tied to earth more than flags or national anthems. Poland to me looked like a famished child and the glassy eyes of a mother with nothing left to feed her children.

One day a Polish nationalist told me that Jews could not be good Poles; that we might become good Cracovians or Varsovians but never true Poles. That comment made me remember something one of our girls had said when she was asked what kind of person she was. She said she was lots of things. Adults tend to overlook that we can be many things at once, even contradictorily.

• • •

Henryk came into my office, as usual without knocking. He knew I would not get mad. He had figured me out quicker than any of the other children.

"Teacher, did you see what's going on outside in the street?"

I was so wrapped up in thought that I had not noticed the sound of footsteps, drums, and music. We went out to the balcony and looked into the distance.

The Germans were marching through the streets with their tanks and cannons as if to drive home the fact that they were the new masters of Poland.

"Their uniforms are nice," Henryk said.

"You know, I have one, from my days in the Polish army."

"Really?"

"Of course. Want to see it?"

He nodded, so I went to my closet and dug around in the back until I found it.

"It's really nice! Why don't you ever wear it?"

"Well, I'm not a soldier anymore, and really I never was. I was a field doctor. I've never shot anyone."

"Wouldn't you shoot one of those Germans?" he asked.

I paused and cocked my head to think. I would certainly have liked to shoot them all, but I knew all too well that it would not fix anything.

I did not criticize others for fighting to get free of their oppressors, but I hated war with all my heart.

"What are you two up to?" Stefa came in and asked, smiling.

"Teacher has unveiled his uniform."

"*Unveiled*? My, your vocabulary is growing by leaps and bounds with all that reading you're doing." She ruffled his hair.

"Thank you, Miss Stefa."

"Could you leave us a moment, Henryk?"

I leaned against the desk as he made his way out of the office. My legs were aching that day.

"So you saw the parade?" Stefa asked. "I heard that Hitler himself is here."

"It's a dream come true for the Austrian corporal, though it's a nightmare for the rest of the world. Dostoevsky said we all eventually get our dreams, but they're generally so garbled we can't even recognize them."

"I'm being serious, Janusz," she said, weary from her endless work and all the anxiety she bore on behalf of the children. She slouched into a chair and crossed her arms.

"I've spent my entire life preparing for what happens next, and this is the first time I'm not doing it. Though that's not entirely true—sometimes I think about what I'll do after the war and when the Germans leave."

Stefa gave me a puzzled look. "What do you mean you're not preparing for what's coming? I just think about tomorrow, next week, the coming winter. How are we going to feed, clothe, and keep these children warm? How are we going to protect them from these beasts? But you're talking about when the war is over and the Germans are gone. It may be that neither you nor I live to see that day."

I sat down and took her hand. It was both sweaty and cold. "I don't know, but I know that we'll think of something. Life is a gift. If we see it as a loan or as an obligation, we'll grow bitter. Every day we open our eyes and find ourselves here is a gift. Don't lose sight of that."

Stefa began to cry softly. She was not a woman given to many tears—and certainly not in public. She was much stronger than she seemed at first glance.

"My dear friend, we're in God's hands. We can't do anything, really, but don't worry. We'll be here as long as he wants us to be, and not a minute more or less."

"Since when did you turn religious?"

"Since there's absolutely nothing we can do but pray."

I gave her a hug and swallowed back my own tears. Together, she and I had built this home with our own hard work, and for almost thirty years we had given our lives to the country's children and Warsaw's Jewish orphans in particular. Now we were foreigners in our own land; even worse, we had become simple pariahs.

"I don't actually want to die," Stefa said, voicing the deeper fear.

"We're all going to, sooner or later."

"I know, that's not the problem; I mean not like this, in their disgusting hands."

"There are no undignified deaths. We all reach the same threshold of life's mystery. Dying is as natural as being born."

We embraced for a few more moments, the solitude of the one mingling with that of the other through the strange connection that souls are sometimes allowed to make. Fleetingly, I wanted to confess to Stefa that she was the most important person in my life and that I never wanted to live far away from her; but, even in moments of despair, sometimes the absurd fear of being misunderstood forbids us from letting our hearts speak.

CHAPTER 9

THE DOORWOMAN'S SON

Fairy tales always have a grain of truth in them, and they teach us many things," I told my precious audience of Dom Sierot's children. Most of them loved my stories. "Let me tell you the story of two boys. They lived next to each other, and both of their mothers were widows. The mothers had helped each other when their husbands died in the Great War. One of the children was blond haired and blue eyed. The other boy was dark complected and had dark hair. I couldn't tell you which boy lived where because this happened a long time ago, and I heard this story from someone else.

"The two boys went to school together every day. They were best friends and were inseparable. They played together after doing their chores, and their mothers had to yell loudly to get them to come back inside for supper. One day, when they got to school, their teacher told them they could no longer study together. They looked at each other, puzzled. It turns out that one of them had a Jewish grandmother, and the grandmother of the other one was Aryan. They didn't really understand what the teacher was saying. He had a silly little mustache, and his hair was combed down all greasy on one side. They went home very sad and told their mothers, and, to their surprise, their mothers also forbid them from playing together anymore. Sometimes they tried to sneak out and play together when no one was looking, but it got harder and harder, and they eventually gave up trying to be friends.

"Now, both of these boys were head-over-heels in love with the prettiest girl in the neighborhood. She had dark skin and blue eyes, or maybe she was blond with green eyes. Anyhow, her parents had a little stand at the corner where they sold candies, cigarettes, and trading cards. Her father had lost one of his arms in the war but could still run the little stand. The mother was so pretty and nice that, since these two boys were friends with her daughter, sometimes she would give them a piece of candy for free. Not long after the boys had been told that one of them was a Jew and the other an Aryan, they learned that the family of the girl was also Jewish. Their mothers forbade them from seeing her.

"When they grew up, the two boys became airplane pilots. One of them fought in the Polish Armed Forces and the other in the German Army. When the war broke out, each boy served his country because they had been told that one of them was Polish and the other German, which meant they had to kill each other. It didn't make any sense to these grown-up boys, but, since everybody thought that way, they fought hard in lots of air battles. Over Warsaw they fought in their hardest battle yet in the air. Without knowing it, they shot each other down, and both planes crashed on a road where their old friend and her family—the ones that owned the candy stand—were going by, trying to escape from the fighting. It's absurd, but that's how the three friends died.

"But don't cry, my little friends. Their bodies were all burned up in the plane crash, but their souls flew free up to heaven. There they found each other again, and they realized that there weren't any differences between them after all. They hugged and got back to playing together right away. They weren't sad because they understood what had happened to them and what will happen to all of us. Many of you have lost your parents, your brothers and sisters, or your friends. But one day we will see them all in heaven."

Some of the children were crying, as were many of the caretakers. I myself was choked up thinking about my own parents. Missing them did not ease up as the years went by. On the contrary, I missed them more and more as the time of our reunion inexorably approached.

The group slowly dissolved until Agnieszka came up with her sad face and red eyes. "Thank you for that lovely story," she said.

I waved off the compliment. "They're just fairy tales."

"But they do my heart good."

Stefa came up, exuding even more nerves than the day before. A perusal of the kitchen had confirmed that our pantries were nearly empty again.

I did not mince words. "The children eat like horses, and our donors are either too scared to give or have fled the city." I had spent the last several weeks trying to squeeze money out of turnips, and it was harder and harder to come by.

"We could go back to that rich old lady," Agnieszka suggested.

Stefa and I raised skeptical eyebrows. The art of fundraising was not simple. That woman was mean and miserly, and softening her up was no easy task.

"It's too soon to go back to her house. We'd better ask at city hall. I imagine there are fresh supplies coming in by now."

"Fine, but we need food before the week is out," Stefa said.

I nodded and shrugged. We had somehow managed to keep the orphanage open for decades, and none of our children had ever gone hungry. It was true that we were facing unprecedented times, but provision would come from somewhere.

"I'll go with you," Agnieszka said.

Stefa frowned. My poor friend suspected that Agnieszka was falling for an ugly old toad like me.

It was pouring heavily when we went out. Now that the electricity was back, the trolleys were working again, and we made it to city hall within twenty minutes. The people we passed in the street wore tattered clothes and walked lethargically with their heads down. Many refugees and those left homeless by the bombs had no alternative to living in the streets or in makeshift wood and cardboard shacks.

We got off, and just as our trolley was moving on, it blew its whistle and stopped short. The brakes screeched, and we heard a deadening *thump*. We turned back and saw a black-haired horse splayed out, its intestines and blood spilling out and turning its belly red. As soon as the carriage driver released the animal's reins, a crowd jumped on the beast. They pulled knives out of somewhere and started carving the animal as it lay dying. One woman made off with the leg, which was nearly too heavy for her to carry. Some men who had been working on a building construction took a full side, and an old man cut out the horse's kidneys. Within minutes all that was left were the ribs, the spine, the head, and a few inedible organs like the lungs.

It was to be expected among a starving population. Meat was prohibitively expensive, and only the rich could afford it now.

Agnieszka and I did not comment on the scene. We just turned and walked inside to where a Polish employee, under the gaze of a German soldier, asked us to wait. Half an hour later, we entered the office of the minister who oversaw the Department of Food and Public Distribution. The man did not rise to greet us but merely motioned to two chairs while he finished a phone conversation.

After a few minutes he said, "Dr. Korczak, it's a pleasure seeing you around here. I imagine you're here, like everyone else, to ask for more food. Barely any supplies are getting through."

"How can this be, minister?"

"The Germans are requisitioning nearly all the basic supplies. They call it 'compensation for the war efforts.' We have no authority. At this point I'm just managing the crumbs they're willing to toss my way."

I was incensed. It was unacceptable for the Germans to use the food of the Polish people to feed their army.

"Things aren't like that with the Soviets," I said. "The Germans are more savage than the Bolsheviks."

"I'll deny saying it, but doubtless that is the case. From what we hear, they're going to annex the vast majority of our country. What's left will be for the displaced Polish population and for relocating the Jews."

"What's the difference? We're all Poles, aren't we?"

The minister held his tongue at my uncomfortable question.

"I feel so sorry for your poor children. The only thing I can offer you is five sacks of potatoes, a few vegetables, a couple boxes of apples, and about fifty pounds of powdered milk for the youngest ones."

That would last us a couple days if we rationed it carefully. "It's not much," I said. "But we'll make it work for now."

"I'm sorry to tell you that on the black market you can get more, but it'll cost a fortune."

"When can we come by to pick it up?"

The minister signed an order and handed it to me. "Come by tomorrow, or else the little we've got left will all be gone."

Agnieszka and I were a bit encouraged leaving his office. We crossed the street and decided to walk back home. The cool air cleared our heads. The city was still a bombed-out ruin, but the streets were starting to get cleaned, and some of the displaced had been able to return to their buildings.

"One of these parallel streets has a few market stands. They might have something at a decent price," Agnieszka offered.

"We lose nothing by trying," I answered, fingering the zlotys in my pocket.

Taking the turn, we found ourselves in what felt like a different city. Peasants and undercover vendors were selling the widest possible array of goods, some of which I had not seen since the beginning of the war. There were eggs, cheese, chicken, pork sausages, and wine. I stopped in several stalls for the mere pleasure of smelling those exquisite aromas, though we could not afford any of it. But the smell itself satisfied me. In my reverie, a child dashed by and pushed me out of his way. I nearly fell on my face.

"What in the . . . ?" I hollered after the child who was bobbing and weaving between the pedestrians that crowded the street. A few seconds later, the heavy butcher from the first stall passed by panting. He called out every now and then for the child to stop but was out of breath. I glanced at Agnieszka, and we followed them.

The little thief ran much faster than the fat butcher, but at the end of the street he was snatched up by some Polish policemen. The butcher made his way to them, panting, and started shaking the child. The boy, who could not have been older than nine, stared at him in terror.

"But I'm hungry," the child whimpered.

"Well stealing is a sin!" the butcher roared, pulling on the boy's ears. "Throw him in jail; that'll teach him!"

By that time I had caught up with the group. The passersby had stopped to watch what was happening. Among them I spotted the heartless mother and daughter who had argued with me over trying to help an injured Polish soldier in their doorway.

"It's the Jewish doorwoman's boy! Those filthy Jews are all thieves. The Germans better give them what's coming to them," the older woman screamed, nearly in my ear. I emerged from the crowd and inserted myself within the circle of the primary actors.

"Let the boy go at once," I said.

The policemen gave me a stunned look. The butcher frowned and thrust his face into mine. "And who the hell are you? Is this your grandson?" he demanded.

"He might as well be. The child has stolen because he's hungry, and hunger isn't a crime."

"My mother has taken ill in the building—what's left of it—where she used to be the doorwoman. We've got nothing to eat, and if she doesn't get help soon, she'll be dead just like my dad," the child said between sobs.

"See?" the old woman from the doorway insisted. Her eyes were bulging. "He's just one more Jew full of lies." Both mother and daughter turned to defy me, but Agnieszka intervened.

"Don't you know who you're talking to?" she said. "This is Janusz Korczak, from the radio."

A murmur ran through the crowd. They had not recognized my voice, but thousands had heard my educational programs for children.

"Dr. Korczak," said one of the policemen with a tone of admiration, removing his hat.

The butcher scratched his greasy, brownish-gray hair under his white cap, then took the pieces of meat the policeman had recovered and left.

"Does anyone else accuse this boy?" the policeman asked.

"Poor kid, leave him be," someone called from the crowd.

"Then we'll leave him to you," the policeman said with a farewell nod.

Then the boy lifted his dirty, tearstained face.

"It's all right; come with us," I told him.

We walked to a nearby stall where I bought two loaves of bread, a few potatoes, and some butter. I gave them to the child.

"Is this for me?" he asked in surprise.

"Yes, sweetie, and for your mother. Take good care of her; you've only got one."

The boy took the food, smiled for the first time, and ran off up the street.

"So you spent the last bit of money you had," Agnieszka remarked.

"Yes, my dear, but for a good cause. Can you think what would've happened to the boy had we not been passing by? Everything happens for a reason. Even the greatest misfortunes can become the sweetest blessings."

Agnieszka put her arm through mine and we walked back to the orphanage, content at having been able to do at least one good thing.

"Why are you so good, Doctor?"

"I'm not good. I'm a selfish, proud man. The trick is that some of what I find pleasing happens to align with what others call virtues. If God puts a starving child in front of me, what can I do? Ignore him? I don't have the stomach for that."

We walked on without hurry, grateful for what the day's outing had sent our way and heartened to see a small light of hope shining in the eyes of one hungry child. I knew he would always remember us. The best lesson we can ever teach is to show love to those around us without expecting anything in return.

CHAPTER 10

A BIRD BURIAL

I remember the first time I was called a Jew when I was young. The pet canary I loved died. I had taken care of it assiduously, and it had been with us for some time. How I loved to listen to it sing. When it died, I buried it in our yard and put a cross over its grave. Our gardener came up and asked what I was doing.

"I want to give my bird a decent burial," I answered innocently.

"A Christian burial? You're a Jew. The cross is for Christians."

I looked at him in surprise. These things had never occurred to me. My parents were not religious. They lived like Gentiles and never taught me Hebrew or bothered to raise me up in any Jewish customs. My grandparents were the same way. They were considered "liberals" and thought that all those customs were a cumbersome holdover from the past. If they'd seen me now that I was in my sixties, perhaps they would have laughed at me. Every morning I gathered the children together for morning prayers. It was completely voluntary, but many did come. They felt the peace of being drawn together in that moment for a common purpose and the comfort of someone looking out for them and listening to them. I hardly knew any prayers when I started this with them but had learned a number over time. Now, after a lifetime estranged from the traditions of my ancestors, I felt closer than ever to my origins. Being a Jew was the worst of crimes.

Let me be clear: I still felt nearly allergic to organized religions in general, believing they were more concerned with the material than the spiritual, with accumulating wealth and power. Besides, Orthodox Jews would not have approved of me as a good Jew. I had always been polemical in that regard. I could not deny that I admired many things about Jesus. I appreciated his love for his enemies, his desire for peace, his mercy, and most of all his optimism. Sometimes Judaism felt too pessimistic to me, though there was a ray of hope for returning to Jerusalem one day.

Each day that passed brought more dire news. The world's winter was approaching its inevitable climax, and the war was impossibly far from over. Things went from bad to worse in Warsaw. There were shortages on everything, and we could not even keep the house warm. Since Hans Frank, the governor-general of Poland, arrived, life had gotten harder for all Poles and especially for the Jews.

Soon after the Nazis arrived, twenty-four prominent Jewish community members were convened into a Jewish council called the Judenrat, presided over by Adam Czerniaków. Yet we continued to suffer increasing humiliation and mistreatment. The first thing that Hans Frank's government did was force Jews to rebuild the buildings that German bombs had destroyed. The work was mandatory, without pay, from sunup to sundown. All Jewish business were ordered to display a Star of

David on their doors and shop windows, and now they wanted each of us to wear an armband too.

Stefa had been working with several tutors on making armbands for all the children. They had to be big and easily visible, a blue star against a white background. In other countries Jews were forced to wear yellow stars, supposedly because yellow is the color of betrayal, so these armbands would prove that we Jews were all traitors like Judas who sold Jesus to his enemies. But in Poland, Frank seemed to prefer blue for some reason.

Every day I thought of my good friend Ludwik Liciński, who had showed me the Warsaw of the poor when I was younger. We thought of it as plucking lovely flowers out of marshy swamps, which is how we saw the ghettos we frequented to rescue the city's impoverished children. He always told me that freedom ended right where fear began, which is why I have never been afraid. What can men do to me? They have no power over the immortal soul. They can punish the body, but my old hide is worth little, and I know it will not hold out much longer.

That cold December morning I went with Henryk to a meeting of the Judenrat. Stefa did not want me going alone. Sometimes the cold would freeze up my joints, and she didn't want me to fall and get stuck somewhere with no one to help me. We headed out after eating and as dark was falling. It was very cold.

We hopped aboard the trolley where only about a dozen travelers were spread out, four of whom wore armbands. I looked at the different styles. A woman with a leather coat wore a silk armband. I could imagine a maid carefully embroidering the blue star with fine thread. It was well done. It shone more like a badge of distinction rather than of scorn. A bit in front of her, a young man, a manual laborer from the looks of him, wore a sloppy one that sagged to his elbow. His look was hard and defiant. In one corner of the trolley, a schoolgirl was trying to cover her band with her backpack. Her eyes were lowered, and her whole demeaner screamed insecurity. Next to her, her blond-haired, blue-eyed mother also had her star partially concealed.

"Why are we wearing stars now?" Henryk asked. Stefa had insisted he wear one so the Nazis would leave him alone. I did not wear mine and had always refused to do so.

"That's a great question. I think the only answer is because they make us."

"But you're not wearing it, Teacher."

"How observant you are, my boy. It's not easy to explain, but we all have something called dignity. Without it, life has no meaning. The Nazis want to take ours away. Does that make any sense? If they succeed, they'll have won the game."

Henryk studied me, thinking hard. Then with his left hand he ripped his armband off and stuffed it into his pocket. I thought about stopping him, but I knew I should be consistent in my actions.

When we got to the building where the Judenrat was meeting, we got off the trolley and headed straight for the chief council's office. The secretary tried to stop us, but I ignored him and entered without knocking. Adam Czerniaków had his head in his hands and his glasses on the desk, but he startled like a hare in a bush at our interruption.

"Korczak, good God, you scared me to death."

"You thought we were Nazis? Calm down, you can spot them from a mile away."

"And to what do I owe the honor of your visit?"

Henryk removed his hat and sat in the chair to my right. "Well, I don't think it's much of an honor. Since the cats have made you the chief of the rats, I'm hoping you'll help us get a little bit of cheese."

"There's nothing funny about it, jokester. Every day that goes by, the Germans add more restrictions. In a few days we won't be able to use public transportation anymore—we might contaminate the Gentiles, you see—or eat in restaurants or walk around the parks. Most of the liberal professions will be closed off to us, not to mention that we're forbidden from moving. And that's just the start."

Czerniaków seemed so desperate that, for a moment, I altered my approach. An engineer by training, he had been one of the first Jewish senators. He was polite and well educated, but he lacked charisma and spark, though it could hardly be easy to negotiate with the Nazis.

"Have you spoken with Hans Frank?" I asked.

"I've requested a meeting several times, but he always sends some lower official in his place. For him, we Jews are a mere nuisance, and they're trying to get rid of us. There are nearly half a million of us here in Warsaw, too many mouths to feed. There are rumors that they'll deport us to Madagascar, and some say they'll shut us up in ghettos. I don't know what the future holds, but I am convinced it isn't pleasant."

"We Jews are still useful to them, no?"

"Not for much longer, Dr. Korczak. They keep siphoning money away from us, which buys us a little more time. But when that runs out, I don't even want to think about what the beasts are capable of."

"We've been persecuted so many times, but we always manage to prevail."

"That's what I'm trying to work toward. The war started four months ago, but I don't think it'll be over in just a couple of years. If we manage to survive to the end and the Germans are defeated, we might have a chance."

I sat up and said with full confidence, "We need help. Our pantries are bone-dry, and it's impossible to get food at the market."

"Everyone needs help."

"But my children need to eat, you see? Our people have to prioritize the children."

Czerniaków looked at me with his slanted eyes. He was dismayed but remained calm. "I'll do what I can; that's all I can promise."

"That's not enough. City hall isn't giving me anything anymore. Most of our donors have fled or are ruined. You're the only help left."

Czerniaków took out a document, filled it out, and handed it to me with a shrug of resignation. "It's not much, Dr. Korczak, but we'll try to get more very soon. The only good thing about the German administration is that it's so corrupt that sometimes a shipment is allowed to go missing."

I glanced over the paper he had signed. It meant at least another month of hope. "Thank you so very much. This is enough for now."

Czerniaków glanced at Henryk as if for the first time, fished around in a drawer, and handed the boy a piece of candy. Henryk looked at me and waited for me to nod before receiving it. "Thank you, sir."

"It's a hard time to be a child." Czerniaków sighed. "But you're the future of our people."

"Mr. Czerniaków," I said, "being a child is always hard, not to mention being a Jew and an orphan. My pupils are true heroes, not like those shoddy figures that make the front page or get written up in history books."

He stood, and we shook hands. We headed out of the office and were about to go down the stairs when someone called after me.

"Doctor! Do you remember me? It's Chaim."

I stared at the man in front of me and through his features just barely made out one of the children who had come to us right after Dom Sierot opened. "Well, good God, what are you doing here?"

"I'm in charge of rations."

My jaw dropped. As a child, Chaim had been a little devil, without question the most difficult student who had come our way. He cared nothing for studies, was disobedient, refused to help the group, and was mean-spirited and unkind.

"Well, I'm so glad to see you. It looks like you've done well for yourself."

"I know I was terrible when I was in the orphanage. I was so angry," he said with a frank sincerity I would never have expected.

"Right you were!" I confirmed.

"But I also learned a lot."

"That's good to hear. We always reap what we sow. There are no bad seeds, just rough patches of land."

"Why are you here? Do you need something?" he asked.

"You know, we're always short on food, especially these days."

Chaim perused the document I was holding and said, "I can get you twice what the Judenrat can supply."

My eyebrows arched in surprise. "Really?"

"Yes, I'm the one who goes after the—shall we say—'unapproved' shipments of food. I won't let those orphans go hungry, even if just for old times' sake."

My former hellion gave me a hug, and I could tell he was encouraged by this challenge. I marveled at human emotions. Only time lets us appreciate what we once despised. "Thank you for being the father I never had."

He walked off quickly, leaving me so surprised and almost giddy that I had to concentrate hard not to trip going down on the stairs. Henryk and I walked in silence. We had gotten more than we asked for. Chaim had been one of my failures. I'd been convinced he would wind up murdered in some dark alley. And here he came like a ghost from the past to save us from a deep, dark pit.

When we got to the street, we noticed that the signs forbidding Jews on public transportation had already been hung. I ignored them, and we got on the trolley anyhow.

Henryk started, "But the sign says—"

"I know what it says," I interrupted, shrugging it off.

"Shouldn't we obey though? You're the one always telling us we need to obey the rules."

"That's true, my young friend, but not unjust laws that are against humane values. God does not ask that of us."

The way back was uneventful, and I watched my beloved Warsaw going by. People hunched over with the cold as they walked by the toppled buildings. It was going to be a harsh winter. The Star of David was now visible in the windows of many stores, and the streets were full of foot traffic since the sidewalks were reserved for Aryans. It was a Darwinian vision of the strongest imposing themselves over the weak in a clear example of the dehumanization of the people of my times. The values and principles that had turned Europe into the birthplace of democracy and human rights no longer mattered, and the human soul held no more worth.

CHAPTER 11

A HOUSE

That day I called together all the children, the caretakers, and the tutors. Nearly a year had passed since the Nazis came to Poland, and nothing had gotten better. Typhus had run its course around the city in recent months, given the deplorable hygienic conditions and insufficient nutrition of the population. It seemed the Germans preferred to kill us off slowly. Their program was designed to weaken our spirits and erode our morale. Few resisted, and those who did disappeared in the night. Some were taken to the concentration camps that had popped up all over Poland. Others were dragged out of prison and shot over the mass graves they had been forced to dig near the cemeteries.

The governor-general of Poland had informed the Judenrat that the Jews would be cloistered within a ghetto fashioned from one of Warsaw's older Jewish neighborhoods. At the beginning of 1940 they had outlawed praying in groups in the synagogue, purportedly to curb the spread of disease. Now, with the same excuse, they intended to enclose Warsaw's 359,827 Jews—though really there were more like 400,000 of us—within an area no larger than 1.3 square miles.

Whenever a new difficulty arose, we convened an assembly—but we had no idea how to explain this situation to the members of Dom Sierot. Summer had been surprisingly calm. We had even managed to have an outdoor summer camp, and now we had to tell the children we would soon have to leave our home to go somewhere we knew nothing about. The Nazis were taking even the roof over our heads that provided a sense of security, however fragile.

Everyone was already seated when I went into our assembly room. I made my way to the front and asked, "What does it mean to be happy? Can anyone explain to me what happiness is? We all want to be happy, or at least that's what we say. But does anyone know what makes a person happy?"

A hand shot up and a child started speaking. "For me, being happy means getting to do whatever I want." Everyone laughed.

A girl stood and said, "I want to be rich. Rich people are always happy. They can buy whatever they want and have nice clothes and eat all their favorite things. I'd have a room to myself with a nice desk. You have to have a lot of money to be really happy."

An older student, whose eyes were scrunched up in thought, offered, "I think that being happy means being around people who love you. I'm not happy because I don't matter to anyone and nobody else matters to me."

A little tyke piped up with, "I want to be big and strong, the strongest man on earth."

"And why is that?" I asked him.

"Then nobody would hit me or bother me."

A shy little girl with black braids stood and worked up her courage to speak. "I was happy when I was with my parents," she said in nearly a whisper. "We were a family. We lived together, and that made me happy."

A sigh ran throughout the crowd. Most of them felt the same way. It was hard enough for kids to be separated from their parents in the best of times, much less during a war.

A wide array of opinions and ideas peppered the next few minutes. When the children's voices died down, I returned to my feet, grabbed my lapels, and offered my perspective.

"Many times we seek happiness in the things we possess, in the people we call friends, in life circumstances, or in our moods. We erroneously conclude that joy means always feeling cheerful, surrounded by everyone we love and having everything we need and want. When I was a child like you all, everything was fine, but I always felt that something was missing. If my mom gave me a bouncy ball, I wanted a soccer ball; if I got a soccer ball, I begged for a bike; when I got the bike, it wasn't long 'til I no longer wanted to ride. The feeling of happiness turned into indifference and then into apathy. I longed for those fleeting moments of being excited—that short-lived feeling of anticipation—but I didn't realize that I was already happy; I couldn't understand my own happiness.

"Usually, when we're really and truly happy, we don't even think about it. We're content to enjoy a day at the beach, an ice cream, a walk with a friend, a Sunday morning breakfast. We don't even notice that these small things are what our joy is made up of. Life in and of itself is an act of happiness. A bird high up on a tree branch looks out on the world and is happy; a rabbit hopping toward its burrow enjoys the cool spring evening; the eagle flies high above the wide sky and is happy looking down on everything from above. Happiness is not about things.

We look for it outside of ourselves, but it's something that's in our own minds. The work of our hearts is to give pure love. Our stomachs hurt if we don't give them food. The heart is the same way: if it isn't full of love, that emptiness makes us unhappy and makes us long for a better time."

My words held the children and their teachers hypnotized. Yet I was so worried about what I had to tell them next and how they might take it. A firm lump had formed in my throat.

"Listen carefully, now. This week we are all going to have to leave our wonderful home here at Dom Sierot to go somewhere else. It might not be as nice and comfortable as this house. We won't have a yard, a garden, a theater, or a library. We'll live really close together, all up on top of one another, and there won't be hot water. It'll be an old place that's very cold in the winter and very hot in the summer. We'll probably long to be back here in our wonderful house. But the walls that you see around us are not our home. The real refuge of each one of us is inside our hearts. As long as we're together, we will keep being happy and belonging to our big family."

Every man, woman, and child was crying, some loudly, some softly. They knew I was right, but none of us wanted to leave our building. It was the nest where our baby birds felt safe.

"Time for hugs! Time for hugs!" I called, and everyone turned to hug whoever was nearby while wiping away the tears. Thus, our assembly ended.

Stefa and Agnieszka came up as the children were leaving the dining room.

"So you weren't able to stop the relocation?" Stefa pronounced her question more like a statement.

I shook my head. "We've pushed it off as long as possible. Most of the other orphanages and children's homes have already been moved into the ghetto. All the CENTOS members are enraged. You know how little the new coordinator does. She's supposed to organize all the charities that help Jewish children and orphans, but she just accuses us of thinking we're special."

"But what about that Aryan school that's near the ghetto? I thought you were trying to get us into it?" Agnieszka asked.

"That won't work either. It's just outside the boundaries. You've heard about the endless disputes about which streets are in or out and where the exact boundaries are. Some people have had to move two or three times. I only managed to get one thing in our favor. The Judenrat promised me we'd have the Roesler trade school building. It's two terribly ill-suited floors on Chłodna Street, but we'll have to make it work."

"At least that's on the south side, where there are fewer people in the ghetto," Agnieszka conceded.

"Right now I'm off to see the place. Everything will be ready for tomorrow. Zalewsky, our ever-valiant doorman, will help oversee the transfer. That man and his family are gems, so helpful to us. I've got a meeting with Zofia Rozenblum, the chief physician of CENTOS. Will you come, Stefa?"

She shook her head, her eyes full of sadness. "I'd rather help the children pack up. It will be so hard on them to leave this place. Agnieszka, what if you went?"

"You don't need my help with the children?" she asked.

"You'd better keep an eye on this old ogre and see that he doesn't get into trouble," Stefa said, cocking her head in my direction.

I adopted a severely offended face that morphed into an ogre's grimace before turning into a smile.

Agnieszka and I set out that November 30 with heavy hearts. Part of me did not want to see the place we were being forced to move into until we got there, but I knew it would be best for me to know what to expect beforehand and help the others prepare. We got there quickly as it was less than a mile from Dom Sierot. That had been one of my arguments to the authorities for letting us stay where we were. We were so close as to practically be in the Jewish zone. Zofia, wearing a black coat and a small hat, was waiting for us at the door.

"Dr. Korczak, I'm glad you've decided to come."

"It's hard to say no when there's an invisible knife held to my throat," I said, unable to hold back.

"You've got one of the best buildings in the ghetto, I assure you. Unfortunately, the other orphanages have not been so, shall we say, lucky."

"I'm not complaining about you, my dear madame. I accept our situation, but don't expect me to be jumping for joy about it."

She pulled out her keys, opened the door, and led us into a musty building that smelled like it had been shut up a long time. Dust lay thickly everywhere, little natural light entered the place, and the heat did not work. The kitchen pipes were clogged with rust, and there were precious few burners. The brief tour left me more depressed than I was even prepared for, but I tried not to let it show.

"Well, it will be . . . enough," I said as we went out to a balcony.

"It's the best spot in the ghetto. They call this southern zone the Small Ghetto. The homes are larger and more comfortable. It's the preferred area for the wealthy Jews." Zofia's voice was dripping with sarcasm. It was true that the street was wide and notably clean, but nonetheless it was a jail.

"Have they already closed the wall?" I asked.

"Yes, the German swine made us pay the costs of construction. It's like making a hanging victim build his own gallows," she huffed.

"Well, it could be worse, right?" Agnieszka offered, trying to hold on to optimism. Zofia and I stared at her. "I mean, the Nazis have invaded the whole of Europe within a year. The United Kingdom is on the point of succumbing. If they do, the war is lost. So what will the Nazis do to us when there's no one left to speak up against them?"

"Agnieszka," I said, "the British don't care a fig for two or three million Polish Jews. The luckiest of our people have fled to the Soviet-occupied side of the country. I would never, ever have imagined that the Bolsheviks would respect human life more than the Germans." This, despite my profound dislike for the Stalinists.

We bid farewell to Zofia and walked around the neighboring streets. Trolleys and cars were still allowed in and out, so we would not be entirely closed in. Agnieszka and I walked the length and breadth of the ghetto, my first time doing so. I had intentionally avoided the place. Something childish in me hoped that if I pretended it was not there, it might go away.

People had set up improvised market stands along the streets, and everyone was walking fast, as if there were actually somewhere to get to. People were desperate to make this huge, abnormal jail feel normal. The Nazis had turned it into our particular hell. Even so, in some sad, macabre way, they had, for the first time, constructed a Jewish society removed from Gentile life. We were persecuted and defamed, hated and despised, shut in and enslaved. Yet, despite it all, God's chosen people—from Abraham's loins, led by Moses, made great by David and Solomon, preserved by the prophets—had united now as one flesh and one soul in the face of adversity and suffering.

CHAPTER 12

THE POTATO CART

Life makes no sense, at least not when examined through a microscope. We are a mere, nearly impossible casualty, the sum of chance and a thousand possibilities. Yet when we look at life through a gigantic telescope that brings the entire universe close, everything seems to fulfill a particular purpose.

Friedrich Nietzsche's Übermensch is not a man but an antiman. He denies everything good and honest that humanity has accomplished over the course of thousands of years. The German philosopher defended the idea that individuals—or rather, a select group of supermen or overmen—were capable of creating their own system of values, since God was no longer necessary in the scientific age. These new supermen, with their powerful wills, would be capable of achieving all that they desired and imposing themselves on the fainthearted and weak ones that Christianity had wasted time protecting.

I do not know why I woke up that morning with these thoughts running through my head. Perhaps I was angry that the Nazis' powerful will was turning the world into a fatuous place that was no longer worth living in.

First thing in the morning I was ready. We all worked together to wake the children for our last few hours at home. We made the best breakfast we could with what we had, hoping to instill one last good memory of the beloved house we had to leave to go to the ghetto. Then we gathered our last things, the children with their little suitcases or bags, the teachers carrying larger and heavier versions, the cart with our precious provisions, and, in my case, a suitcase with three changes of clothes and a handful of books. I had to leave behind my most valued earthly possession: my library.

My books were the hardest material thing in the world for me to let go of. Yet, that morning, in our short march to the new building, I felt like Zeno of Citium, who argued that there was no greater freedom for a man than to untie himself from all that binds him to the world. Unfortunately, before we arrived at our new destination, I had already fallen back into the arms of Epicurus. I had always tried to enjoy life in both the big moments and in the small things. I did not want to turn my back on any of it. Plus, I loved thinking about Epicurus's famous garden, where he taught philosophy to Athenian men and women, rich and poor, nobles and plebians, respectable citizens and famous prostitutes. I was moved by one particular section of his *Letter to Menoeceus*. I had memorized it as a boy:

> Let no one be slow to seek wisdom when he is young nor weary in the
> search thereof when he is grown old. For no age is too early or too
> late for the health of the soul. And to say that the season for studying

philosophy has not yet come, or that it is past and gone, is like saying that the season for happiness is not yet or that it is now no more.

"What are you thinking about, Dr. Korczak?" Agnieszka asked, noting my absent look. I was walking hand in hand with Henryk, who had been crying since we left Dom Sierot. The boy had been particularly fond of the garden.

"Little Henryk, don't cry. We're going to live the adventure of our lives. Do you remember the kinds of stories that are in pirate books? Treasure hunts always occur in exotic, remote places. No one's ever done anything amazing without leaving home first."

Henryk lifted his head and gave a weak smile. Then I handed him a little treasure map I had sketched the night before to entertain the children when they got to the new house. My goal was to help them accept our new quarters.

"When we get there," I went on, "would you like to be the keeper of the treasure map?"

Henryk took the piece of paper in his hands as if it were the most precious gift in the world and smiled for real this time. "Thank you," he said, his big eyes open wide.

"Thank you," Agnieszka echoed.

"You're welcome, Agnieszka. I'm trying to make the situation as least traumatic for them all as possible. I was thinking about nonsense when you asked. Just imagine, in the midst of all of this horrible drama, I've been worried about my books. But I suppose they'll know how to look after themselves."

"Of course you'll miss them. We all need to have things that keep us grounded here on earth. Otherwise we'd be a bunch of hot air balloons just floating around."

"Yes, my friend, the lightness of existing is difficult to embrace, but, you know, what ties us to this world—or, at least, what ought to—is very different. Love is what gives weight to life. My books are not actually what's important. It's my love of them that is."

We were coming up on the outskirts of the ghetto. At that point in time there was still freedom to enter and exit at will. In fact, there was rather a long line to get in, as many merchants and farmers wanted to prey on the desperation of the inhabitants and sell their products at marked-up prices.

"That's true," Agnieszka answered. "Love is what ties us to the world."

"I often wonder what all these world leaders can be thinking. They are so worked up about acquiring fame and fortune. Do they really not understand that those who always want to climb higher and higher end up the victims of vertigo?"

"I don't think I follow what you mean."

"Hitler, Stalin, or Mussolini, the great men of our time, the conquerors of peoples, the supermen who have created their own morality and have imposed it on the whole world—at the core they are all lightweight. They're at the top, floating over us, but without real weight. They can't love because love always means renouncing force. They violate the masses whom they subjugate with their false, populist words."

"From what you're saying, the only thing that makes life make sense or gives it weight is love."

"Yes, I believe that's so. But not just any love: true love, which is always a burden, but the heavier the burden, the more fulfilling life will be. Why do we consider *Romeo and Juliet* a beautiful love story? Because they loved each other to the point of death. People nowadays split up over any little thing. Everyone wants to be free, but they are slaves to their egos.

"The Nazis are the greatest example of this. Look at their ostentatious uniforms. They want to instill fear and elicit awe, so they put on costumes. But beneath their gray or black bomber jackets, they are just normal people. Mediocre shopkeepers, miners who are lashing out at the world that up to now has denied them nearly everything, frustrated street sweepers and trolley drivers. Their officials are even worse. They are so lightweight that I can almost see them floating, even flying, above our heads."

We were coming to the checkpoint. Since Agnieszka and I were at the head of our column, the German sergeant asked me where we were going, who we were, and all those ridiculous formalities the Germans love to insist on. After I explained everything, he allowed us to proceed. It would have been quite funny had he forbidden it. I stayed with Agnieszka at the entryway. I had decided to wear my Polish army uniform that day, my own small attempt to provoke the Nazis and show that we Jews also knew something of histrionics and could wear uniforms just as flashy as their own.

When our provisions wagon arrived pushed by Zalewsky, the sergeant ordered our doorman to stop.

"What's inside?" he barked, but Zalewsky did not understand German.

I answered for him. "It's our provisions. We have two hundred people to feed, the majority of them still young and growing."

"We requisition all food. You can't bring in anything more than what you can carry."

I looked at him indignantly. There was no way he was keeping our food. "This food is for the children and under no condition can I allow you to take it away from them."

"Dr. Korczak, I'm just following orders. If you want to lodge a complaint, you'll have to go to the office of the Gestapo."

The mere whisper of that name struck fear in the hearts of all who heard it. In thirteen months of German occupation, we had learned that the Nazi police organization, together with the SS, was the darkest part of the unimaginably dark Nazi machine.

"So we can keep what we carry?" I confirmed.

The sergeant nodded. We unloaded as much as we possibly could, but even so, over half the supplies remained in the requisitioned cart. We trudged and sweated the rest of the way to our new building, deposited the food in the pantry, and called the children together in the main hall.

"I've got to step out in just a moment, but I'm leaving Stefa in charge of the treasure hunt. You'll have to tell me later who wins. Henryk has the map, so you should pay attention to him."

The boys and girls dashed toward him and started reading the clues. Stefa came up to me. She knew what had happened at the entry to the ghetto.

"Are you mad? The Gestapo are heartless. No one can 'lodge a complaint' against them. For them you're just a miserable Jew."

"Today I'm in my best Polish officer garb."

My joke did not amuse her, but the children were pulling at her to get the game started, so she let herself be drawn away, making no attempt to disguise her concern.

"Should I go with you?" Agnieszka asked.

"I'd better go alone. Zalewsky, I'll walk with you and your family out of the ghetto."

Our doorman looked up in surprise. "We're not going anywhere. We're staying right here with you."

"The ghetto is for Jews, and you're a Christian."

"The children, the teachers, and you are our family. We can't leave you alone."

"This is madness! No one wants to stay here. It's dreadful! Look what's around you."

"But you yourself taught me that our home is not a building; it's the heart of the people who love us. We love all of you, and we want to share your fate."

I hugged this man. I had never seen a heart grander than Zalewsky's. "But, friend, your family will be in danger."

"I don't understand the world anymore, Doctor. But I do understand what you're doing with these children. Please don't ask me to leave."

I wiped my eyes and saw that he, too, was crying. I had never seen him in this state before. The breadth of his compassion—of shared suffering—was beyond anything I had ever witnessed. They wanted to suffer alongside us. Then I quoted one of my favorite passages of the Gospels: "Greater love has no one than this: to lay down one's life for one's friends."

I marched out of our new building more determined than ever. Zalewsky had revived my belief that good can overcome evil, and I was not afraid of walking right into the heart of darkness.

The building of German administration offices was on a wide street. The entryway was flanked by enormous square columns that led to a small patio. As I approached, two soldiers cut me off.

"Good day, I am Dr. Janusz Korczak. The Gestapo has confiscated a cart of supplies, particularly potatoes. I am the director of an orphanage and have come to request the return of our supply cart."

The two soldiers looked surprised at the ludicrousness of my request. "Wait here," one of them said.

The tallest soldier went up to a corporal, who went to a sentry box with a telephone. He must have called someone, because five minutes later, a soldier came out of the building and asked me to follow him. I had walked by this building countless times but had never been inside. We went up several flights of stairs, which the soldier took with quick ease while I huffed and attempted to keep up.

Finally he led me down a hall and into a small office. A German secretary glanced up but made no overtures to greet us. After knocking at the door, we went into a state department office, as prior to the war this building had been a Polish government building.

"Herr Commander, Dr. Korczak needs to discuss a matter regarding the requisition of a cart."

Josef Albert Meisinger, the head of SS and SD police, was about to receive a Jew into his office. The comedy nearly outweighed the tragedy.

A frown creased the commander's imposing and terrifying face. The hair behind his receding hairline was cut extremely short, and his square jaw and straight nose made him the poster image of the Teutonic warrior the Germans were so fond of.

"Professor Korczak."

"No, Herr Commander, I am Dr. Korczak."

He stood and came up to me, studying my uniform with curiosity.

"And Captain Korczak."

"Indeed. In the Great War I served in the Russian army and later with the Polish army, but as a field doctor."

He made a complete turn about me, as if examining me from every angle. I tried to stay calm, despite the enormous pressure building in my chest.

"My assistant tells me there has been an incident with a few sacks of potatoes."

"That is correct, sir."

"Well, sit down, and let's see what can be done."

At that moment I began to relax ever so slightly. The Nazi commander settled into his seat like a satrap in complete control of the situation.

"The children need to eat. They are orphans, and—"

"We've taken a cart of potatoes from an orphanage?" he interrupted, disgruntled.

"That is the case, though surely it was in error."

He frowned again, picked up the phone, and made a phone call. He spoke for a few minutes with someone, then hung up furiously. Before speaking again, his cold glare dug into me.

"Herr Dr. Korczak, you are the director of a Jewish orphanage, correct?"

"Yes, sir, just as I was telling you."

"Why are you not wearing the Star of David?" He stood and began walking toward me.

"I see no reason to."

"You see no reason to? Who the hell do you think you are? You're a Jew, aren't you?"

"Yes, Commander, at least as far as my birth goes, yet . . ."

"Don't try to manipulate me with your Jewish nonsense. Get on your feet."

The commander was much taller than I was. He stood in front of me. His teeth, somewhat discolored, seemed like wolf fangs when he began shouting. "You are not a Polish official! You're a Jew!"

And with that, he ripped the braids off my uniform and then the badge over my chest and threw them to the floor. I remained calm and did not close my eyes, flinch, or give any sign of fear.

"You'll be going to jail at this moment for being out of compliance with the laws of the German state by not wearing the Star of David."

"But this is not Germany, Commander."

"It is now, by conqueror's right!" Little flecks of spit shot out as he shouted.

"And the potatoes?" I calmly insisted.

His eyes were alive with hatred. He slapped my face several times until I finally folded and fell to the floor. He called for his assistant.

"Take this vermin to Pawiak prison. Tell them to lock him up until they hear otherwise."

The soldier grabbed me unceremoniously, and, barely back on my feet, we left the office. As we walked toward the yard where a van would transport me to the jail, I thought back to my early morning musings. Those Aryan gods, coarse and vulgar, uncouth and cruel, were, at their core, so weak. They could cause great pain, but they were as lightweight as feathers or windblown leaves.

For them, life was a useless sketch through which to imprint their senseless brutality and show the world that they were the bosses. For me, life was a perfect, beautifully framed painting, full of meaning and hope. For them, life was prosaic and frivolous, ever so light, whereas for me it was so heavy I could hardly take a step without feeling the mud stuck to my feet.

CHAPTER 13

CHESS MATCH

The night I spent in jail filled me with calm. For the past five or ten years, I had not been able to sleep well. Insomnia ran in my family. But, there in the jail, I was not awoken by the moan of a sick child, the crying of the smaller ones, Stefa's cough, or the jolt of worrying about having everything ready for the orphanage's activities the next day. That night my dream took me to a dark, mysterious text from the prophet Zechariah that I had never fully understood but always been fascinated by. Apparently, Joshua was the first high priest after the Jews returned from captivity in Babylon, and he was behind the rebuilding of the temple. In the book of Zechariah, there is a text in which Satan begins to accuse the high priest Joshua before God, and then God answers Satan:

Then he showed me Joshua the high priest standing before the angel of the LORD, and Satan standing at his right side to accuse him. The LORD said to Satan, "The LORD rebuke you, Satan! The LORD, who has chosen Jerusalem, rebuke you! Is not this man a burning stick snatched from the fire?"

Now Joshua was dressed in filthy clothes as he stood before the angel. The angel said to those who were standing before him, "Take off his filthy clothes."

Then he said to Joshua, "See, I have taken away your sin, and I will put fine garments on you."

Then I said, "Put a clean turban on his head." So they put a clean turban on his head and clothed him, while the angel of the LORD stood by.

The angel of the LORD gave this charge to Joshua: "This is what the LORD Almighty says: 'If you will walk in obedience to me and keep my requirements, then you will govern my house and have charge of my courts, and I will give you a place among these standing here.'"

I was in the middle of this macabre conversation when loud knocking from the guards woke me. I was sharing a cell with a Czech businessman who had tried to swindle Hans Frank, the governor-general of Poland.

"Mirka, are you awake?"

"Who could sleep with the sound of your snoring, Doctor?"

With some difficulty I got down from the top bunk and sat beside him.

"I slept like a baby."

"You're not afraid."

"Of what, exactly?"

"I've been told this is one of the worst jails in Poland."

"What would you say if I told you a secret? This jail has reminded me of old times. The czarist empire locked me up for defending my country's independence. At that time I was a mere lad, and now I'm an old man. I wasn't afraid then, and I'm still not."

"Of course, but you've not been accused by the governor-general."

I looked at the man's chubby face. His nose was thin and pointy like an arrow tip. He wore gold-rimmed glasses, and his curly brown hair was somewhat long. He was in the same business suit he had been wearing when he was arrested, as if to indicate he would not be there long. His tie hung from his neck like the hook of a fish caught red-handed.

"Swindling good ole Frank," I chuckled. "Selling him the guaranteed way to get even richer, a solution that would turn water into gasoline. How could he fall for something like that?"

Slumped on the bed, Mirka's ample belly fell into several folds. His week in jail had barely begun to thin him down.

"Have you ever seen Hans Frank?" he asked me.

"Only from afar."

"My good doctor, his face is common enough, one you'd forget five minutes later, but his eyes—his eyes are something else. They are as cold as icebergs through which his soul has been sucked out. He's a lawyer, though he respects no law."

"And have you ever met one that does?" I prodded to lighten the mood.

"The man has been by Hitler's side from the beginning, and they sent him here as a prize for his evildoings."

"And you thought you'd toy with a man like that?"

"Well, it was somewhat of an accident. I've always been in this business, shall we say. My father was a swindler and a counterfeiter, and my grandfather before him. It all started on the train coming from Prague when I met an officer who turned out to be tight with Frank. I was going after him, and once he fell for it, he said the governor could get me a load of gold for the invention, and I couldn't resist. When I met with Frank, my legs were shaking. I was standing before the most powerful man in the East, and I played my part perfectly. Just as I was walking away with the money, someone sent background info on me from Prague, and the ruse was up. It's a pity. I could've retired."

The story fascinated me. It was unbelievable but exactly the kind of thing that would happen in our crazy day and time.

A guard approached. "Dr. Korczak? The captain wishes to see you."

They led me out of the cell and through endless halls but did not handcuff me. I suppose I did not emanate the threat of danger. We left the main building and headed for another nearby. It was very cold, or at least I felt cold during that 1940 autumn. They took me to the office of the captain, who turned and looked at me in surprise.

"Do you remember me?" he asked. Of course I did. He was the officer who had defended me from the German soldiers, the one with the sick chauffeur.

"Yes, of course," I said, smiling.

The captain held out his hand to shake. I was struggling to recall his name—Neumann or Newman.

"And how did you find yourself here? Never mind, I take that back. I've already seen that you've got guts. Yet, in these times, bravery is more dangerous than cowardice."

"Oh, I think that's always been the case."

"That may be," he replied, "which is why the heroes are dead and the cowards become generals."

His comment surprised me, but not entirely. I suspected that quite a number of Germans did not agree with what was happening in Poland. I looked around his office and spied a marble chess set on a lovely carved wooden table.

"Do you like chess?" he asked.

I nodded. He brought the set over and then his chair. He set the white pieces on my side and motioned for me to play first.

"Why did you choose the black?" I asked.

"Does that need explaining?"

We both smiled at that. I moved my knight, and the captain studied the board thoughtfully.

"It's incredible that we're still playing this game after some fifteen hundred years. I think it was the Hindus or the Persians that came up with it," I said, glancing up from the board.

"The Persians invented it."

"No, the Indians from India."

"It's a cruel game. One side must win with the king in checkmate."

I nodded. "There are winners and losers."

"Yet in life," he said, "sometimes everyone loses. At least in chess someone wins."

I was surprised at the exhaustion I saw in his face, as if the war had sped up the aging process. "What did you do before the war?" I asked.

The captain thought for a while, as if the year before were many decades back to when he was a mere mortal. "I think I've always been a soldier. It's a family tradition, stretching way back into Prussian days. I always saw uniforms at home and was raised on the values of honor, discipline, and giving your word. My father, Alois Edmund, was an infantry commander and was angry life had not let him at least become a field marshal. His father had been a general. Now I'm a captain, and I see the world breaking down little by little.

"I always admired my father, though we're very different. When I

109

was young I thought he was weak for following the profession of his ancestors. He was a marvelous horseman and would have been an excellent painter, but his Teutonic blood would not let him develop his art."

"A painter, like your leader." I could not help myself, detecting that the captain was no great fan of the führer.

He smirked. "I fight for Germany. I thought it could be great again, but not at this price."

"I don't follow you, Captain."

"Have you heard of the city of Częstochowa?"

I did not answer. We had all heard about the indiscriminate killing.

"At that time I was in the Forty-Sixth Infantry Division. We had captured the city and had taken a few prisoners. A few Polish partisans offered a petty attack from nearby house windows, and the German soldiers responded by firing their guns and killing some two hundred people within minutes. They were on drugs, not in their right minds. Our troops have gone through the war thus far doped up on amphetamines. That's the true source of the courage and strength of the glorious German Army."

"The attack sounds like a coincidence. Drugs and alcohol are poor counselors."

"No, things didn't stop after that first massacre. Several thousand people were later rounded up in Magnacki Square near the cathedral and ordered to lie facedown. My superior ordered the men and women to be separated. Any man holding a knife—even a razor blade—was shot on the spot. The rest were sent to the church, but with no warning the soldiers opened fire on them. Hundreds were killed, and many were seriously wounded. I asked our lieutenant colonel the reason behind this attack, and he explained that this was not a normal war. This was annihilation because we needed space, and there were too many Jews and Poles."

The captain's face creased with his horror over the events. He went on. "I'm not a religious man, but, my God, I'm sick at everything that's going on. This isn't war; it's massacre."

"All wars are but massacres, Captain; don't be deceived."

We kept at the chess match until he had me in checkmate. "Well, that's the game," I said.

"No, it's not over." He stood and scribbled something down, then asked his secretary to type it. After signing, he handed it to me.

"What is this, Captain?"

"Orders to release you."

"Thank you. I did not expect this."

"It may not be a favor. Sometimes living is the worst condemnation. Tomorrow both you and your cellmate were to be shot."

"And can he be saved as well?"

"No, that's impossible. The Czech scammed the governor-general himself."

"Do you believe in the power of dreams?"

"Freud is a Jew, so all his books are banned," he said sarcastically.

"Well, last night I dreamed that, like the high priest Joshua, from the days when the Jews were returning from captivity in Babylon, I was being accused by Satan before God, but God defended me."

"A man of science like yourself believes in such superstition?"

I looked at him with compassion. His soul was clouding over. How long until the darkness would have it fully?

"Sometimes a few pawns are the price of saving the king," I said.

"Then your God is worse than my führer."

I was not one to defend God, but his comment stuck with me. I held his eyes and put my whole heart into the simple words: "Thank you."

A soldier led me out to the street where he just let me go. It was not yet noon. I was rather dazed. I thought about Joseph, son of Jacob, when he was set free from jail while the baker had been executed by Pharaoh's men. Why did life follow such an arbitrary course?

I made my way on foot to the gates of the ghetto and walked down the busy streets to the orphanage. The first one to spy me was Henryk, who started hollering with joy, and they all ran and nearly bowled me over in greeting. Amid the hugs and smiles, I thought again of the captain's words: *Sometimes living is the worst condemnation.* I did not want to die, at least not like that, but there were moments when I thought death would be a sweet gift.

CHAPTER 14

LITTLE ISRAEL

Many times I have come upon children lying dead on the sidewalks on my way back to the orphanage after exhausting visits to beg the ghetto's wealthy-yet-fearful inhabitants for donations. Even here in the ghetto the differences between social classes are scandalously real.

One morning when I set out, a boy was begging in his usual spot. I had watched him grow thinner and less attentive, his glazed eyes staring out at either nothing or at eternity. His hand was always stretched out mechanically, and his hat was shoved far down over his eyes. He was usually drenched from the snow that had been falling mercilessly for two straight months. I would give him a coin or two, though it was not enough to buy food. Since Gentile shopkeepers and entrepreneurial peasant farmers who did business with Jewish misery were no longer allowed in the ghetto, food prices were higher than ever. The soles of the beggar boy's shoes were worn out, and his shins were so thin that they looked like bones wrapped in brown leather, the brown that skin becomes when the body's organism wears out through starvation. Sometimes I gave him a bit of bread, but I knew I should have taken him home with me.

That day was particularly bad. As the weeks went by, little Israel was turning into an inferno. Our ancestral customs required us to take care of our own, but people were turning their backs on their own family members. Desperate to get enough for themselves, parents were abandoning their children; family members cast out the elderly they could no longer maintain and who were merely a drag on the rest of them. Mothers were willing to walk away from their husbands and children for the promise of food; others sold their bodies in exchange for a handful of corn, a bit of black bread, or a pad of butter. The worsening situation was very difficult on our spirits.

I felt the weight of the world on my shoulders. I felt guilty for having abandoned all the sick children when I stopped practicing medicine; I felt guilty for having ignored my earlier passion to go to China and help the children there; I felt guilty for wasting the chance to do something meaningful with my life. All of the pain around me made me feel helpless. My joy was gone, and almost all my hope as well.

The first visit that day had worn me out. My faithful sidekick, Henryk, had come with me. I could see fine, but my legs often betrayed me. Malnutrition was stealing the little muscle mass I had left. At sixty-something I looked like a decrepit old man, a skeleton about to die.

Our first visit had been to see the rich old bat for whom Agnieszka had played the piano the year before at the woman's mansion. She lived just two streets down from the orphanage. Despite the difficulty of finding livable conditions in the ghetto, Mrs. Goldstein had a lovely two-thousand-square-foot apartment with pleasing views. She still had her housekeeper and some of her furniture. By that time, what was normal in the ghetto was for a family of five or six people to be crammed into one small room; meanwhile this spinster lived at her leisure. She was waiting in luxury to die, thus proving that money could make life better even in hell.

We rang the doorbell and went up the elevator to the top floor. The housekeeper opened the door and led us to a parlor where she set out coffee and pastries. We looked at the offerings with feverish desire but left everything untouched until Mrs. Goldstein appeared. Once the coffee was poured, we took our time savoring each sip and bite.

Seeing the assiduous attention we paid the food and drink, Mrs. Goldstein said, "Yesterday we got a box of Danish pastries and a packet of Colombian coffee."

"Ah, I had almost forgotten the taste of butter," I said, delighting in the cookies that nearly melted in my mouth.

Beside me, Henryk was ecstatic. After the coffee, he drank a full glass of real milk, which was a coveted delicacy in the ghetto. Then he sat still, watching Mrs. Goldstein with curiosity.

"So," she began, "this is the son of the woman who brightened my day by playing my beloved piano. I couldn't bring it with me. The Germans wouldn't budge on that."

"Yes, ma'am. Henryk is my trusty sidekick and goes with me most places."

"I haven't left the house since they forced me to live in this pigsty. I only got a slightly roomier place thanks to the German ambassador. I've still got a few contacts in my country."

"I wonder if you could use any of those contacts to help us," I mused, sipping on the delicious coffee.

"They advised me to get out. They were ready to stuff me onto a ship for Sweden or a train to Switzerland, but where am I going to go at my age? I'd rather death find me near my kin. At least the Jewish cemetery is inside the ghetto. You, sir, should get out. You're still young enough."

I chuckled, wiped my mouth with the cloth napkin, and looked at the flowerpots on her terrace.

"This is all that I have left of the garden I loved so much. Can you believe this?"

"I've got a few pots on my windowsill. Now that we can't even leave the ghetto, I want more than ever to walk through our parks and the forests surrounding Warsaw."

Mrs. Goldstein kept watching Henryk, who was now onto another cookie.

"Eat whatever you want, but don't eat too much. You can make yourself sick," she said with a kindness rare to behold in her.

"We need more food," I said. "The winter is harsh already, and it's only December."

"I know. I can see the snow through the window. Do you think I don't care what's going on outside? I think about it often. I'm not a selfish old rich lady, but there's nothing I can do to change things."

I didn't want to argue. At least three families could have comfortably moved into her apartment without encroaching too much on her privacy.

"It pains me to be so blunt, but we need money," I said.

"I don't have much left! And don't think you're the only one asking me. There are other orphanages in the ghetto, not to mention the hospital, the soup kitchens . . ."

"Yes, I know, and we're grateful for all that you do."

Mrs. Goldstein closed her eyes. She was more sensitive and expressive today than I had ever seen her.

"I don't recognize my own people anymore. All this cruelty—it's simply not necessary. You already know how I feel about Jews and Poles; I think they need a firm hand. But this is terrible."

She called for her housekeeper to bring a small blue cashbox. She opened it with a tiny key that hung around her neck and handed me a large wad of bills. "Will you pray for my soul when I die?"

Her question caught me off guard. "But of course," I said.

"None of my family is left to pray a Kaddish for me, and I don't want my soul to wander eternally without rest."

So, at heart, the old bat was as Jewish as the rest of us whose grandparents and parents had renounced their faith to integrate into society. In her heart of hearts, she still belonged to Israel.

As we stood, I sensed that this would be the last time we would see each other. She took my hand and said, "When I die, I'll leave something for your children. Get them out of here. Hell is just beginning. I've got several friends in the SS. They don't know what to do with us, but they'll let us die of illness, hunger, and cold, that much I can assure you."

"What God wills," I said, kissing her hand.

"Boy, take a handful of cookies for your friends," she told Henryk.

Back on the street, we had warm, full bellies and the sweet taste of cookies still in our mouths. We walked toward our second stop, an older couple who lived nearby. Anyone who still owned anything lived in the southern area, the Small Ghetto. I did not venture much into the larger area of the ghetto unless dealing with paperwork demanded it.

This wealthy couple owned several nightclubs and cafés in the ghetto. Thanks to the corruptibility of the Ukrainian guards and Jewish police, they managed to source alcohol and other substances despite the restrictions.

They lived in an apartment above one of these locales. They must have been around seventy years old, and before the war they had managed several upscale cafés in Warsaw. The woman opened the door to us. She was still attractive, though her skin was less vibrant and her large green eyes less bright than I recalled. She had a round face with high cheekbones and was thin rather than gaunt. The rumor was that her husband had married her from out of a brothel, but in reality she had been a leading ballerina at the Polish National Opera.

"Do come in, Dr. Korczak, and your young friend." She led us to a parlor where her husband was counting bundles of cash. The thin, closely shaven man stood to greet us. He was balding except for one red patch and wore round glasses.

"What a nice surprise," he said kindly.

The house was unusually warm, and we actually had to remove our coats and hats to get comfortable. That was not something Henryk and I were accustomed to anymore.

Once we were settled, I did not beat around the bush. "I don't like to be a mooch, but you know how things are." I was weary of buttering donors up.

"You bet I do. This damned Waldemar Schön wants to starve us to death."

I knew he was talking about the Nazi official most directly in charge of running the ghetto. "Why would something like this occur to him?" I mused. "Cheap Jewish manual labor is helping him, not to mention making all of them rich. They are forever needing more soldiers, and German manual labor is running short."

"Nazis don't think practically when it comes to Jews," he grumbled. "After taking our money and stealing our possessions, all they want with us is death. At first they thought about shipping us off to Madagascar, and then they thought up the solution of ghettos. What's next?"

I shrugged. I had more urgent matters to tend to than our eventual future. The number of children in our care was now over two hundred.

The man sniffed and continued. "Irena was here yesterday. Do you know her?"

"The Polish social worker, yes, of course. She does all she can for us. She's gotten us several typhus vaccines, and thanks to her none of us in the orphanage has gotten sick yet."

"She's doing wonderful work. I only wish more Varsovians were like her."

"Many are indeed helping us. Children from inside the ghetto are slipping out through the bars in the wall to get food that people offer us."

"That's true enough, but I've also seen just as many, if not more, taking advantage of our misfortune."

His words surprised me. From all appearances, he did not seem to be facing much misfortune. He had to be the richest businessman in the ghetto.

"I'm not going to give you any money." The man's brusqueness left me speechless. He went on, "You'll just lose it paying the high prices on the black market. I'd rather give you twenty sacks of potatoes, two sacks of flour, eight gallons of oil, butter, and a bit of sugar and honey. How would that do?"

I was even more speechless but managed to splutter out, "Wonderful!" That amount of food was worth far more than money.

"I'll send it tomorrow with my men." In a fit of joy I hugged the man, who stiffened in surprise.

The day could not have gotten better. Henryk and I were euphoric on our way back to the orphanage. But then we saw something that froze our blood. Two women were begging on a street corner. I did not recognize them at first. They were so gaunt and dirty that they were hardly a shadow of their former selves. But then I really saw them: it was the older mother and daughter pair that I had run into on two unfortunate occasions, first with the injured soldier on their doorstep and second with the Jewish boy who had stolen food from the market.

I went and stood before them. They returned my stare, still retaining their haughtiness.

"So you're Jewish?" I asked, incredulous.

"No, we aren't," the daughter said, as argumentative as I had previously experienced.

"Then why are you here?"

"They say my paternal grandparents were Jews, so that's why they've locked us up in here with the rest of you."

Her sneer left me aghast. How could she keep up this charade in her present condition? I felt sorry for them. I elbowed Henryk. "Could you give her the cookies?"

His shoulders sagged, but he pulled out the bag and handed them over. The two women tore into them with disgusting ferocity. Their bony faces made their eyes stand out in a deranged way. They did not say thank you.

As Henryk and I walked back, I mused on life's ironies. Those women were terrified of being recognized as Jews and had lived their whole lives as Gentiles. They had become viciously anti-Semitic and despised their own blood.

When we reached our street, I saw the bony beggar boy lying down. He looked to be asleep, but his rigidity told another story. I went up to him and touched his freezing hand. His fingers were stiff.

"Can you hear me?" I asked, but there was no answer.

Oh, the impotence of holding a dead child. I embraced him and wept, rocking him like a baby while people passed by without so much as a glance. Henryk was watching me with a puzzled look, unsure why I was reacting so strongly. I recited the Kaddish right there in the midst of the indifferent foot traffic. The Nazis were beating us. They were taking away the only noble, beautiful thing each of us has: our compassion and mercy. When anything goes, nothing is worth it anymore.

CHAPTER 15

BLUE-AND-WHITE ARMBAND

The art of wearing a blue armband was about the same as wearing a fancy outfit. Some wore it carelessly or with indifference; others, with pride, like it was a seal that suddenly restored their lost identity; and most wore it with shame and humiliation, even though it was practically meaningless inside the ghetto since everyone wore it. What few understood was that here, in the ghetto, we were in an endless race to survive. We wore the emblem like medalists striving to reach the finish line first, though for us the goal was to reach the finish last. Life never stops being a desperate race to death. And what for most is the end is for others the beginning of a new reality.

If I had asked most of the people walking feverishly around the ghetto why they did not commit suicide, they would have explained that what kept them tied to life was not much, but it was enough: love for a son or daughter, an elderly person who needed them, hoping to see their beloved again, some gift or other that mysteriously kept at bay the worst of the hopelessness. That is why we heard so much music in the ghetto. It was like an unending concert, like the *Titanic*'s orchestra that made the last few seconds more pleasant for the shipwrecked wretches who knew there was no escaping their fate.

"Teacher, are you all right?" Henryk asked. That child could read me at a glance.

"No, I'm not," I admitted, leaning against my desk. My room was much smaller here than on Krochmalna Street where Dom Sierot originally was. I had only kept two or three objects from my youth, and they were all I had to help me not forget that there had been another life. I felt like a stranger inside my own body and could hardly recognize myself. The death of that frozen child in the street had been the thing to weaken my resolve. I was convinced that things would continue to get worse and worse.

"I've been to war. I've seen suffering, pain, and sickness. These tired old eyes have seen a mother begging bread for her dying son; I've heard the desperate cries of a father who had no medicine to give his children; I've seen the grief on the face of a woman who knew her husband was gone but refused to leave the body and clung to him like a lifeboat. But what's going on here is different. We're not at war, at least not a conventional war. The Germans simply want to erase us from the map. I can assure you they're not the first to try it, but I'm afraid they just might succeed."

"Don't talk like that, Teacher. You always smile and tell us not to give up hope."

"Do you want to hear a sad story?" I asked.

"How about a happy one instead?" Henryk tried.

"Not here, at least not this one."

"All right." He sighed. "You always tell good stories."

"When I fought in the war, they sent me to Kiev and put me in charge of four centers for lost or displaced children. The poor devils were divided into several different cabins and homes outside the city. That winter was really something else."

"Worse than winter in Poland?"

"Much worse, I promise. I worked seventeen hours a day. Twice a day I made the rounds in each of the four orphanages. I walked in the snow, sinking in up to my knees and shaking nonstop with the cold. I put eyedrops into eyes that were oozing pus; I put iodine on mangy feet. I tried to console them as best I could and cure their wounds. I was hungry and exhausted all day long. We were so cold we stole wood from a nearby forest, and the ranger would shoot at us with his pellet gun.

"One day, when I couldn't stand it anymore, I bought a big, round loaf of bread. I sniffed it a long time, then broke it up into tiny pieces and devoured it all. While I was enjoying it, I couldn't stop feeling terrible. There were hungry children on the other side of the wall. If I had shared it, each one would have gotten hardly a bite. I justified it by thinking that if I, who was taking care of them, didn't have any strength, there would be nobody else to take care of them. But that wasn't true. I was just being selfish."

"Don't feel bad," Henryk said. "That's normal; you were really hungry."

"Something like that happened here the other day. Before I got back to the Small Ghetto, I saw a stand selling sodas. An incontrollable craving for a soda came over me, so I went and bought one. Immediately a gaunt, starving child came up to me and asked for a drink. I looked at him and then at the soda and finally handed him the whole bottle. I walked away but was unhappy with myself. I hadn't felt compassion for the child, just a mixture of fear and repulsion. Doesn't that seem strange?"

"I don't totally understand," Henryk said.

"Poor child, of course not. What happened to me was that I was being tormented by guilt. Guilt is not a good thing. It accuses us, condemns us, and delivers a very harsh sentence. My teacher Wacław Nałkowski always said that 'We mustn't lightly sacrifice the lives of individuals to achieve social goals; the individual who thinks and feels is too expensive a material.'"

Henryk's eyes opened larger in his effort to follow me.

"What I want to tell you is that you have every right to have a good time and be happy. You have the right to a warm bed and tasty food, to take a bath and wear clean pajamas, to think about happy things and have good dreams at night. Don't let them make you live with the bare minimum for yourself and for others as if to prove Jesus's point that 'The poor you will always have with you.'"

We both started when Stefa knocked on the door. We were so engrossed in my musings that we had not heard her approach.

"Maryna Falska is here," she said.

That brought me up short. We had not seen each other since 1936 when she gave in to anti-Semitic pressure and asked me to step down from directing her Aryan orphanage.

"What does she want?" I asked.

"I don't know, but I told her you would see her. You can't stay mad at her forever, much less in our present circumstances."

After a heavy sigh, I asked Stefa to show Maryna in just as Henryk slipped out. Maryna had been a very close friend, one of those you hate all the more for how close they were. She stood looking at me, surely surprised to see me so decrepit, though I have always managed to underwhelm people with my appearance.

"My dear Janusz," she said, coming up to hug me. But I stood quickly and held out my hand. "Oh, so you're still angry with me?" she asked, shaking it calmly.

"You betrayed me as very few have, because I can count on one hand the number of people I actually count on."

Her face clouded over. She still carried herself with distinction, her personality filling the room and giving off a light that was hard to resist. There was hardly anyone else like Maryna. "I made a bad mistake, and I ask your forgiveness a thousand times over. But this isn't the time for reproach. Life is more important than misunderstandings and past wrongdoings."

"Maryna, you rejected me for being Jewish, and at a time when I hardly identified at all as a Hebrew, but you were better than that."

Her eyes were brimming with tears, and my pride began to falter. I had imagined this scene so many times over the past few years. But I changed the course of how I had envisioned it. "Never mind all that. I'm so glad to see you again, even though it's here and in these conditions."

"Irena got me permission to make a visit. That woman is working so hard for the children; all the social workers are."

I nodded in agreement. "If we had more like her, the ghetto wouldn't be the hellhole it's become. There's not enough food or medicine, orphans are starving to death in the streets, and the Judenrat can't get more supplies. And Poles who try to sell us food on the black market face stiff fines."

"We're all aware of the situation. Your friends on the other side are doing all we can. We haven't forgotten you or Stefania. You two are valuable people, and when this terrible war is over and the Nazis lose, we will need you to help rebuild the country."

"Do you really think that will happen? The Nazis control all of Europe."

"The British have been bombing Germany for weeks. The Germans are no longer untouchable. It won't be long before the United States and the Soviet Union get involved, and then the Nazis will fold."

I shook my head. "I don't know much about geopolitics, but I can promise you it won't be easy to defeat the Germans. Hitler has riled up his fanatics to the point that they'll do any and everything for the Third Reich. One more winter in the ghetto and they'll be carting us away in pinewood boxes."

"You're as bleak as ever. That's not going to happen. You and Stefa are coming with me, right now. I've got false papers for you and a place for you to hide out. And, if things get worse, we can smuggle you to Sweden."

I took a step back, shocked at her proposal. For a moment my head spun at the possibility. But she was crazy to think I would leave the children. "But, Maryna, I can give you two hundred reasons why I've got to stay. Would you abandon the children of your orphanage to escape? They're the reason we exist."

Her head dropped, recognizing the weakness of her plan before my determination. "But you can't sacrifice yourself for nothing."

"For nothing?" I asked. "Two hundred souls, two hundred boys and girls whose only sin is to be Jewish—nothing?"

Suddenly she embraced me. It took me off guard, but my arms reacted, and I held her tightly. I could feel her body shaking with sobs, and I, too, cried.

"I don't want you to die, Janusz, not like this."

"We're all going to die. Whatever time the good Lord gives me on this earth, I'll live out like the rest of my existence, savoring it to the last drop, enjoying the children and Stefa. But there is one thing you can do for me."

She pulled back, her eyes bright and her face starting to regain its composure. "Anything, Janusz."

"I know there are shortages outside the ghetto, too, but I need you to get us food and medicine, and for you to get a few of our children out of here, some of the youngest ones who won't survive much longer without better care. Talk to Irena; she'll help you figure out how."

"Of course, we'll do the possible and the impossible. But please save yourself too. Poland needs you. Men like you are irreplaceable."

"If I saved myself, I wouldn't be Janusz Korczak. The Nazis can steal our freedom, health, dignity, and even our future, but I have to be the watchman for the children's happiness. They'll be happy 'til the last breath. There's something that can't be replaced by bread, a glass of milk, a present, or even the prettiest clothes: love. That's what we'll keep giving them, and we'll teach them to smile in the midst of the horror and not let their joy be taken away."

Maryna hugged me again. We did not know if we would see each other again, but we did not bid farewell. Friends are never truly separated. They are connected forever by the bonds of the past, the time that cannot be stolen from them and that will return every time suffering or loneliness evokes it.

PART II
LIVING FOR AN IDEA

CHAPTER 16

THE SMALL GHETTO

That morning I went to the window and looked out at the wall and the guards, most of whom were Ukrainian or Lithuanian. *What made them sign up with the SS?* I wondered, knowing I would never have an answer. Then I looked at my flowerpots, where I had planted plastic flowers. Even the illusion of life growing in this frozen place of death was pleasing. The rooftops of my beloved Warsaw were covered with snow.

Christmas felt strange this year. We were all hoping it would be over quickly and maybe 1941 would bring better times. Despite the shortages of everything, the teachers had prepared what gifts we could. We had been wrapping them all week and putting them beneath a makeshift fir tree, since a real tree was impossible to come by. It was strange for Jews to celebrate Christmas, but we were also Poles, and we liked singing carols and the idea of looking out from a warm room onto snowy streets.

There were a couple thousand Christians in the ghetto. With their absurd racial laws, the Nazis had condemned people with no connection whatsoever to Jewish traditions to live and die among us simply because their parents or grandparents had been born Jewish.

The morning of Christmas Eve, I walked to All Saints Catholic Church. It was one of three churches inside the ghetto walls. Father Marceli Godlewski had been the parish priest there since 1915, had founded a Christian union, and had been working for Warsaw's poor for the past twenty-five years. He had also supported National Democracy and, before the creation of the ghetto, had been outspokenly anti-Semitic.

The church was one of the prettiest buildings in the ghetto. Two towers stood atop semidetached rectangular columns in the stone facade. Three archways, two smaller flanking a larger central one, indicated the main sections of the chapel. The Virgin and representative images of all the saints figured prominently in the classical frontispiece.

At the chapel entrance, half a dozen beggars had their hands outstretched to the believers who came for confession or mass. I went inside and immediately felt the reassuring quiet that large Catholic churches always exude. The world seemed to stay put at the threshold. It was a cold and gray day, but the light of candles overcame the darkness inside the building.

I made my way to the sacristy, a place I was familiar with. Father Godlewski and I had been together on radio programs about poverty and had had more than one discussion about anti-Semitism.

"Dr. Korczak," I heard a voice call from the confession box. Father Godlewski stood and came up to me. He was tall and robust, with clear eyes and ruddy cheeks. At first glance he seemed stern, but people soon learned that behind the imposing exterior was a heart that beat for others.

"Father, thank you for being willing to see me so quickly. I know you're swamped with preparations for Christmas."

"Well, Christmas is all about hope and salvation."

I nodded. "Both Jews and Christians are longing for the Messiah."

"Let's go to my office," he said.

The chapel was empty at that hour of the morning. I supposed the ghetto's Catholics were preparing for their vigil later that night and the special foods for the following day.

Father Godlewski's office was as austere as he was, with just a crucifix and a few books, mostly liturgical and religious in nature. The priest put away the holy oils he had been carrying and sat into his worn leather chair.

"I've always secretly admired you," I said. He smirked, thinking I was mocking him. "No, I'm serious. You fought for independence and defended the city's workers tooth and nail. You started the Association of Christian Workers, which allowed thousands or even tens of thousands of workers to get a pension, get legal help, and access childcare for their children. I think Jesus would be very proud of you."

He bowed his head, then spoke. "I know that look. I've seen it many times, Doctor. You're still reproaching me for my anti-Semitic ideas. You're not the first to be surprised that I stayed in the ghetto once the walls were built. There are some two thousand Christian souls here who need a pastor, but there are also some three hundred thousand Jewish souls that are just as needy as the Christians."

"I still remember your article in *Pracownica Polska* where you urged Polish women to only make purchases in stores run by Poles, not by Jews. But aren't we also Polish? Aren't we as human as you? Do Jews not suffer as much as Christians?"

He lowered his head again. Then he propped his chin on his hands and said with a disarming gentleness, "The Polish people have always been hassled by various enemies. Everyone wants a piece of this land. The Austrians, the Czechs, the Russians, and the Germans have always wanted our fertile lands and the magical forests of our ancestors. We've been destroyed, massacred, and vilified. The Germans think we're of simple and weak character; the Austrians write us off as indolent and the Czechs as superstitious and overly pious; and the Russians—they're the worst—have always seen us as mere slaves. Poland was being reborn, and we needed to recover our dignity and emphasize what brought us together."

"But we are Poles too."

"I know—I know that now. Did you know that before the war I was about to retire? I'd spent my whole life fighting for the good of others, and I'd built myself a house in Anin. I'd be there reading and planting my garden now, contemplating God's beautiful creation and letting my weary bones rest. Instead, with the help of Father Czarnecki and the bishop's support, we feed about one hundred people a day in the soup kitchen, and just as many sleep here at night. We don't turn anyone away, Jew or Christian, baptized or not. Finally, here in my late seventies, I understand the true worth of human life."

His words moved me. He was not apologizing but rather testifying to the power of love over hatred and rage. That priest had become a minister of souls for whom surnames, customs, and creeds had ceased to matter.

"I want to ask you for something."

His weary, serious face was open to me, and his eyes held the brightness of an indomitable spirit. "Anything. Your people are the family of my Lord, Jesus the Jew."

"We need to get some of the children out of here and to somewhere safe."

"But how?"

"Convert them into official Catholics, then take them far away from here. Save them, Father."

He reached for my hand and grabbed it tightly as tears streamed down his face. "Forgive me for having sown hatred and not love among my people. I'll never be able to undo what I did, but if I save one life, even one, it will have been worth the attempt. I cannot go before the judgment seat of Christ without trying to save some of the least of these."

Hand in hand, brotherhood was forged in the tears we shed. We were two Poles, two men, two human beings both weak and impotent, scared and decrepit, and holding on to the most beautiful gift God had given us: the capacity to love so much that our hearts ached with the overabundance of compassion.

"I'll get as many out as I can. I'll sign birth certificates and ask the Franciscan Sisters of the Family of Mary to care for them in my house in Anin. They'll take better care of the little ones than this old man can."

"Thank you, Father, thank you," I said, squeezing his hand again.

When he lifted his head, his eyes were two bright chips of sky shining with hope. Each single human being saved was the entire human race saved.

CHAPTER 17

LORDS OF THE GHETTO

What is a human being? I wondered that Christmas Day. The simplest and bitterest answer, given our current context, was that humans were executioners. "Man is wolf to man," as the astute Hobbes popularized in *De Cive*. He was not making a negative statement, though, but rather describing the savage beast we all have inside us—the capacity to survive by pure instinct, just as those who lost human sensitivity adapted well to a place like the ghetto. Conversely, this logic dictates that the well-educated, the highly skilled, the sensitive, and the humanized are overcome and swept away to an early death by the masses.

Hobbes believed that peace and social unity could actually be achieved. What would he have thought if he had lived to see the Warsaw ghetto? Every social contract had been ripped up and stomped on, and there was no discernable human or divine law at work in the place. What would Hobbes have had to say about this?

These were strange early morning thoughts when everyone else remained asleep. In a few hours we would pass out the modest gifts we had managed to put together. Everything was strange in the ghetto, new and unsettling.

I closed my eyes again and tried to get back a few more moments of calm, though old age does not allow true serenity. There are always thoughts, memories, and regrets barging in, making you bemoan all that you never achieved and now recognize that you never will.

After our party, or rather, the very modest celebratory change in routine, I was scheduled to go with a former pupil to meet the "lords of the ghetto." That is how he described them. There are always masters and lords, even in hell. Perhaps they would help us get through the winter. Food was always running short, and the children were weak. I put my diary down. Later I would need to ask Henryk to make a clean copy. He and Agnieszka were the only ones who could make out my sick old doctor's hen scratch.

I stood and looked out the window. The guard was close enough that I could wave, but I dared not. I just studied him for a while and wondered at his background, what his parents were like, if he had a wife and children, and what he thought when he saw the children begging in the street and people keeling over from hunger and cold with no one to help them. I figured that, like all of us, he had ways of justifying what he was doing. His kids were also probably hungry. After all, it was war, and the Nazis were the new masters. If you could take advantage of the situation and survive, it was better to obey the ones that fed you. The war would end, and this guard would go on with his life. This job would become a story to tell about long ago, like counting cattle in a barn or slitting their throats later at the butcher.

I got dressed slowly. It was increasingly challenging for me to get my pants on, button my shirt, and get the knots of my tie straight. These efforts tired me out, and I had to pause for deep breaths before going on with the laborious tasks of normal life.

When I went by the dormitories, everyone was still asleep. Down in the living room, I found Stefa arranging the last few gifts under our makeshift tree.

"Good morning, Janusz. How did you sleep?"

"Poorly, but I'm not complaining. I've got a bed, a blanket, a room of my own—much more than most!"

"Well, Merry Christmas!" Stefa said to drive the gloomy thoughts away. Her approach worked. She got me remembering back to Christmases past, when my parents and grandparents were still alive and the world was still a beautiful, friendly place. I thought about the excitement of Christmas Eve, snuggling down into soft blankets and thinking about the presents the next day would bring. The excitement of childhood must be the secret to a long and happy life. Those memories were enough to make me forget my present aches and worries.

A few minutes later, the room was full of Dom Sierot's teachers and caretakers. Their bony faces and jaundiced skin showed the wear of the past few months. I seized the moment to encourage them.

"We sleep and dream of better days but wake to find ourselves here. Yet here, where we serve, we are doing all we can to make better days for the children. We're in this world to serve one another, to give our very last breaths for our neighbors. True happiness is not found in the savage struggle for power and ambition. The eyes are never satisfied with seeing nor the ears with hearing, but every time we bring a smile to a child's face, our lives have been worth it. In a few minutes they'll come downstairs, weary from hunger and misfortune, from being locked up and separated from their parents, from the stench of death all around that anesthetizes our souls. We labor to give them back their hope; but we cannot give what we do not possess. Therefore, be full of hope this morning. May your joy overflow because you do what you do out of love and service for the weakest ones. And when negative thoughts come to steal your peace and joy, don't let them make a nest in your minds. We can't avoid those kinds of thoughts, but we can keep them from controlling us."

Everyone started clapping, and I saw optimism ripple like a wave across the living room, lighting up our little world again.

We broke up to go tend to the children, helping them wash and dress. These little routines saved us from indolence and provided an outlet of logic in the vast abnormality of our lives.

An hour later, after a slightly special breakfast because I had managed to find enough milk and chocolate powder for everyone, we sat around the great tree.

"Please, Dr. Korczak, tell us a story," one of the youngest children asked. Then everyone chimed in.

"Very well, but I thought you would want your presents first."

"Story! Story!" all the children chanted.

The tutors settled down into their spots, and I began one of my oldest tales. "I don't know if you've heard the one about Artaban, the fourth wise man."

"I thought there were only three," Pawel interrupted.

"Well, no, it turns out there were four. Besides Melchior, Gaspar, and Balthasar, a fourth magi came up from the east to bring his presents to the Messiah who had been born in Bethlehem. Artaban brought no gold, incense, or myrrh. What he brought were expensive, precious stones, like rubies, diamonds, and jade. He had agreed to meet up with the other three magi at a certain spot where they would all head for Israel. On his way, this fourth wise man came upon a poor, sick, tired old man who needed help, and Artaban decided to see what he could do.

"After spending a few days with the old man, Artaban got back on the road, though he knew his friends would've already gone ahead. By the time he got to Jerusalem, Jesus and his parents had already fled to Egypt to escape the slaughter of the innocents that King Herod had decreed. When Artaban saw what the Romans were doing to the children, he tried to stop them, so they arrested him and locked him up in a dungeon for thirty-three years. He grew really old during that time. When he got out, he heard the rumor that they were going to kill Jesus in Jerusalem. So Artaban went to Jerusalem with the only jewel he had left, a ruby. Right then he came across a woman in the street who was about to get sold as a slave to pay off one of her father's debts. Artaban gave her the ruby so she could buy her freedom and then went to Golgotha, where Jesus was being crucified between two ruffians.

"Artaban knelt down before the dying Jesus and apologized for not bringing him any of the gifts he had intended to give him as a baby. Then there was a huge earthquake, and a rock hit the old magi on the head. He fell down dying at the foot of the cross. That's when Christ raised his head and said, 'Artaban, I was hungry and you gave me something to eat, I was thirsty and you gave me something to drink, I needed clothes and you clothed me, I was sick and you looked after me, I was in prison and you set me free.' With his very last strength, Artaban asked, 'When did I do all that for you?' And Jesus answered him, 'Whatever you did for one of the least of these brothers and sisters of mine, you did for me. Now come with me to the kingdom of heaven.'"

The children, who up to that point had been in rapt silence, started cheering. Then Henryk stood and hazarded a serious question.

"Is Jesus the Messiah we were waiting for?"

His question had me in a tight spot, but I smiled and answered, "For many people, he is, but Jews believe the Messiah is still yet to come. What do you think?"

He wrinkled his nose in thought, then shrugged and said, "I don't know much about the prophecies or the laws, but Jesus's words remind me of that phrase from Leviticus, 'Love your neighbor as yourself.'"

The adults all raised our eyebrows and nodded, impressed. The children cheered again.

"Well," I said, standing back up and raising my voice above the clapping, "we'd best get to the presents that the magi have brought!"

The tutors called the children up one at a time and handed each a little packet before the boys and girls scurried back to their seats. Anticipation lit up their faces, but they dutifully waited until each child had a gift.

After all the gifts had been opened and duly delighted over, I went to the foyer and got out my coat. Agnieszka came up to ask where I was headed.

"A former pupil, Chaim, wants me to meet some of the smugglers. We don't have enough to eat, and we won't make it through the winter in these conditions. The Judenrat has too many orphanages and abandoned children to look after as it is."

"I'll go with you. The ground's frozen, and you might slip."

"I'm an old fogey, but I can still get around," I answered wryly.

"I wouldn't call you *old*, just *stately*," she said kindly.

So we set out in the cold that bore through our coats and into our bones. We both wished the snow would let up for a bit. It did not take long to get to one of the clubs that Chaim frequented. We waited at the door, as only the very wealthy were allowed in such sites, which served wine, champagne, and other delights that the rest of us mere mortals could only dream about.

"Dr. Korczak!" Chaim exclaimed from behind us, grabbing me in a big hug. After I introduced him to Agnieszka, he said, "I hope you're both doing all right. Things certainly are difficult. We're using children to sneak out and buy products on the outside, and we've got people manning the sewers that go under the walls and the buildings that are right on the border. We pay off the guards heavily to keep quiet, but even so there's not much to be gotten in the rest of Warsaw."

"It certainly will be a challenging Christmas for Poland," I said.

"I was out a few days ago. People couldn't find firewood or coal. Most of our basic products have been diverted to Germany or to the armies around here. It's better in the Soviet sector, but getting across the border is no small feat. It seems like the Nazis are preparing something against the Russians."

"Indeed?"

"Everyone's talking about it."

"Ah, well. And who did you want me to meet?"

"The most powerful man in the ghetto," he said in the lofty way he sometimes used.

"Is it a member of the Judenrat?"

"Certainly not! Those poor devils are just Nazi slaves."

Chaim started walking down a side street and knocked at an iron door. A few seconds later, a thick man with wide shoulders opened it and led us up a dark, narrow stairway into a large, brightly lit area. The comfortably furnished room stunned me and Agnieszka. Expensive furniture, nice paintings, and all kinds of utensils and things were stacked everywhere.

A man sat in a leather chair in a dimly lit corner of the room. "Dr. Korczak," he said. I tried to make out the figure but could barely see his face. "Good afternoon. I believe we met once before."

"Well, the ghetto is a small town," I answered.

"Quite so, just rather densely populated. Many won't make it through the winter. The Germans have recently reduced the permissible calorie count for each individual."

"It's beyond my understanding. I thought many here in the ghetto were working for them; we're their new slave labor."

"Oh no, Doctor. We're mere scum to the Nazis, rats to be exterminated. But they've decided to take their time and go about it slowly. Forgive me, I've not introduced myself. I'm the chief of police, Józef Andrzej Szeryński."

"So you're the famous Józef Andrzej Szeryński."

"My real name was Josef Szynkman, back in our former lives when we were all still men," he said with a sarcastic bite.

I was intrigued. "And what are we now?" I asked as I took a seat beside him, and Agnieszka sat beside me.

"Now we're just beasts, as someone like yourself knows better than anyone. It's mere survival. But being a human being is much more than that, wouldn't you agree?"

"Perhaps; who can say?"

"I like your style. You tell people what they want to hear."

I smiled. "Only when I need something from them."

He burst out laughing at that, and his men followed suit from the corners of the room. I felt like I was in a poorly made film about the Italian mafia.

"I was a policeman, a colonel with the Polish police, then an inspector. I changed my name and turned my back on my people. Ironic, isn't it? I was even in favor of persecuting the Jews. And now I've got to live with them and keep the peace."

"It's like putting the fox in charge of the hens," I said lightheartedly enough. But my stomach churned in the man's presence. He guffawed again.

"You should do stand-up at the nightclubs! You'd make quite a living. You've got the humor of an old rabbi."

"I suppose it's never too late for a career change, but you're aware that I've got an orphanage with two hundred children and a number of adults to look after."

"Mmm, you're quite well known in the ghetto, something of a celebrity. Our Chaim here was a student of yours, I believe. He speaks quite highly of you."

"Chaim was someone to watch out for back in the day, and, seeing his present company, it seems he might not be all that different now."

The commander of the Warsaw ghetto's Jewish police force stood and started pacing. "We can help your children, though I'll need two or three of them to come work for me. There are plenty of thieves trying to get food on their own, but they don't know how to negotiate. Fur coats are highly valued on the outside, and many old Jewish ladies are still holding on to theirs. I'll ask you for something very simple: convince the old dames to part with their furs, and we'll get food for them and for your orphanage."

I was ready to stand up and leave, but I held back a moment. The business disgusted me, but, after all, it was just about some meaningless coats. I could help several families as well as the children under my care. What I could not swallow was putting some of my students in imminent danger as Szeryński's gophers.

"I can get you the coats, but I can't allow my children to work for you. They would be completely lost on the outside."

He frowned darkly but eventually held out his hand.

"Deal."

"Deal," I answered, shaking his hand.

Leaving the building, I felt like I had sold my soul to the devil. Chaim walked us to the end of the street. When we were alone, Agnieszka grabbed my arm to steady me. "Don't feel bad, Doctor."

"Don't call me 'Doctor,' Agnieszka!"

"I'm sorry, sorry. Your mission is to keep these children safe."

"Even if it means making deals with that sort?" I spat out.

"We're not heroes. You told me yourself, Janusz. We're just simple human beings trying to survive. He's got food, and you've got the means."

"Do you know what he does to vagabond children or the ones he catches selling things? He beats them to death. The man is a beast. I've just made a deal with a monster."

My friend placed her hand gently on my face before we resumed our walk back to the sad building of what was now Dom Sierot. The time for great ideals had ended. Soon enough we would all become monsters, our own executioners, and we would not deserve to survive this infernal world that was just a caricature of the one we'd known a mere year and a half ago. I looked up at the patch of sky between the buildings. Snowflakes were streaming down on us. How I wanted to be like Artaban and hand my whole life and soul over to a higher being. But the truth was that God seemed totally absent from the ghetto, despite the pleas of thousands of people day and night.

CHAPTER 18

TYPHUS

Most people lived crammed together, six or seven people to one room. To say that living conditions were bleak would be an understatement. There was little soap, and often the running water just stopped as the network of pipes deteriorated from lack of maintenance. More and more buildings had no water at all, much less hot water or heat. In the most run-down buildings, the elderly and weakest could hardly move around, and people resorted to tossing their garbage out the windows. The stench was unbearable. The conditions for typhus were ideal.

The leaders of the ghetto were very troubled. The outbreak was one more excuse for the Nazis to further restrict the flow of workers and goods in and out of the ghetto. Yet the more they isolated us, the fewer provisions we had, and the number of infections skyrocketed. We did all we could to keep Dom Sierot's children safe from illness, but it was increasingly difficult.

Typhus, a bacterial disease, spread through lice. As soon as the first wave hit, we shaved all the boys, but it was trickier with the girls. We kept their hair shorter and inspected them daily; yet in a place like where the Nazis had locked us up, it was impossible to be fully rid of lice, fleas, and ticks.

All the tutors and Zalewsky pitched in to help fumigate the building, but the wretched little pests reappeared a few days later. It seemed we could not get rid of them. We had no medicines, nor was there an effective treatment against the quickly spreading plague given the lack of hygiene, poor nutrition, and overcrowding.

That morning as the tutors carefully scoured the girls' hair with the fine-tooth combs to hunt down any new lice, Stefa gave me a message. Adam Czerniaków, the chairman of the Judenrat, wanted to see me. I put on my jacket, glanced at my poorly shaven chin, and straightened the knot of my tie. I ran into Agnieszka as I was going downstairs.

"Where are you off to, Doctor?"

"The Jewish Council summoned me. I suppose it's about the problem of the lice and typhus, as schools have always been the pests' favorite haunt."

"Shall I go with you? There's supposed to be a shipment of cheese coming today, and I was told there would be a portion for the orphanages."

I waited for Agnieszka to get her coat, and we headed for the Judenrat. As we walked, I was thankful that the beggars and the infirm calling out on the streets were not slumped over dead on the sidewalks. Every time I saw a child begging, my heart went to pieces. I could not care for them all. I had to stay strong for the children and the people helping us. Yet each day wore me down more in body and spirit.

The building where the Jewish Council met was in the Small Ghetto not far from Dom Sierot. We entered and went upstairs to Czerniaków's office but were told the meeting would be in one of the larger rooms to accommodate all the directors of schools.

We passed through the glass doors into the hall where many directors were already seated in a mismatched array of chairs. I nodded to one after another. Most of us had known one another for years. In our present circumstances, we were in an unfortunate competition for the scant resources available, and many thought that, given my renown, Czerniaków favored Dom Sierot. I knew that was not the case.

Only the front row had available seats. I would have preferred to slip by unnoticed in a back row to avoid the arousal of pathetic envy and jealousy that showed up even in a place like the ghetto. If we could not join together in a situation like this, when could we ever? We Jews had often been accused of being too individualistic, incapable of thinking about anyone other than ourselves. I figured that surviving nearly two thousand years without a country, state, or army to protect us proved otherwise.

Maria Rotblat, who directed an orphanage for girls, stood and cleared her throat.

"Members of the Judenrat and orphanage directors," she began, "I'm grateful that we have been called together in this emergency meeting. Things are getting worse by the day. In our building we have two cases of typhus. We've isolated them on our own, since the Jewish hospital is overrun. The only way to stop the epidemic is to act as soon as possible. I imagine that the German authorities aren't keen to see the plague spread across all of Warsaw, Poland, and even to Germany."

Murmurs ran throughout the crowd, and Czerniaków, with his formal, polite mannerisms, rose to speak.

"My esteemed directors, here we are again in a difficult position. The German authorities are asking for a list of those who are ill, including all those in the hospital and clinics as well as those who remain in their homes. Yet we fear that their intentions are to do away with these individuals."

The room grew restless as the chairman updated us. "About twenty thousand cases have been reported, though we have reason to think that the real numbers could be as high as eighty to one hundred thousand."

Ringelblum, a historian in charge of documenting statistics, handed the chairman a sheet of paper.

"Well," Czerniaków continued, "the exact number is one hundred and ten thousand infected. The situation is desperate. At this rate of infection, within a few weeks the entire ghetto will be sick, and I'm afraid of what drastic measures the Nazis will take." Like the rest of us, Czerniaków was growing more tired and discouraged as the weary months of ghetto survival rolled on.

Ludwik Hirszfeld, a bacteriologist, stood. We were fortunate to have such an eminent epidemiologist among us. Sometimes I wondered how the Poles and Germans could ignore the quality of human capital concentrated in the ghetto. Thousands of us had so much to offer the world, but they had eyes only for our Jewish blood, which, they felt, tarnished their cobbled streets and cities.

"The only way to change the situation is for the Germans to increase our food rations and allow us to repair the ruined pipes so that each area has running water again, which will help us get the homes of the elderly cleaned up as well as common areas in buildings. We don't have beds for the ill, or enough resources, but we can at least improve the sanitary situation. Furthermore, we must cordon off buildings with high rates of infection and get rid of the lice there. Schools are one of the focal points of concern, which is why we have called you all together here."

As soon as he was finished, my legs shot me up like a wound spring. My body had reacted quicker than my mind, and it took me a moment to gather my thoughts. All eyes were on me. "My dear colleagues, this is not an easy situation to deal with. The conditions of our overcrowding are deplorable. There's not enough food, and things are likely only going to get worse. New Jews and even Gypsies from other parts of Poland keep arriving, yet resources get more and more scarce. No matter how many orphanages we have, there are still dozens of children out begging on the streets, and many more stealing or risking their lives leaving the ghetto to bring back food. Our schools don't have enough resources, and since our students aren't yet part of the workforce, they're not allowed the same food supplies as other inhabitants receive. We need help. We're desperate. The only way to stop this is for Jews from other parts of the world to send us aid and for our esteemed chairman to increase the resources set aside for schools. Children are our future, but they're also the present. Without them, there's no hope."

There was a timid response of applause, but the brows of most directors were deeply creased. I continued, "We have to help all of our children and, if at all possible, get them out of here. The only way they're going to survive is if we create a network outside the ghetto to rescue and hide them."

A long silence ensued. I had said words that were forbidden wherever the Nazis were presumed to have spies. And spies were to be expected, given that many Jews would sell out for an extra ration of food for their family. For its part, the Judenrat was walking a fine line of staying within the bounds of what the German overlords considered "legal." The council hoped to thus outlast the war and for the Nazis to grow tired of us and perhaps send us somewhere far from Europe.

"Are you crazy?"

"Who would take care of our children?"

"Most Christians despise us."

The murmuring spread throughout the crowd. It seemed a good time to make my exit. Agnieszka followed me out the door. "Where are we going now?" she asked.

"We should go see Irena. I think she's our one chance."

That social worker was the shortest ball of fire I had ever met. If anyone would be willing to change things, it would be her.

CHAPTER 19

IRENA, THE ANGEL
OF WARSAW

Irena Sendler was like an angel for us, especially once typhus started to spread in the ghetto. She was also just a typical Polish woman. She had blond hair, soft features, and mischievous eyes in a rosy face. Of short stature, she retained a childish and innocent air about her at around thirty years of age, which helped her slip by unnoticed by most. She had been very active politically in the thirties while studying law and Polish literature. She was smart and well educated but tended to keep her opinions to herself and avoid the limelight. At the Free Polish University she studied social work with Helena Radlinksa. I had known Helena for years. Though I had given up any Marxist tendencies ages ago and did not share Helena's leftist ideas, I always appreciated her valiant work among the disenfranchised. Irena was one of her most illustrious disciples.

The first time I saw her was right at the beginning of German occupation. A group of Varsovian social workers was falsifying documents for Jewish families to secure them the social protections the new Nazi state denied them.

I knew where to find Irena in the ghetto. She was at one of the welfare centers that provided assistance to many Jewish families. Agnieszka and I went into the small room and sat among a dozen others who were waiting to be seen. We watched Irena kindly tending to one client after another.

While we waited, I leaned over and spoke softly into Agnieszka's ear. "I think the best thing is for you to take Henryk and get out of here before things get worse."

"But where would we go? The Germans have taken over half of Europe, and they'll soon have the whole world."

I took off my hat and scratched my bald head. She was right, of course, but anyplace was better than the ghetto.

"Irena can find you somewhere safe to hide at least until the war is over."

"What about the rest of the children? If all the tutors leave, how will you and Stefania manage?"

"Over the years we've found ourselves in many difficult situations. Plus, we're old. We're on our way out anyhow. Sacrificing our lives for our children is the best way I know to go."

"Dr. Korczak," Irena said, coming out of her office, "how nice of you to come see me." I stood and shook her hand.

"It's not a courtesy call," I said.

"I imagine not! Let's go to my office," she said, glancing around to make sure the waiting room was empty. Then she closed the curtains and led us to into her office where we sat around a shabby desk. "Forgive me for making you wait, but I thought it best to see you alone. The Gestapo has many eyes and ears in the ghetto. It's always wise to take precautions."

"Yes, I'm generally too lax in that regard," I admitted. I tended to trust anyone who came along and deep down did not much care what might come of it.

"We don't have that luxury anymore, I'm afraid. We're not fighting the czarist authorities or Polish bureaucracy anymore. Now we're dealing with the most sadistic murderers history has yet produced. Helena—you know, Radlinska—is in hiding in a convent, but she's helping me organize the aid to the ghetto."

That surprised me. "I knew she was a Jew, but I presumed she had managed to get to Sweden." Helena was one of the most important social workers in all of Poland.

Irena shook her head.

Agnieszka piped up, "You're wearing the Star of David?"

"I consider it an honor," Irena said. "I'm not a Jew, but many of my very good friends are."

"Irena," I began, taking off my glasses to clean them, "you know how ugly things are getting. As the war goes on, conditions are only going to get worse. I know you've helped many children and have put them in hiding at convents and with Aryan families in the countryside. I'm afraid for Dom Sierot's children."

She frowned and nodded. "It's not that simple, my dear doctor. The Germans and their Jewish guards are watching every corner. Earlier on it was easier to jump the wall at certain points or slip through the sewers, but they've found nearly all of our outlets."

"There's got to be a way."

"The only ones who know how to get in and out are the mafias who traffic certain goods on the black market. Abraham Gancwajch's Group 13 is really the only one who could do what you're after."

"I know that rat; he's not to be trusted. He'll do anything for money but wouldn't bat an eye at turning us in," I said. Just saying his name out loud made me nervous.

Irena shrugged. "My boss, Jan Dobraczyński, suspects all of us. If he finds out we're smuggling children out of the ghetto, I don't know how he'll react. It's possible that your students might be safer inside the walls. The situation outside isn't pretty. The Germans take all the food, and people are starving."

"But the typhus, the overcrowding . . ."

"I promise that we'll have a meeting soon, and I'll get back to you with an answer. We've got to be fully prepared before we take any children out."

"Do you know Father Marceli Godlewski? He could help."

"Oh, of course, of course; he's one of our collaborators." With that, Irena stood up and took her coat. "I've got to meet some people. If you want, we can keep talking on the way."

Agnieszka and I stood and followed Irena out toward the gate near the Dworska hospital, which was just outside the ghetto boundaries. It was one of those anomalies resulting from the hasty division of the city between Jews and Aryans.

The friends Irena was to meet were just finishing their shifts at the hospital and coming back to the Jewish zone. Irena was to join them for a rare outing to a nightclub to wash away the day's labor with a drink. Irena, Agnieszka, and I stood watching from just behind the police checkpoint. Out there life seemed to be continuing its normal course, heedless of what was happening inside the walls. It was odd to look out at that other world where people still had a measure of determination and control over their monotonous lives, while every day we debated the point of continued existence. Irena waved at her colleagues. At the head of the group was Dr. Ludwik Hirszfeld and Ala Gołąb-Grynberg, the head nurse. The rest of the medical personnel followed close behind.

Twarda Street, where we stood waiting for them, had undergone significant changes. Before, it was a clean and busy street, known for its impressive buildings where the bourgeois lived their happy, carefree lives. But the Germans had put their stables and a warehouse of food and wine there to mock us on the route Jews formerly took to the Great Synagogue.

But then half a dozen SS soldiers marched alongside the group of doctors and nurses, who hung their heads and attempted to carry on unnoticed. Things happened fast. Without warning, one of the soldiers slammed the butt of his gun into the chest of a young, spectacled doctor. He let out a cry and fell to the ground. The soldiers guffawed and began kicking him while the rest of the group simultaneously drew back and picked up their pace like insects trying to escape a trap.

The scene enraged me, and I took a step forward, but Agnieszka grabbed my arm. "We'd only make things worse," she hissed.

Loud commands in German broke the medics' silent hurry away from the scene. A corporal ordered all the doctors and nurses to line up. Two of them helped their fallen colleague to his feet. The colonel—an alcoholic by the looks of his yellowed teeth and reddened skin—grinned and ordered them to start jumping. Some of the older ones lost their balance and fell to the ground, where the delighted soldiers set about kicking them.

Just then Captain Neumann came walking down the street right in front of the police checkpoint where I still stood with Irena and

Agnieszka. He paid no heed to what was going on but then glanced toward us bystanders. He caught my eye and saw my consternation. At that, he stopped, turned abruptly, and barked at the colonel, "What is going on here?"

The soldiers immediately jumped to rigid attention. Only the colonel seemed unaffected. "Just having a bit of fun. Isn't that allowed? Or are you a friend of the Jews?"

"You doubt my patriotism? It's a matter of pragmatics. The Reich needs Jewish manual labor. If their doctors get sick or injured, who will treat the Jewish workers? We must use our heads, colonel."

The colonel's only response was to salute and then go off with his men.

Captain Neumann glanced at the doctors and nurses and respectfully asked them to return to the ghetto. Before moving on, he raised an eyebrow at me in farewell, as if to say, "See, we're not all a bunch of small-minded savage brutes like the SS."

Irena ran up to the group. Ala was dabbing at the superficial wounds the young doctor had sustained. Her eyes were pinched in a grimace over what had just happened. "I don't think any of us is up for the cabaret anymore," she said.

Dr. Hirszfeld shrugged. "Arek's cousin, Wiera Gran, is singing tonight, but she'll be there tomorrow as well. Dr. Korczak, it would be an honor to have you join us. How about tomorrow night? We all need to escape every now and then, don't you think?"

The thought of going to a nightclub did not appeal to me in the least. Everything I hated about the ghetto would be there: the Jewish aristocracy and the gangsters who profited from the people's misery like detested parasites.

Agnieszka answered, "It would be our pleasure to join you.

Lighthearted fun in times like these is its own act of rebellion against the Nazis."

I cocked an eyebrow at her in surprise but said nothing. She had every right to be happy and have a good time, even if it was only for a few hours.

"It looks like we'll be joining you," I told Irena.

"We'll keep talking about our projects then," she said, flashing her girlish smile.

Agnieszka took my arm, and we made our way back to the orphanage. I could not help asking her why she had accepted the invitation.

"It's simple. In the cabaret we'll find the people we need to get the children out of the ghetto," she said.

I chewed on the idea the whole walk back. We had to get the children out at any cost. There was no other option.

CHAPTER 20

A HAPPY CHILDHOOD

The older I got, the more I remembered my parents. Somewhere along the way I'd heard that when you say the name of the dead, you bring them back to life in a way. Happiness had always evaded me, but childhood was the closest I got to having it. I was a solitary, taciturn, self-absorbed boy with a head bursting with ideas and always spending my efforts on lost causes. When I heard Gypsies singing Christmas carols in exchange for coins, I lost myself wondering about the injustices of life. Helping others never actually made me *happy*; it just held the *unhappiness* at bay. Now that I had real reasons to despair in the ghetto, I sensed I had wasted a lot of time worrying about things that never happened. Perhaps that is just part of the human condition.

When I was seventeen, I tried writing a novel and titled it *The Suicide*. The protagonist hated life because he was terrified of going insane. At the core, the scared boy in my book was none other than Janusz Korczak. My father's illness, his insanity, and his death had impacted me irrevocably. At that time I had not yet learned the fine line that separates sanity from derangement.

I never felt particularly loved. I knew my parents loved me, as did my grandparents, but none of them ever expressed affection. Not being loved and not knowing you are loved are pretty much the same thing, which led me to write *How to Love a Child*. While we work ourselves silly giving children things or teaching them math, the only thing children actually need to be happy is to feel loved.

In previous times orphanages were like jails or barracks. But in my time they had become like nursing homes. The children complained about everything even though they had all that they needed. This led me to wonder where we had failed. We gave them things, but they wanted our time and, most of all, our affection.

The morning after that meeting with Irena, I went up to Leon's bed. He had been with us for four years and had taken ill. His sallow skin proved the poor state of his health. Yet the saddest part was that, behind his extreme weakness, his rage, frustration, sadness, and longing were plain as day. He was like an old man recalling the past with a halo of sadness over the years.

"Why don't you take another bite?" I encouraged him.

The boy looked at the plate of food on the bedside table and shook his head. "That's not my food," he said, frowning.

"Not yours? Then whose is it?"

"Julian's."

The day before, Julian had died. He had been sick for a long time, and he and Leon had been inseparable.

"Julian's no longer with us, Leon. He's gone on to heaven."

Leon shrugged. "Do Jewish boys go to heaven?" he asked.

"Of course," I answered.

He perked up a bit. "To the heaven where Aryan boys go?"

"Yes, well, there's only one."

"Then I don't want to go. They treat us like dirt. I don't want the same thing to happen in heaven. It's their fault that Julian's dead."

"Children aren't innocent, but none of what's going on now is their fault. The adults have done this."

"Why do they hate us so much?"

I was thoughtful and took my time answering. It was a question I often asked myself. "I think it's because they don't know us. At their core, racists and anti-Semites are poor, ignorant souls. Fear is what makes hatred, and fear comes from not knowing people."

The boy studied me through feverish eyes. I did not know how long he had left. I had seen so many of our children die that I was somewhat numb to the reality by that point. I put my hand on his forehead and muttered a prayer between clenched teeth. The possibility existed that all this suffering might have some purpose, some meaning. That was one of the reasons that had brought me to a measure of faith. I refused to believe that existence was just snuffed out and that we turned into nothing more than dust. Perhaps for people who had been happy and successful, the world made sense, but what about the millions who died shortly after birth or who had not known even a moment's happiness? And did the deplorable actions of those who had turned the world into an inferno just go unpunished? And what of those who had given themselves in body and soul to others? My family had never practiced the Jewish faith, and I cared little for organized religions and all the ceremonial rites. For me, talking with God was like breathing, a nearly unconscious act.

Suffering is the cornerstone of the conscience. Life begins in the most absolute desperation. Leaving the warmth of our mothers' wombs, we are born into a cold, threatening world. We get hungry and feel scared at the infinite space beyond the welcoming belly that fed us and kept us safe.

I was lost in such musings when I heard Stefa give a long moan. I ran as fast as my rheumatic legs would take me into an adjoining room. There my dear friend was kneeling at the bed of Amalia Wittlin, one of our nurses. She had been sick with tuberculosis for months but recently had started to improve.

"What is it?" I said, putting my arms around Stefa. She lifted her head, her eyes full of tears, and said, "Good God, when will the nightmare end? I can't take it anymore!"

"Calm down; breathe. Nothing happens without a purpose."

She pierced me with an incredulous look. "What's the purpose behind the death of a young woman who spent her life helping others, while those brown beasts parade around the city torturing us? God has forgotten us! It's been two thousand years—our people constantly persecuted. It won't stop 'til we have our own land. No one wants us, Janusz."

She was right, of course, but I had to keep morale up for the whole house. My consolation came at night with a smidge of vodka and reading poetry.

I hugged Stefa 'til she was calm. It did me good to feel the closeness of another breathing body. There is nothing worse than soul deadness. Tears welled up in my eyes, but I held them back. It was not that I was ashamed to cry; crying was natural. But I did not want others to lose heart.

"Let's go have a spot of what they pass off as coffee here," I coaxed. "It'll at least nip the hunger in the bud."

We went downstairs. The kitchen was still empty at that time of the morning, like the rest of the building. It was my favorite time of day.

The coffee pot was soon whistling, and I poured two cups. We sat, and I stared out at the street awhile. The strip of sky we could see was leaden gray.

Stefa had stopped crying and was staring dully into her coffee. "None of it makes any sense. Life, death—none of it."

"You're sure?"

"Just look around us. The Nazis have caged us in like animals. They exploit us and are waiting for us to disappear. Why keep trying?"

I took a sip before answering. The warmth of the mug felt so good in my hands within our freezing house. There was no money for coal, and even if there were, no coal was to be found in all of Warsaw or, most likely, Poland itself.

"The problem is that we believe we have the right to exist. We think life owes us something, so we strive to fit in. Freedom is scary, like childhood terrors. So we all take on the roles that society gives us. I was to be a Jew, a doctor, a Pole, a father, and a husband. I didn't meet any of those expectations, and therefore I've never fit in. But in the anomaly that is my life, I've discovered something tremendous: the feeling of existence doesn't come from inside us. It's external. We need to connect with that 'something' to discover true meaning. If we don't, we get driven away and fall into meaninglessness."

"Oh, friend. I've always felt like my life had a purpose, but these days, with the way things are . . . I often dream about Palestine. To be honest, there was only one reason I came back." Stefa took my cold, bony hand, and I started shaking. "Janusz, we've been together for a lifetime. I've never asked you for anything. I've been content to be at your side like a little bird who builds its nest in a big leafy tree. Being at your side makes me happy."

I shuddered involuntarily, not because I was unaware of how deeply

Stefa cared for me but because I did not feel worthy of her affection. I took a deep breath and said, "I never thought I'd find someone to help me escape the loneliness. You've been the light brightening up all these years. Now I regret that you came back. You've come to hell itself to save me from myself."

We stayed there awhile, holding hands and letting the minutes go by slowly until the hustle and bustle of the children filled the house and we returned to our painful reality.

CHAPTER 21

CABARET

My grandfather always said that living a whole day honestly was harder than writing a book. After writing many books, I could corroborate his statement. But I had never felt dirtier than that day in the cabaret Café Sztuka. It was not the only club inside the ghetto. Melody Palace was more glamorous, and there were a few professional theaters with performances in Yiddish and Polish. The most famous venues were on Leszno Street, not far from Dom Sierot's building.

I waited for nightfall, when the world turned into an inhospitable place. Agnieszka had put on her best dress, and I wore a suit jacket that hung loosely on me. Age consumes us until we nearly disappear. We set out arm in arm down the lonely, frozen streets toward the cabaret. Two huge bouncers at the door controlled who was allowed in, though the club was so expensive that few ghetto inhabitants could even try.

After going down a dark hallway, we found ourselves in a large, well-lit room. Round tables were arranged around a circular stage. There was a piano and a small orchestra on one side and a curtain on the other, where the different actors and singers stepped out.

Through the haze of cigarette smoke, I caught sight of Irena's hand waving at us. We went to the table where she sat with Dr. Hirszfeld, Ala and her husband, and Irena's guest, Adam.

"I'm so glad you could join us," she said.

Agnieszka smiled. "A little distraction won't harm us."

"Nearly everyone I see here is a Thirteen guard, a smuggler, or a delinquent of some stripe," I said, settling in next to Dr. Hirszfeld.

"They're the only ones who can afford a bottle of champagne or a plate of real food. We've only got enough for substitute coffee, not even enough for a beer." Hirszfeld was right. The only ones in the ghetto who had enough money to have a drink in the club were somehow tied to the mafia.

Suddenly there was music, and three actors emerged onto the stage. The master of ceremonies wore an elegant black suit against which his bright-white armband with the Star of David shone out.

"Welcome to paradise and the inferno, depending on your perspective. The best cabaret in the Warsaw ghetto, where we can forget about everything around us and look on the bright side. Better times will come!" the MC with luminously white teeth and a huge smile declared. "The ghetto ends where the smiles begin. When you come through those doors, you've got to forget everything else and learn to laugh again. The future doesn't exist, and our only weapon for survival is humor. And that is something Jews are experts at. Our humor is a mix of pain and joy. In here, the only way anyone's going to die is by laughing!"

The crowd chuckled and applauded. After an outrageous dialogue between two actors, one of whom was dressed as a Nazi, the MC introduced the beautiful Wiera Gran. She took her time climbing onto the stage and making her way to the microphone. She looked to the man who sat at the piano, then said, "My dear audience, tonight I want to sing a love song everyone knows."

The sweet melancholy of her voice mesmerized me. For those few minutes, there was nothing in the world but the music and "Lili Marleen."

For a blissful moment, we remembered the way everything was before—and we all longed for our return to normalcy.

A voice behind me broke the reverie.

"Good evening, Doctor. I didn't expect to see you here tonight." Immediately I recognized Chaim, my former student.

I stood and hugged him. "Some friends invited me," I explained.

"You know that the worst of the ghetto—even of all Warsaw—is here." I shrugged in response. He went on. "How are the children? Do you need anything?"

"Ha, well, they need everything, in fact. Things are much worse than last year."

"Damn this war!" he spat out. Then, "Excuse me," and he went up on stage as the singer stepped down to take a drink of water.

Chaim addressed the crowd. "My friends! We're here to forget the harsh realities of the ghetto, but we are honored to have among us tonight the great Dr. Korczak whom you all know well. His poor orphans are having the devil of a time, and I'm begging you all to be generous. Could the band play something cheery, and I'll pass my hat around."

Chaim made his way to all the tables, shaking his hat and flashing his mischievous smile. When he finished the strange collection, he returned to our table. "Here you go, Dr. Korczak. I hope this helps get you through for a while."

"Thank you, Chaim, really and truly, thank you. Yet we need more than money." I motioned for Irena, and she slid over dubiously. She did not trust the likes of Chaim.

"Why don't we step out for a bit?" Chaim suggested. He took us through one of the emergency exits to a dark alley. It had started to rain, but we were covered by a shallow tin roof. The raindrops drummed above us while my former pupil leaned against the wall and lit a cigarette. He offered me one, but I declined.

"So exactly what is it you need? I already introduced you to my boss. I can tell him it's not enough, but he doesn't have much of a soft spot for orphans."

"We need a different kind of help. The children are getting sick; the ghetto is getting more and more dangerous; soon there won't be enough food for everyone, and more people keep coming. If starvation doesn't kill us, then diseases will."

Chaim took a deep breath and exhaled milky white smoke that stretched up until it dissipated in the rain.

"I think I see where you're going. It's crazy. The Nazis might look the other way if they catch us sneaking in food or drink, but no one tries to get people out. You've got to understand, it's too dangerous."

"But living here every day is too dangerous! We have to give these kids a chance at life!"

"Not so loud! The whole ghetto is crawling with Gestapo spies. What does she have to do with all of this?" Chaim nodded toward Irena. "Isn't she a nurse?"

Irena sneered at him. He was exactly the kind of guy she despised: a mafia henchman who enslaved the poor and sowed violence everywhere they went. "I'm a social worker, not a nurse."

"What's the difference? I don't know you. For all I know, you're a spy."

"I've been fighting the Nazis for months. You're just a two-bit thief, a juvenile delinquent."

"Hang on, let's all calm down," I moderated. "With what we're facing, it doesn't matter who we were outside these walls. Now we're just simple Jews trying to survive." They both took a deep breath, and the tension abated. "Irena is constantly coming and going along with some of her colleagues. We've got to find a way to get the children out, starting with the youngest ones. Yes?"

"My boss isn't going to like it. Like I said, the head of the Jewish Order Service is not known for his compassion."

"He can't know anything about it. Don't you see? If he discovers us, he'll hand us over to the Gestapo."

My eyes were locked with Chaim's. I could still see that small, scared boy that the police brought to Dom Sierot all those years ago. He somehow intuited what I was thinking. His ironic expression changed, and he put his hand on my shoulder and said, "We'll do what we can. That's a promise."

We went back into the club and I sat down next to Agnieszka. I could no longer focus on the music or laugh at the MC's jokes. My head was spinning with how to get our children out of the ghetto and give them a chance to survive, though surviving even one more day was becoming something truly miraculous.

CHAPTER 22

A VISIT TO THE CITY

War in this time was no more than lazy shooting. There was none of the careful taking aim and intentional trigger pulling like in the Great War. Now it was all about fighting for ideals, but those who wielded the guns closed their eyes before shooting, fearing death at their core. Before, armies fought for a king, a flag, an anthem, and even for a faith. Now their only goal was domination, even though most of the Germans in Poland were mediocre shopkeepers, toothless manual laborers, and sad peasants.

The Prussian army no longer existed. A few officers played at being true Teutons, but they were a mere shadow of those warriors. Armies gave up before even fighting. When they had to face the Soviets, then they would see what they were really made of.

The Russians wanted to mix and crossbreed humans to create one single race, though first they aimed to exterminate the bourgeois, dissi-dents, and priests. The Germans wanted to unite all the sheep into one fold, but only those with the same eye and hair color and the perfectly Aryan skull shape.

Irena was in her office. Light was waning, and I was eager to get going. My body was shaking, and my hands were sweaty. We had been making plans for months to get all the networks and contacts just right. Everything had to work perfectly for us to get a child out. Father Godlewski had joined our clandestine project and had made arrangements with nearby convents and parishes, but there was still one missing link.

"Doctor, we can go now."

I stood and nearly lost my balance.

"Are you all right?" Irena asked.

"It's just that my conspirator side isn't highly developed," I joked. The truth was that I was a terrible liar and could not playact when it came to real life. It was one thing to write plays and even direct them, but the stage itself had always been too large for me personally.

We walked toward All Saints Church, which enjoyed a privileged position in the ghetto: one of its doors opened onto the Aryan side. We arrived after the five o'clock mass. The priest was still in his robes. One of his collaborators took us to the sacristy and asked Irena to wait outside.

"Janusz, I think this will fit you," Godlewski said, handing me a black cassock.

"You want me to wear that? Please, Father, it seems sacrilegious, a joke of bad form."

"Don't think that the Nazis have much regard for priests, but it's more than for Jewish doctors," he quipped, removing his outer robe and stole. Shaking my head, I slipped the cassock over my suit and then put on the black coat Godlewski held out for me.

"Father Korczak," he said. I looked in the mirror that hung on one wall. It was true; I really did look like a parish priest.

I turned and smiled. "If someone on the street asks me to pray for them, what should I do?"

"Just smile and do this." He showed me how to cross myself and give a simple blessing.

A smile lit up Irena's face when we walked out of the sacristy. "Not a word about this to anyone. Is it really necessary for me to go? I'm not afraid of dying, but I don't know that now is a good time."

We both chuckled, and Godlewski went to the back door. It was not typically watched, but there was always the chance that a guard would see us. We had our papers all in order and the perfect disguise, but this was scarcely a guarantee against the unpredictability of the Nazis.

We walked briskly through the door to the avenue, and I felt instantaneously free. The streets outside the ghetto were cleaner and less crowded. At this hour, people were returning home from work, and the trolleys were packed. We got onto one and were surprised to find seats at the back. Looking out the window, I felt like a kid on his first trip to the big city. Irena let me enjoy the moment for a while before speaking.

"Don't think that things are peachy out here. It's worse and worse as the war drags on. Spring isn't even enough to cheer people up. The Germans now have Greece and the Balkans. Russia's all they've got left to conquer. I don't think they're too worried about Great Britain."

"Then there's the United States, though I doubt they'll get into the war. They certainly won't lift a finger for us. Europe is Hitler's private reserve," I said with deep skepticism. The only thing that might stop the Nazis was an error in overconfidence.

Irena nodded. "I'm really worried. People all over Poland are literally starving to death. Warsaw is a facade, a stage, but hunger is everywhere, and thousands died from the cold this winter. If things don't change, next winter we'll lose hundreds of thousands of Poles."

"That's what's been so hard for everyone to accept. When the Nazis came and took out the intellectual and political elite, most looked the other way. Then they came after us and the Gypsies, and most people stayed quiet. And now it's the entire country. Only a miracle can save Poland."

Irena nodded again, her typical smile clouded over with concern. I went on, "But better times will come. I've lived through the Russo-Japanese War, the Great War, Polish independence, and the fight against the Bolsheviks. We Poles are stronger than what we may seem, and we're used to surviving. The Germans think we're too peppy, but that's just because they're so serious; and the Russians think we're too weak, though they're just hiding their own inferiority complex."

"From your lips to God's ears," she said.

We got off at the last stop. The trolley riders dispersed quickly, and we walked along the emptying street toward the building where Irena's boss, Jan Dobraczyński, would be waiting for us. Most government workers had gone for the day, and we climbed the stairs with little light. At the end of a long hallway, Irena stopped and knocked at a door. We entered without waiting for an answer and saw Jan leaning over his desk. A weak lamp cast only the faintest light on the papers he was studying. When he sat back in his chair, his face was in the darkness.

"Irena, good evening. To what do I owe this honor?"

Irena was clearly nervous. Up to that point, her boss had not been willing to collaborate, though he had turned a blind eye at a few oddities he had observed.

"I'd like you to meet a friend of mine, though he's well known throughout Poland. This is Dr. Janusz Korczak."

Jan cocked his head, his eyes flicking between my face and the cassock. "I wasn't aware that you were a priest," he said, getting to his feet and holding out his hand.

"I'm not." I shrugged. "But this sort of thing is necessary for wandering beyond the walls of the ghetto."

His eyebrows rose even higher. Many people did not know the Old Doctor was a Jew. "Well, you've certainly got my attention now."

I began, "The situation inside the walls is worse and worse every day. I don't know how we're going to get through this year. There's little food or medicine, running water and electricity are continuing to fail, the overcrowding is terrible, and the Nazis are indiscriminate in doling out punishment and death."

"Yes, my social workers keep me abreast of the situation. Dr. Korczak, I can assure you that things outside the ghetto are not much better. We simply don't have the capacity to help any more families. Children wander the streets begging—"

"We haven't come to ask for food or medicine. I'm dealing with that in other ways. It isn't pretty, but we are surviving. No, Irena and I want you to do something else for us."

Jan leaned against his desk. The weak light was enough to show the cold indifference on his face. Here was a professional welfare worker whose managerial heart had hardened after years and years of service to society. I despised such bureaucratic agents, but this was not the time to let my anarchic side loose.

"Well, then, how can we be of service?"

"My children will die by the dozens if we don't get them out of the ghetto."

Elbows on his desk, Jan propped his head in his hands. "You're asking me to do something illegal?" He shook his head. "If—when—we're caught, the Germans will wipe out the entire welfare network in Warsaw. Then thousands of families would be without food or resources."

"They're children, for God's sake. Irena and I will take care of almost everything. The only thing you have to do is get us the documents to forge and alter the records of deceased children so we can give a new identity to the children we smuggle out."

"No, I'm sorry, Doctor, but I can't risk everyone for the sake of just a few."

"A few? The day that people like you chose to look away while the first person was ruthlessly killed, we were all condemned to die. A single life is of infinite value."

Jan stood and pointed at me, "I don't like your tone! I've given my life to Poland for years and every day put up with all sorts of humiliation. I could have slipped off to a country farm and done nothing; but here I am, fighting for Warsaw."

"Let's all calm down," Irena intervened. "Janusz is just worried."

"That doesn't give him the right to judge me," Jan spat out. His face was strained. I could tell then that it was hard for him to turn us down.

"Forgive me; I'm so sorry. The situation in the ghetto is desperate. I've lived through many crises and wars, but until now I've never seen such disdain for life as what the Nazis practice. It's a matter of life or death."

"The Gestapo is ordering all the beggar children in the city to be rounded up. We know that the mafias use kids to get food into the ghetto. Soon enough not only will you not be able to get kids out, but the Nazis will just send them all back in once they're caught, unless they do something worse. Believe me, we're doing all we can."

"Well, it isn't enough," I said, getting to my feet.

"I admire your work as a pedagogue and speaker, but leave the social work to us," Jan said, but I was already walking out of the office. I did not say goodbye. Irena followed and grabbed my arm when we got to the stairs.

"Look, Janusz, the meeting didn't go like I hoped it would, but Jan is a good man. I know he'll think this over. We have to tread very lightly at every step. I already told you, we aren't ready to get any children out. Maybe by this summer or the fall."

In silence, then, we went down the stairs and waited for the next trolley. We were the only ones on board. The streets were empty when it started off a few minutes later. Near the ghetto, some soldiers stopped the trolley, and two Nazis came on board.

"Documents!" they barked. We handed our papers over and held our breaths.

"What are you doing out this late?" the corporal asked.

"The Lord's work never stops," I said.

He frowned and turned to the other soldier. In German, he said, "It's a priest with his niece. The priests are all a bunch of corrupt fools. We should take them in and teach them a lesson."

I stood and answered in German. "This woman is a social worker, and I'm a parish priest. We're out here trying to help people and now just want to get home. What is your name?"

The corporal looked at me indignantly. "Who do you think you are?"

"Are you not religious?" I asked, matching his indignant tone.

"Well, my family has always been Catholic but . . ."

"Well, then you understand how we're always to help our neighbors, corporal . . ."

"Fischer, I'm Herman Fischer."

I made the sign of the cross, and he automatically bowed his head to receive my blessing. The two soldiers got off the trolley and told the driver to keep going.

Irena and I let our breaths out slowly. It was my first time to function as a priest, but I had saved at least two souls that night, both Herman's and my own.

CHAPTER 23

THE TROLLEY

As people age, they become a conglomerate of diffuse traits. Old people all look the same: we lose our hair, get dark age spots, and surrender our facial features to the weight of wrinkles. Our eyes sink deep into their sockets as the skull seeks to make its harrowed presence increasingly felt. Our shrinking, weakening muscles become a thin pillowcase over our aching bones. I was never strong and robust, but now, when I looked down at my spindly legs, I wondered how much longer they could carry me around.

That day I woke in good spirits, though there was no particular justification for optimism. The food situation had gotten slightly better. The governor-general, Hans Frank, had appointed Heinz Auerswald as the replacement ghetto commissioner. Auerswald believed in using

Jews as a workforce and therefore increased the food rations enough to halt all-out famine.

We could already feel the approach of summer. Soon the heat would come and bring with it the stench of the refuse piled all around. It would make the air all but unbreathable. But that morning the pleasant sun and a soft southern breeze made me feel alive again. I closed my eyes and enjoyed the sensation of the warmth over my face. Then I watered my plants, real ones now to replace the fake flowers that had sustained me through the winter. I had not seen any other windows in the entire ghetto that had flowerpots hanging from them.

After coffee, or what passed for coffee, I finished getting ready and headed out for a walk. In the Small Ghetto it was still possible to walk without being smothered in a crowd. I approached the stretch that divided our Jewish jail into two sections. Sometimes I liked to stop and watch the Polish citizens that passed by, glazed with indifference as they looked out from busses and trolleys toward their Jewish countrymen. Most were manual laborers or office workers, but sometimes I also saw mothers taking their children to school or retirees who had nothing better to do than take a turn about the town.

I could not stop myself from studying a child who was on the other side of the ghetto, sitting with his head propped against the lamppost. I had seen him there before, begging for bread from the unresponsive passersby. Sometimes I took him something to eat. I knew he was begging for his grandmother who was ill and was the only family member he had left. He had told me that before the war they lived in a big house on the outskirts of Warsaw. His grandfather had been a well-to-do Russian businessman but had fled the country during the Bolshevik Revolution. His father was a well-respected lawyer, and the boy, as the only heir, would inherit the family wealth. Yet the Nazis had taken his

father and grandfather away—to a firing squad, the boy supposed—
and then had seized the house for a German officer to live in. He'd
entered the ghetto with his mother and grandmother, but his mother
had quickly succumbed to illness, and now his grandmother was all
he had.

Someone did toss him a crust of bread from a window, but the child
did not respond. I wanted to cross over and see how he was, but there
was no point. Before long his inert body would be in one of the wagons
carting off the day's cadavers.

I swallowed my tears and looked back at the trolleys. I recognized a
former colleague from my days in the city's children's hospital. Our eyes
met, but I doubted that he would recognize me after all these years. Yet
he turned to keep looking and then waved at me, his face contorted with
emotion. The horror had ceased to be anonymous for him. It had taken
on familiar eyes and facial features—mine. So it was real to him in that
moment. The rest of the time, for those who glimpsed us from the trolleys, we were no more than strangers, poor devils they were powerless to
help. But for that doctor friend I was Korczak, the buddy he had shared
many a beer with after a long day's work.

I was about to head back, and in a much more dismal mood than
when I had come, when I saw the most peculiar thing.

In those days trolleys had a driver and a ticket seller, who would
stand at the back of the car. The ticket seller was separated from the rest
of the passengers in a small metallic stand. The one I observed had a
round face, small eyes behind glasses, and short hair. He started throwing big round loaves of bread over the wall. Every twenty yards or so he
would toss one out, and people in the ghetto would flock to it, ripping
it into a dozen pieces at least. The SS guards noted that something was
happening and stopped the trolley. The passengers stirred nervously. The

soldiers had not seen who had thrown the bread and started questioning the passengers, but most had no idea what was going on.

"If you don't tell us who was doing it, we'll take you all out of the trolley. You see those Jews over there? Well, it'll go worse for you," a soldier barked in German.

One of the passengers, dressed in black, pointed to the ticket seller, who hung his head. The soldiers dragged him out of the trolley and threw him to the ground. The conductor glanced out the mirror at his unlucky partner and started up the trolley.

"You dog! What are you doing feeding the Jewish swine?" the soldier demanded.

Just then an officer walked up and asked what was going on. He went up to the ticket seller and forced him to his feet. "Why have you done this?" he asked.

The man was trembling with fear. He had lost his hat, and his tie was twisted. "I pass by the ghetto dozens of times a day, and it breaks my heart. They're God's children too."

"God's children? They're dirty rotten Jews. And you're wasting good food on these vermin."

Everyone watching was paralyzed. We knew what the Germans were capable of. But the ticket seller kept on. "A lot of them are children or old people. What harm have they done?"

The officer pulled out his pistol and held it to the man's temple. "Rats are rats, whether they're babies or old sacks. If you feed the rats, they'll end up devouring us all." The officer grabbed the man's neck and shoved the pistol into his forehead. "Let this be an example to anyone who wants to help the Jewish swine!"

And he pulled the trigger. The man's head exploded, spewing blood on the officer and the gray street. A terrible silence followed, and everyone on the street quickly made their way elsewhere to escape any further violence. I turned back for the orphanage.

On the way, I spied a tiny red flower blooming between the curb and the cobblestones. There it was, life trying to make a way in the midst of the horror. It always did; that is what it was made to do. Standing before our building, I looked up at my window to where my little garden sparkled against the gray facade. I smiled. That was one thing the Nazis could not take from me. The world was a terrible place, but every spring the flowers would cover the fields of the earth, promising summer's harvest before autumn slowly muted the colors for the thick blanket of winter's ice and snow.

CHAPTER 24

GET KORCZAK OUT

I had never before seen a man with a suit made out of newspaper. Summer had arrived with a vengeance of heat and no running water. I studied the poor devil dressed in newspaper and wondered what could be next. What else was there to see in this world? The answer was soon in coming. A messenger arrived that morning bearing a letter from the chairman of the Judenrat. I opened it and was surprised to find myself summoned immediately. So I put on a lightweight shirt and jacket and headed for the Jewish Council's offices. I was glad not to have to go through the Great Ghetto that day. I had ventured out of our side the day before, and it was not enjoyable. Conditions had worsened notably.

I went straight to Czerniaków's office. He did not look good. He waved me in dispiritedly, and I took a seat. I had always preferred to keep my distance from politicians and secure the support our orphans needed through other means.

"Dear Korczak, thank you for coming on such short notice."

"Of course. Yesterday I walked the length of the whole ghetto. Have you seen how bad things are out there?"

"Have I seen—do you think I'm blind, man? Twice now we've barely skirted a full-fledged famine and calmed the typhus outbreak, but I don't know how much longer we'll be able to keep up with the Nazis. You know they've invaded the Soviet Union? And they started from their position in Poland? The Jews in that area have had it slightly better than we have, but now they're being wiped out on a large scale. And to feed the German soldiers and aid the USSR front, Jewish rations will be reduced even more."

That was disheartening to say the least. We were barely surviving as it was with the subhuman rations. Further decreases would mean death to tens of thousands of people before the end of 1941.

Czerniaków went on. "We can't get by without the food aid from the Joint, but if the United States declares war on Germany, the JDC won't be able to operate in Polish territory."

I was familiar with the American Jewish Joint Distribution Committee. It had started in 1914 to help Jews living in Palestine under Ottoman rule and since then had come to the aid of Jews in Russia, helping Jews flee Europe for the United States for nearly thirty years.

"Why are you telling me all of this?" I asked, puzzled.

"We're helping a few prominent Jews get out of the ghetto. Not many, just a handful that the country can't afford to lose. The world needs people like you, Dr. Korczak."

"I'm an old man, and my strength is gone. Your efforts are better spent getting as many children as possible out of here," I said, indignant.

How was the value of a human life to be measured? Did culture or status make one person more valuable than a beggar child or an illiterate woman?

"Janusz, the Nazis are exterminating all the Jews in their path to Moscow. There have been massacres in places like Lvov, Radziłów, Palmiry, and Szczuczyn, some of them started by Polish nationalists."

I had nothing to say. It was not that I had not expected this. But I felt the urgency of time running out and our impotence to save the children from this hell. Irena and her collaborators had been shoring up details for months, but soon enough there would be nothing left to save.

"No, I'm sorry. I cannot leave my children," I said, standing to shake his hand before leaving.

I turned everything over in my head on the walk back. Evil struts about openly and unencumbered, while we must seek out good wherever it is hiding. Evildoers go about their nefarious business in plain sight, and society is forced to react to their insanity, whereas the just strive to do what is necessary without being noticed. It had to come out into the light—everything that was going on in the ghetto, what the Nazis were doing, what Polish Aryans were doing, and what even Jews were doing to one another.

CHAPTER 25

ACTING THE PROPHET

Though I was already aware of this notion, one thing the ghetto made very clear was that human life was expendable. After our brief time on earth, we disappear into the dust cloud of history. Our flowerless tombs will wilt quicker than new-grown May grass that is yellow by July. Fields of wildflowers that fade by fall prove that our existence is passing and ephemeral.

When I had crossed the invisible mile marker of turning sixty, with my body worn down by the misfortunes and trials of life, I no longer held any illusions about the world. Traveling to Palestine with Stefa had been my last great gust of happiness. The only thing that mattered to me during the fall of 1941 was getting our children out of the hell that the Nazis had concocted for us in Warsaw.

People say things can always get worse, even in a place like that.

Running Dom Sierot in the old trade school building was, to say the least, uncomfortable. But then the authorities adjusted the boundaries of the ghetto, our new and terrible country. In the changes, we were forced to move into the old trade union building on Sienna Street. It was smaller and in even worse shape. After the days of packing, moving, and getting settled, we were all so frustrated and uncomfortable that I decided we would put on a play. The children needed something to focus on and keep them engaged, and the tutors needed something to motivate them. It was so hard to keep a positive outlook in our circumstances. News from the Russian front was terrible, the situation in Warsaw continued to be terrible—everything was terrible. It was anyone's guess how many of our children would survive another winter. The Nazis were proving invincible, and our hopes of their eventual defeat were succumbing to the brutal reality of the war.

My young friend Henryk helped me raise Dom Sierot's green flag. We had made it in the early days of German occupation. On one side it bore an embroidered chestnut tree flower and on the other, the Star of David. We flew it daily as part of orphanage life.

The rest of the children applauded. Then they went off with their teachers to practice for the next day's performance. I had invited our few remaining donors, hoping that they would be inspired to renew their commitment to the orphanage.

"Teacher, thanks for letting us do a play," Henryk said with his sweet smile.

"It's the job of every educator to keep his pupils' spirits up," I answered. I always dodged compliments, not out of pride but rather a certain shyness.

"But I see that you're sad behind your smile," Henryk said. His comment took me by surprise. I sat right in front of him and met his eyes. He went on, "It's hard to live without my dad and far away from my grandparents. All I've got is my mom. I smile, too, even when I'm crying inside. Encouraging the people we love is the most important job in the world, I think. That's why I like clowns so much."

"And what do you think of our new home?" I asked, waving my hands to encompass the building.

He frowned, and his mischievous eyes flashed. "It's a shithole! It's nothing compared to our nice house outside the ghetto and way worse than the first one inside. There are no real bedrooms. This room is big, but it's damp and cold. Plus, it's not just us. They serve soup here too."

We shared part of the building with one of the charity soup kitchens, but it was the best that the Judenrat had been able to offer us. And to make matters worse, the number of children kept increasing while food rations decreased. It was a fatal combination.

The next day our students were ready for the performance. A few of Dom Sierot's friends and donors sat in the first few rows. The rest of the seats were filled by the poor souls who came for their soup and two or three passersby who wandered in off the street. The ghetto was no longer replete with cultural offerings like it had been this time last year, when music and theater offered an escape from the daily hell.

I had chosen Kahlil Gibran's work *The Prophet*. Gibran was a Lebanese author, and I had read his book some twenty years before and knew it had been adapted for the theater. Gibran was a Maronite, but his writings were a mixture of Hebrew, Christian, and Muslim cultures.

Igor, our talented little Communist, was playing the role of the prophet, the protagonist. First the narrator came out onto our improvised stage and said in his sweet, soft voice:

Almustafa, the chosen and the beloved, who was a dawn unto his own day, had waited twelve years in the city of Orphalese for his ship that was to return and bear him back to the isle of his birth.

And in the twelfth year, on the seventh day of Ielool, the month of reaping, he climbed the hill without the city walls and looked seaward; and he beheld his ship coming with the mist.

Then the gates of his heart were flung open, and his joy flew far over the sea. And he closed his eyes and prayed in the silences of his soul.

But as he descended the hill, a sadness came upon him, and he thought in his heart:

How shall I go in peace and without sorrow? Nay, not without a wound in the spirit shall I leave this city. Long were the days of pain I have spent within its walls, and long were the nights of aloneness; and who can depart from his pain and his aloneness without regret?

Too many fragments of the spirit have I scattered in these streets, and too many are the children of my longing that walk naked among these hills, and I cannot withdraw from them without a burden and an ache.

And the audience was thus drawn into the enthralling narrative. As I watched the performance with delight, I found myself pondering. Why had I not fled like so many others? What was it that really kept me bound to this small army of desperate beings? People tend to hold on to life with all they have, but I felt that my duty was to remain like the captain of a sinking ship. It was, of course, love. Love is what tied me to these children, the kind that is given with no expectations of anything in return. I thought about how Gibran's prophet said that the only way to really live is to make a temple and a religion of daily life. I, who had been a skeptic for so long, had come to understand that God was in everything. I recommitted to giving myself to the children with joy for whatever time I had left with them. Sacrifice was not enough. I had to invest my whole heart and soul.

The room erupted in applause when the performance was over. There was happiness painted on everyone's faces, the ease of momentarily forgetting the hardships and pains of life. The children were grinning with joy like they had before the ghetto. While desolation continued its march to destroy the world we knew and loved outside Dom Sierot, the small, beautiful things of life had filled the room. Right then I let go of the past, of their pasts, of what these children could have become— doctors, teachers, the benefactors of society, and perhaps a few thieves in the mix as well—if there were no war. Life does not stop; it keeps unfolding toward the future and leaving yesterday behind.

CHAPTER 26

FRIDAY DINNER

The cold had begun. People selling firewood lined the sidewalks. With the scarcity of coal, many people broke down their furniture for wood to feed their stoves and heaters. If our confinement lasted much longer, it seemed to me that we would end up disassembling the ghetto and leaving it an empty waste. In the stalls selling firewood, entire families would be there—parents, children, grandparents, an aunt or uncle—to exchange their former dresser or table split into stove-sized pieces for a loaf of bread. No one wanted money anymore, as paper money was worthless. Most people had already hocked any gold, silver, and jewelry they had brought into the ghetto. Within a few short months, the accumulated wealth of generations had vanished. Sometimes it felt like years, entire decades that we had been locked up, but it had really only been a year. The desperation made the slow agony feel endless.

It was Friday, and before I was scheduled to have supper with one of our benefactor families, I needed to make a few home visits. Several families wanted to send us their children, as if we had room for any more.

The first building was in the northern part, in one of the poorest and least maintained areas of the run-down, dirty ghetto. Class differences had slowly started to disappear. I smirked to think of how proud Marx would be: we were finally approaching equality. We were all equally poor, miserable, and desperate. Perhaps for the first time in history, money, class, and family background did not matter. We were a people united by misfortune and destined to demise.

I climbed the dirty stairs, confirming my knowledge that many in the ghetto lived in even worse conditions than we did. I was out of breath as I struggled up to the fourth floor, and I wondered if my heart would beat right out of my chest. I continued to grow weaker and to tire more easily. My one physical luxury was a drink of vodka to warm me up and relax me before bed.

I knocked at the discolored door. Instead of a lock, a cord stretched from an open hole in the door to the adjoining wall. I thought of how much cold air must blow through that hole. Before the war, not even the poorest neighborhoods had doors like that. A woman as rail thin as the rest of the ghetto's mothers untied the cord and opened the door to me. Her sunken, wrinkled cheeks could not fully hide that she had been beautiful. But now the only thing bright about her face were her green, catlike eyes.

She led me down a long, dark hallway to what was once a nice parlor. The doorways off the parlor were covered by curtains and led to separate living quarters. Each was one bedroom where an entire family lived. Most of the inhabitants were too weak to stir from the beds. Their loved ones allowed them the luxury of dying on a mattress, covered by a blanket and dreaming of food.

The family I had come to see was in the parlor. We sat down, and a man with a long beard joined us.

"Thank you for coming, Dr. Korczak. We would never have called you if we were not in such a difficult position. This is our old house. We sold jewelry. When I say 'old,' I mean from before, which seems like hundreds of years ago. Until the war began, this was a grand home. We had servants, one of the best pianos in Poland over in that corner, and fine china plates in the cupboard. Now," the man shrugged and gestured to the mattresses on the floor, the chimney, and the three chairs, "this is all that's left."

The man was so downcast that all I could do was nod and give a murmured acknowledgment of his statement. He wiped his tears and called for his daughter, Renia. She was very short for her eleven years, not having had the nutrition necessary for her development. The poor dear did not even look up. She stood beside her father, who put his hand on her shoulder. My heart sank. The child was so sad, like a snuffed-out candle.

"You're very pretty, Renia. You have your mother's eyes," I said. She gave a half-hearted smile.

"We can't feed her. It's been five days since any of us has eaten. We have nothing left to sell. My wife and I are planning to lie down and wait for sleep to take us. We hope to open our eyes to eternity."

The mother was weeping as her husband spoke. The girl seemed like she was hardly hearing anything.

"Your daughter is still young. You've got to keep trying for her sake," I said in frustration. Parents should never give up. They owe it to their children.

"I've tried to work at the factories and bring home anything I can, but they send me away for being too old and unskilled. I'm only forty, but the hunger has aged me."

Many of the arms, clothing, and other factories were being moved to Germany or Belarus. It was too long a journey to ship supplies from Poland to the Russian front.

"I'm sorry, but I don't know that we can take Renia."

The woman grabbed my hands. "I'm begging you. You're her only hope."

"You don't have any other family here?"

"Our relatives live here in this house. They paid us rent for a room. For the first year in the ghetto, we made do, but now we simply have no food." Her voice trembled dryly with hunger and grief.

I looked around and saw a piece of furniture with the only door that seemed to still be intact in the place.

"May I?" I asked, moving toward the dresser. I tried to open it, but it was locked.

"What are you doing?" the man asked, getting to his feet.

"I need to see what's inside."

"There's nothing of value."

"Then why is it locked?"

"We're not the only ones in the house anymore. People steal everything, and it's dangerous to leave things lying about." I yanked at the door, and the wood creaked. "Wait!" the man called out. He came up and unlocked the door. There was food inside, not much, but enough for three or four days if they rationed it well. There were also some small blue velvet bags. I opened them, and even in the dim light, the diamonds were shining.

"That's our life insurance. Please, keep our daughter just a few weeks. We're getting false documents soon and will be able to get out of this hellhole."

I understood then. The daughter would hamper their escape. They could not take her with them. It would be too expensive to arrange papers for her and go all together to Finland or some other place. I chucked the things back in the dresser and slammed the door shut.

"I'm sorry, but I cannot help you. Over two hundred people are depending on me. All the best as you get out of here and return to your pretty little life."

I turned back to the hallway, but the woman grabbed my arm. "Doctor, you can't do this to us! You're sentencing us to death!"

"All of us here have a life sentence. From the moment we're born, death starts chasing us, and he always, always catches his prey."

I went down the stairs as quickly as I could and could still hear the woman calling after me when I got to the door.

It was late now, and I needed to be at the home of the wealthy family who had invited me to dine. I walked back through the ghetto to one of the few areas that still retained something of the charming Warsaw from before. A handful of houses were clustered at the end of a street next to a church. I opened the gate to the empty front yard and went up to the porch. An elderly woman answered my knock. Incongruous with her servant's dress, she carried herself as a lady.

"Dr. Korczak, the master is waiting for you."

Intact furniture gleamed on the recently polished floor of the foyer. The housekeeper opened the double doors to the dining room, where the table was prepared for Sabbath. The owner of the home, Natek Ojbel, and his wife, Krysia, were in a small adjoining room, sitting on blue armchairs before a crackling fire.

Natek stood and held out his hand. "Dr. Korczak, I'm so pleased you've come. We hardly ever have visitors these days."

"Thank you for the invitation," I responded.

"Let's go in to the table. Our dear Anna has prepared a delicious meal."

The smells wafting in from the kitchen testified to the delicacies available in that house. I thought of my students and felt guilty. None of them would get to enjoy a dinner this fine even in their dreams.

We remained standing behind our chairs, and Natek began singing the *Eshet Chayil*, then the *Shalom Aleichem* to ask for the protection of God's angels. Then he spoke the blessing over the wine.

"Cheers," he said, and we each took a cup and drank. The taste nearly knocked me backward. It was real wine, perhaps French. Then we washed our hands and shared the bread. At that, conversation began.

"Well, Dr. Korczak, the world has certainly gone mad, hasn't it? When they forced us into this living hell, I thought God was punishing me for my many sins but things would go back to normal within a few months. The Germans have always been reasonable stock. I cannot understand this fanaticism. I know the Jews have never been their favorite allies, but our money and our gold are just as good as anyone else's," Natek said.

Krysia, who had not yet spoken, passed me a salad plate.

"Do you think the Nazis will beat the Russians?" Natek continued.

It was not necessarily the question I would have expected, but I said, "From all accounts they're advancing mile after mile each day and not encountering much resistance." I took a bite of the fresh vegetables. My senses were nearly intoxicated with flavors and textures I had not tasted in so long.

"And now it's the battle for Moscow. If the capital falls, the rest of the USSR will cave within time. Part of me is glad. I've always despised the Bolsheviks. If the Nazis eliminate them, that will be one good thing they've done for the world."

I gave a noncommittal movement of my head while taking small bites of the various meats and sauces arranged carefully on the table.

"The war might be over once the Nazis beat the Russians, but I don't see how that's going to help us any." My dismal comment ruffled Natek's grasp toward optimism, and he frowned.

"Well," Krysia interceded, breaking her silence, "the important thing is that our children are safe in the United States. I don't think Hitler will make it that far."

I had known the Ojbels since before the war. I had tutored their son and daughter to make money for the orphanage, and the millionaire had always been generous to our cause.

Natek turned a searing look to his wife.

She continued, "We should've gone with them when we had the chance. Our New York family would've welcomed us with open arms."

"Foolish woman! Everything we have is in Poland and Germany."

She winced and spat back, "And now belongs to the Nazis."

"In a manner of speaking. I sold it to Aryan citizens, but that's just a front. We'll get it back when the tide changes. Where do you think all this comes from?" He encompassed the house, the food, and their comfort with a wave. "From the generosity of the Germans?"

Krysia pursed her lips and returned to silence.

"I'm sorry, Doctor, sometimes my wife pushes me to the limit. Giving birth to our children is the only good thing she's done in her life, though she spoiled them. The oldest is at Harvard, and our daughter is at a boarding school for girls. It's been three years since we've seen them, but we write letters. I can't run away and leave their inheritance here. What would happen if we all just up and left everything we have like rabbits scared by every little shadow?"

"A man is more than his inheritance, and the greatest legacy we can give our children is our love."

The man's chin lifted in defiance, and I repented of my words. I was there because I needed his help. The poor do not have the luxury of pride if they want to feed their children, and I had over two hundred of them.

"Love is a feeling and doesn't feed anyone's belly; isn't that right, Doctor?"

"Of course, it's intangible, but it brings deep joy."

"And will your orphans survive on love?"

I thought about that for a moment.

"Love nourishes their souls. People without love are already dead, though they don't yet know it."

Natek dropped his napkin lightly on the table and went to a desk, opened a drawer, and returned to the table. "I can't give your orphans any love, but this is a coupon you can take to the food distribution center. It's a week's worth of food. I don't expect your love or the children's."

I pocketed the precious piece of paper and asked, "Then why do you share with us?"

"Just because I believe in you and your work. God gave me the ability to make money, and he gave you the ability to love, and I like to think that I can love through you even though my heart feels nothing."

I nodded and thanked him, and the conversation meandered for the rest of the meal.

After bidding the Ojbels good night, I walked back to Dom Sierot feeling ridiculously wealthy. Anyone could have money, and many people would amass large fortunes, but I had two hundred children whom I loved and who loved me. I was undoubtedly the richest man in the Warsaw ghetto.

CHAPTER 27

THE "JEWISH GESTAPO"

What is freedom? The question had always disconcerted me. From an early age I had the uncomfortable sensation of being a mere pawn in a cosmic chess match. Does freedom really exist, or is it an idea invented by human beings? What is free will, and did I have it? Was I truly free as a human, or was I the slave of many? I would have liked to think there is a place, a country, where we can be truly free. Jesus said that knowing the truth would set us completely free. But which truth? Ours or the Nazis' or the Aryan Poles' truth? For them, we were disposable garbage, a pseudohuman plague to be exterminated. Could I be the master of my destiny, of my entire being, of my future and still face my executioners?

The Jewish people were slaves in Egypt, where Pharaoh mistreated us. We were his prisoners, and yet I wondered: Were my Jewish forebears ever happy? I imagined that even the most desensitized servant had moments of happiness. It was like that in the ghetto. There were terrible days where you could see an elderly rabbi murdered right in front of his children; and the next day you could have a marvelous time playing hide-and-seek and telling jokes with the children.

How I wished our overlords were benevolent and kind and let us live in peace. They could have maintained decency and been respectful when depriving us of our freedom, filling us with fear, and denying us our rights as human beings. That was an option. After all, some slaves are happy enough and full of laughter; and many free men weep in anguish over what to do with their lives.

I always wondered how the Israelites reacted when Moses showed up. Maybe he forced them to be free. A people group that has lived enslaved for some time no longer knows how to live in freedom. Eventually our people did come out of Egypt, though I was not convinced that Egypt ever came out of them. Moses went up the mountain and brought us the law. The commandments gave us an identity, but they also limited the ambition of freedom because sometimes we desire freedom at others' expense. That is what had happened with the Nazis: freedom for them implied the destruction of my people because the Germans desired what was not theirs and what did not belong to them.

I jotted these reflections down, then set my diary aside. The new building was much more dreadful than the first. We had set it up the best way we could, but we were crammed together in uncomfortably tight quarters. I drank a little of the watery coffee substitute and put my jacket on in search of warmth. Winter was just around the corner, though autumn had already been darker and colder than usual.

"Doctor, may I speak with you?"

I turned and saw Rundowa, one of our tutors. Her face was so thin, and her eyes were ringed with dark circles. She was wearing her best dress and holding her coat.

"Where are you off to so early?" I asked. She took a step forward and lowered her head. When I heard her sobs, I placed my hand on her shoulder. "What is it?" I asked. "Are you unwell? Look, don't ask me how, but I came upon some Danish cookies, and there's one with your name on it. I usually keep them for the children, but you're one of our best teachers."

She slumped into a chair and took the cookie but stared at it as if unsure what it was for.

"I'm not a hero," she began. "I've done what I can, but I can't take it anymore. This week one of my youngest students died, and my cousin died just a few days ago of typhus. I don't want to die. I'm too young."

"I understand. I'm a decrepit old man with hardly any strength left, but you're young and have your whole future ahead of you. But you know how things are right now. The war is still going on, and every day means less food. The elderly die of cold in their beds, and pregnant mothers lose their babies. It's a terrible world we've been given."

"I'm going to try to escape. I've been talking with a soldier from Belarus. I think he likes me, and he's promised to get me out. He's waiting for me at the Chłodna Street gate."

"Are you sure? I don't think they'll let a Jew out."

"He's going to hide me in one of the supply trucks. I wanted to say goodbye to you. I can't say goodbye to the children. I know I'm abandoning them, and I feel terrible about it."

She hugged me, and I did not know what to say. She had every right to be happy and to try to survive this horror. I walked her to the door. It was still dark out.

"I can't let you go alone; it's too dangerous. Muggings and robberies—it's always getting worse. The world seems to be losing the few shreds of dignity it has left," I said as I put on my coat. I accompanied her down the dark street. Most of the streetlamps were out, and the Germans cared only about keeping the perimeter of the wall lit up. It was a short walk to the gate, where several cars were parked and guards were standing around.

"God keep you," I said, kissing her forehead.

She smiled and walked away slowly, her shoes clacking against the cobblestones. She had not gone far when a soldier took her suitcase and hurried her into the back of a truck. I smiled hopefully. Perhaps she could get away and be saved. I was turning to walk back to the orphanage when a voice called out in German, "Open the truck!"

The driver stopped at the control point, got out of the cab, and opened the back door. A German guard shone his flashlight inside. From where I stood, I could not see inside, but his shout told me all I needed to know. "Get out immediately!"

The soldier who was helping Rundowa went up to the guard and said something in his ear.

"No, you Slavic pig!" The German had his gun trained on Rundowa. "Papers!" he screamed. "Show me your papers!"

Rundowa got out of the truck and stood trembling before the guard, holding out her papers.

"Where do you think you're going, you dirty Jew?"

The guard smacked Rundowa with the butt of his gun, and she crumpled to the ground. The Belarusian soldier jumped him, and two other guards ran up. The first yelled, "Kill that traitor!" The two guards grabbed the Belarusian, threw him against the wall, and opened fire. The gunshots ripped through the silent night, and he fell dead before the flashes had been absorbed into the darkness.

My friend screamed and held out her arms to him, but her lover did not respond. She was still on her knees. The German guard took a step back and aimed at her. Rundowa hung her head and started praying. A single bullet pierced her skull, and she fell forward. Her body sank into the mud. It had been raining for several days, and puddles had gathered in every little hollow, turning the street into a quagmire.

There was a fierce pain in my chest, and it was hard to breathe. I tried to move, by my legs seemed to be paralyzed. Primal fear had invaded all of my members. At least she had tried to do something. The ghetto was falling apart, and it was increasingly impossible to survive.

The guard looked up and saw me. He pointed at me and fingered the trigger. I blinked, feeling almost liberated for a moment. He pretended to shoot like a child playing cops and robbers, then laughed heartily.

I lurched to get my legs moving and left as quickly as I could. I wanted to see Irena. I wanted to get the children out of the ghetto as soon as possible. I had just turned a corner when I ran into two members of the Thirteen, a group everyone knew was collaborating with the Nazis to make life harder for Jews in the ghetto.

"What are you doing out at this hour? What were those gunshots?"

"I've got to go," I said, not slowing my pace. One of them grabbed my arm and jerked me back.

"Hey, old man, we asked you a question."

"I don't know anything, and I'm heading home."

One of them lifted his nightstick and with no hesitation popped me on the head. The blood came immediately, and it hurt more than I thought possible.

"What are you hitting me for? Your lot no longer has power; Czerniaków stripped you of your authority. You're just a bunch of corrupt Jews exploiting your own people."

The man raised his arm to strike again, but his companion stopped him. "Don't you see this is that doctor Korczak? Gancwajch told us not to touch him."

They helped me to my feet, and the one who had hit me held a bandage to my head to stop the bleeding. "Where can we take you?" he asked.

Since their expulsion from the Jewish ghetto police force, the Thirteen had focused its efforts on controlling usury and the black market. They had a monopoly on ambulances and horse-drawn carriages and were one of the most corrupt arms of Jewish authority.

"I can make my own way, thank you," I said and walked away as briskly as I could to Irena's office. She was already there and jumped to her feet when she saw me.

"What happened?" she exclaimed, seeing my bloody face.

"It's nothing. I ran into a couple Thirteen thugs."

"Ugh! I hope those vile collaborationists get what's coming to them someday." She took out rubbing alcohol and cotton balls and started cleaning off the blood, taking care around the wound. Then she bandaged it with a fresh wrap. "You can't afford for this to get infected, Janusz. With the lack of medicines, any little scratch could become fatal."

I sat back and let out a deep sigh. Immediately the scene of Rundowa's death flashed before my eyes.

"What's going on?" Irena pressed. "You're paler than usual."

"A few years ago I thought that nothing I witnessed could really touch me. I've already been in two wars. But what's happening here—there's no name for it." I tried to breathe deeply, but the panic spreading through my body allowed no room for the air. Irena rested her hands heavily on my shoulders.

"Easy now, Janusz."

"But you won't go on to say, 'It's all right; things will get better,' will

212

you? It's what I do all day long, though I know things are coming apart at the seams."

Irena moved in front of me and leaned against her desk. "Our informants have told us that in an SS meeting the Nazis decided on a plan for the Jews. Plus, we know they're up to something in Chelmno. Hundreds of prisoners go in alive but are soon dead."

I did not answer. What could it all mean?

Irena drove it home. "They're eliminating them," she said simply.

"Who? The elderly and the sick? The Germans can't feed all of Poland's Jews. They're sending all the food to the Russian front."

"No, Janusz, they're killing healthy people."

"Please, please, we have got to get the children out of here," I begged.

"We can only take out the Polish families that look more Aryan and speak Polish without an accent."

That ruined the chances for at least half of our orphans. "My children speak Polish, but Yiddish is the first language of many of them."

"Make me a list of the eligible candidates."

"I can't choose between who should live or die!"

Irena gave me a look of heartrending compassion. "We may be able to save them all, but we have to start with the ones who can blend in after we get them out. Your children are orphans, but we need to start with children who have parents."

"I don't think you know our people well enough. Most Jewish mothers are not going to just let their children be taken away. Jewish parents aren't going to want their kids housed with Christian Poles or in monasteries."

"That's why I need you, Doctor. You can convince them to let me take their children to safety."

This was not what I had intended, and I doubted that the families would pay me any heed. But I would have to try. It was still saving the lives of children, even though they were not my own.

I stood and nearly lost my balance from dizziness.

"Are you sure you're all right, Janusz?"

"No, but it's not because of the blow. It's called old age, and I can tell you it's wretched."

Irena smiled and helped me into my coat. "You're still in good shape. You don't look a day over sixty."

"And you're a brownnoser."

I waved goodbye and headed for the Dom Sierot on Sienna Street. The shattered face of Rundowa flashed before my eyes. I smacked my forehead to chase it away, but it stayed. I would have to live with that image the rest of my life.

CHAPTER 28

THE GYPSY

One day I had to go to Pawiak prison, where male prisoners were held. Female prisoners were in the smaller building next door called Serbia. Agnieszka had offered to go with me, but Henryk had been sick with a fever, and I told her not to leave him. The best medicine for any childhood illness is always a mother's love and affection.

As I walked through the little plaza at Mylna, I was pressed on all sides by the crowd. People were moving about aimlessly. Christmas was not far off, and the hustle and bustle reminded me of people out finalizing their shopping before the festivities. I felt strangled. I have never liked crowds, and especially not a sea of frightened, desperate faces milling around with no place to go.

Sticking close to the buildings as I walked helped me keep my balance and avoid getting trampled. I noticed a group of boys clustered in front of a shop window. I turned and saw it was a tea shop. It was not fancy. The glitz and glitter had disappeared from the ghetto streets as the equalizing force of decay spread relentlessly. But the people inside wore clothes that were less threadbare, and their cheeks were not sunken. I could still see the fear of hunger and death in their eyes, though. The door to the shop opened and nearly smacked me in the face. A man in a suit and wearing a ridiculous bowler hat sauntered out. Seeing the hungry faces of the boys, he threw a coin into the air. The biggest boy in the group caught it and ran off. The rest returned to the shop window, hoping for a sugar cube or a pastry crust.

I sighed and marched on. You could not take two steps in the ghetto without seeing some misfortune or taking an emotional blow. I could not get used to the daily horrors. As I approached the Gestapo prison, one of the most feared places in Warsaw, I noticed people pushing and shoving to get out of the way of something. An SS truck was coming down the road, and we all knew what that meant.

"Clear the road!" the driver yelled impatiently. Those right in front of him tried to move, but there was no space to go since the people all around were already pressed tightly against the walls and the buildings.

"Spawn of Satan!" the driver yelled again. He pulled out a pistol and shot the head off a woman close to his window. At that, people found a way to scatter, and the driver revved the engine. The truck hit an old man and rolled right over him. Relief coursed throughout the crowd as the truck finally drove off. I continued on my way.

With an uncustomary friendliness, the SS guard at the prison door asked, "What brings you here?"

"I'm here to see Captain Neumann," I said.

The soldier studied me, then went to the sentry box, made a call, and returned a few minutes later.

"The captain's not in his office. Try again tomorrow."

"It's important, and I need to speak with him."

The guard shrugged, looked off into the distance while thinking, and then gestured to somewhere farther off. "Sometimes he goes by the Britannia Hotel to relax."

I had heard about the bar at the Britannia where the Germans would gather to shirk their executioner role as long as the drink lasted. I thanked the soldier and made my way to the old hotel. I doubted they would let me in, but sometimes fate has a strange way of unfolding. There was a German soldier and a guard who was not Jewish. At least, he was not wearing an armband.

"Where are you going?" the one dressed as a concierge asked me.

"I need to see a German officer."

"Jews aren't allowed into this bar. It's just for Aryans."

The German soldier puffed on his cigarette and watched us.

"It's quite urgent. Please, let me in."

The man was tall and dark, with a black mustache and gray-streaked hair. "I already told you, Jews can't go in."

"And aren't you a Jew?"

"No, I'm Romani."

I knew there were a number of Gypsies in the ghetto, but I had not come across any before.

"Romani," I nodded. "I've had a few Romani children in my orphanage."

The guard or concierge—it was hard to tell—raised his eyebrows. His uniform was tight against his well-defined muscles. "An orphanage?" he said. "We Gypsies never abandon our children. We're not like the Poles or the Germans."

"This is true, but these children lost their parents. Their wagon crashed into a truck, and the parents were killed on the spot. The authorities brought the three children to my orphanage." My account seemed to calm him. He took me aside and asked who I was looking for. I said the name, and he went inside. A few minutes later he returned and motioned for me to follow him through a door off the alley. We went through the dressing rooms of the singers and dancers into a dimly lit private room. I heard the captain before I saw him.

"What are you doing here, Doctor? These aren't necessarily ideal times to be getting the attention of the authorities."

"Ah, but when is?" I joked. Humor was my method of dealing with the pressure and stress of each day.

"I miss our chess games, though an American prisoner named Nosjztar is a worthy opponent."

"Nosjztar, from the JDC?" I asked, surprised. She was on the committee helping get American aid to the Jews.

"Yes, the very one. She's quite well educated and interesting. I'm only over common prisoners and a few terrorists."

"But why has Nosjztar been arrested?"

"Haven't you heard? The Americans have declared war on Germany, so they can't have organizations in Poland. Now they're our enemies."

His words heartened me. If anyone could stand up to the Nazis it was the Americans. But we had thought the same thing about the Russians, and the Germans were on the brink of finishing them off.

"Don't get excited. The United States is a big country, but their army is small. Well, and to what do I owe the honor of your visit? I doubt you came to challenge me to chess."

"What I'm going to ask you is pure insanity, and you'll probably have me locked up again."

"I'd love to, Doctor."

I sat beside him. Just down the hall, a group of dancers was swaggering across the stage as the Nazis sang out their decadent old songs. The music was loud.

"I need papers, you see: permission to go and come, ration cards, identification."

The captain picked up a glass of champagne and downed it in one gulp.

"You're aware, of course, that you're asking me to commit high treason."

"What I'm begging you to do is to help defenseless children. I understand that suspects are taken to jails and that the Nazis are trying to consolidate their regime here, but the children themselves are innocent."

Neumann refilled his glass and held my eyes. "You're all a bunch of filthy Jews. Why would I put myself at risk? I've got a family waiting on me in Germany."

"That's exactly why. Could you look them in the face and know that you helped murder hundreds of innocent children?"

Anger flashed in his eyes, but he merely took another sip. "You're quite bold, even suicidal; but I imagine that in desperate times one is willing to risk his queen."

"Checkmate!"

"I'm not promising anything. It's not easy to get documents without anyone noticing. Come back after New Year's. The Gypsy will be watching for you."

"Thank you," I said, barely containing my relief and joy.

"Maybe I'm feeling generous because it's almost Christmas. But just this one time, and I'll deny I ever knew you."

As I got to my feet, he held out his hand. I had never shaken a Nazi's hand before.

"I'm glad we've met," he said. "In this infernal war, meeting good men is the only thing that keeps one from going insane."

I chewed on his words as I found my way out of the hotel. I did not think of myself as "good." I knew what was in my heart and soul. The once crowded streets were now nearly empty. It was almost curfew, and everyone hid inside before the police started their rounds. The darkness felt comforting that night. I knew we might live to see another day, and my children might be saved.

CHAPTER 29

THIEVES

We had been dreaming about food for too long. Hunger was distorting us all. Christmas of 1941 would be like never before, as conditions were so much worse than the previous year's ghetto Christmas.

That morning I had been going over our rations, trying to stretch the meager supplies in our pantry as long as possible. We shared the building with a community soup kitchen, and we had reason to suspect that some who came to receive aid from the ghetto authorities were stealing from us. Since we had moved onto Sienna Street, several utensils had gone missing. People in the ghetto would sell anything they could to survive. But lately it was flour, rice, and beans that were disappearing little by little.

I was so wrapped up in my calculations that I did not notice Agnieszka come up. But as soon as I saw her face, I knew something was wrong.

"What's going on? Are you unwell?"

"No, I'm fine. It's Henryk. He wasn't in his room. I've asked all the other children, and they tell me he left early this morning with Józef."

"With Józef? I didn't know they were friends. Józef is much older than Henryk."

"It turns out Józef has been sneaking off for a while now. We think he's leaving the ghetto to find food."

"Why hasn't anyone told me?" She shrugged. I was incensed. I had already told the ghetto's mafias to leave my children alone. "It's too dangerous to be crossing the walls. The police and the SS are taking the children they find begging out in the street."

Agnieszka was crying quietly, at a loss. "I don't know how Henryk got talked into this."

"Your son is too caring. He realizes the straits we're in and probably went out thinking he could help. We've got to get word to Irena. She may be able to find him and bring him back."

We hurried to Irena's office and walked right by the long line that stretched down the street. When we barged into her office, she looked up in surprise from where she was speaking with a family.

"What in the world is going on?" she asked. Seeing our faces, she asked the family to step outside for a moment.

When we were alone and the door was closed, I got right to the point. "Agnieszka's son is outside the walls. We think he escaped with another one of our boys to look for food. Henryk is small and can get in and out of the gaps in the wall easily enough."

Irena took down her coat and purse from the hook.

"I'll go with you," I said as we walked out of her office. Irena gave some instructions to her coworkers, and we went out to the frozen street. The sky was heavy with clouds that promised snow. The next day was Christmas Eve, but we all knew there was nothing to celebrate.

"You'd better wait at the orphanage. It's not safe for you, Janusz."

"I can dress as a priest."

"No, I'll go alone this time."

We walked with Irena to one of the gates and watched her walk off. There was nothing to do but go back to Dom Sierot and wait as the minutes dragged by. Finally we could not stand it anymore and returned to the gate where Irena had left. After a very long time, we saw her coming back, alone. Agnieszka let out a choked sob.

"I'm sorry, I've looked for them everywhere but couldn't find them," Irena said.

I hugged Agnieszka and tried to comfort her. "Maybe they didn't leave from this spot; they could get back in somewhere else."

Biting cold fell over the city with the afternoon shadows. Once all the light was gone, it was bound to start snowing. As we plodded back to Dom Sierot, we spied Józef running ahead.

"Stop, you little devil! Come here!" I hollered, and he obeyed immediately.

"Dr. Korczak," he said tremulously.

"Where's Henryk? We've been looking for him all day." Józef cocked his head as if confused about what we were asking. "Look, Józef, we know you're sneaking out of the ghetto to scrounge up food and money, right? And today you took Henryk with you, yes?" I knew all the faces guilty children put on to feign innocence. I crouched down and looked him straight in the eyes. "Do you remember your mom? Well, Henryk's mother is worried. You don't want her to suffer any more than she already has, do you?"

He looked down and said, "Come with me."

Józef led us through streets I had never been down before. The little thieves knew the nooks and crannies of the ghetto better than the Jewish police did. We got to a run-down building that must have been a casualty of the bombings early on in the war. We climbed the rickety stairs to the roof, which allowed a perfect view of a good part of Warsaw.

"Henryk and I went to the train station. You can get a lot of money there, and the bartenders often throw out leftovers and rotten vegetables. You can find some real treasures in the garbage bins. Sometimes you eat it up right then and there, and other times you take it back to the Thirteen. They give you food rations and other things for what you bring them. I told Henryk all about it. He was worried about his mom, saying she was too skinny, and he wanted to get her some chocolate."

I could feel Agnieszka trembling as the boy prattled on.

"We got out through a little hole over there," he explained, pointing. "It's getting hard for me, and I don't know how much longer I'll be able to use that spot, but Henryk got through no problem. We stuck our armbands in our pockets and walked calmly down the street like nothing was happening. The truth is, it's not much different outside the walls anymore. A few months ago it was like a different world, everyone so much cleaner and shinier."

"Go on," I prodded him impatiently.

"So we were in the station, and a guy gave us two coins, and a woman gave us some bread. We waited 'til the restaurants closed, and we dug through the trash. There wasn't much good stuff today, though. We were heading back home when a man in a really nice suit offered us some chocolate. At first we were excited, but he said we had to go back to his house to get it. I told Henryk it was a bad idea, but he really wanted it. We got to the gate. It was a really nice house, fancy and clean looking, something you don't see in the city anymore. We were going up the stairs, and the guy put his hand on Henryk's back. That scared me. I grabbed Henryk's arm, and we started running. We were coming here and were almost at the wall when a policeman started chasing us. I dashed through the hole and started pulling Henryk after me, but the policeman was yanking on his legs, and he got him."

Józef's bravado had dissipated. He slumped to the ground and started crying. I hugged him, and we stayed like that until his breathing calmed down. I looked up to see Agnieszka swaying with her hands covering her face.

"What are we going to do, Janusz?" she moaned.

"At least it's the Polish police. It would've been much worse if the SS or the Gestapo had taken him. We can hope they've sent him to the center for juveniles since they caught him begging. I've got some contacts there. I'll ask Irena to take a letter."

We went back down to the street, and I sent Józef home. Then Agnieszka and I retraced our steps to the welfare office. Irena's shoulders slumped when she saw us.

"So what happened?"

I summarized our encounter with Józef, scribbled out a letter, and handed it over to her. Then we went back to Dom Sierot to rest. The children were finished with their studies and activities. I often wondered how they still had energy to learn under these conditions and how it was that not all of the teachers were trying to get out by any and every means.

Stefa fixed something like hot coffee, and we the teachers sat around a table with a small brazier to warm us. With Christmas Eve coming, I could not help but think of Jesus's parents looking for somewhere to stay in Bethlehem before Mary gave birth. Stefa, Agnieszka, and I waited up all night, hardly speaking. We were nodding off around dawn when we heard a noise at the door. Agnieszka and Stefa dashed down the stairs, and I followed as quickly as my stiff joints allowed, all of us a bundle of nerves. Agnieszka flung the door open, and Henryk flew into her arms, his face so dirty as to be hardly recognizable.

"Thank you," I said, choked up, to Maryna Falska. My old friend stood there next to Igor Newerly.

"Comrade," Igor said, embracing me, "it hurts me to see you like this."

It was wonderful to see this friend who had helped me on so many occasions. We had so much in common. He had studied at the Free Polish University but had always been connected to the Communist Party.

"How did you two get in?" I asked, incredulous.

Maryna flashed her ironic smile. "It's easier to get in than it is to get out."

"Could we speak alone, Janusz?" Igor asked, his hand on my shoulder.

I led him and Maryna to an empty corner. I got out three chairs that had seen better days, and Igor started talking.

"Life is a constant struggle. First it's the Russians; the czarists had us trapped in their unlivable system. Then it was fighting to get the Varsovian bourgeois to help the disenfranchised and the working class; and now the worst nightmare no one could have ever dreamed up: the Nazis."

"But you've never given up, and that's admirable," I said.

"Giving up has never been an option. We can't just lie down and make the Nazis' job easy, can we?"

I smiled, heartened by my old friend's fighting spirit.

"I'm in the Resistance, but there aren't a lot of us. Until people are at the end of their ropes, most aren't willing to take a risk."

I nodded. "I suppose that's human nature."

"Yes, but, damn it all, Janusz! This time we're all going down. We're making weapons. I hope that '42 will be the year of liberation. The

Yankees are in the war now, and working with the Russians, they'll chew Hitler's bunch up and spit them out. It's just a matter of time."

"May God let it be so!"

My avowed atheist friend rolled his eyes. "Listen, Janusz, we want you to come with us. We've got papers for you. The Germans have something massive up their sleeves. We've got a mole in Auschwitz who sends us reports on what's going on over there."

"Auschwitz?" I asked, confused.

"It's a Nazi concentration camp. They're expanding. We think they're planning to liquidate all the ghettos in the country. Living conditions in those camps are even worse than in the ghetto. You won't survive it."

"Igor is right," Maryna said.

"I can't leave the ghetto without my children. Nothing has changed since the last time we talked about it, Maryna."

Maryna shook her head. "But we can't get two hundred kids out at once. We don't have enough contacts for that."

I hung my head. On the one hand, my natural survival instinct was intense. All we had here was the ground beneath our feet. On the other hand, who was I without these children? They had kept suicide, insanity, and despair at bay. I needed them more than they needed me.

I shook my head resolutely. "I can't; I'm sorry. I know that you've risked so much to find a spot to hide me and then come here to get me. I'm truly grateful, but I'm not worth all that. I'm just a run-down old doctor who doesn't have much time left."

My two friends nodded and stood. They were not angry, just very sad. They knew this would be our last goodbye.

"Friend, I hope you know what you're doing. I've never found anyone with a heart as big as yours. I admire you and envy you. I wish I had your capacity to love," Igor said.

"You know that I love you," Maryna added.

"And I too. Forgive my shortcomings. I have such bad character."

I walked them to the door. A few paces down the street, they turned back to wave. My weeping started as I watched them trail off. The tears were not for my refusal to go with them. On the contrary, I wept over memories of the life we had shared together. We had fought a thousand fights side by side and lost many of them, but we had stuck with one another—even in the years of silence with Maryna, I always knew she cared for me.

A cold drop fell on top of my bald head. The sky was swarming with tiny snowflakes, and soon a thick white blanket would coat the streets. How I wished it were God scrubbing the world clean from the filth of the Nazis and their diabolical war.

CHAPTER 30

MORE THAN

HOPED FOR

That winter I thought a lot about Jerusalem. I'd never thought I would come to love that land so much or ever understand so deeply what it meant to be a Jew. I had always felt deeply Polish. Only bloodline tied me to the ancient people group I had neither chosen nor could escape. But in Jerusalem I discovered that, no matter how much we may deny what we are, deep down we know we will always be that thing. Now I was a Jew, an admirer of Jesus, a cursed Pole, a sick doctor, and a pedagogue in hell. I had finally discovered who I really was.

After the scare Henryk gave us, his mother did not allow him out of her sight. The children fashioned Christmas decorations for the building. It still looked strange to see a group of Jews celebrating the birth of

Christ, but what we were really celebrating was hope. For us, Christmas meant we were still here together. The task of decorating livened up all the teachers and tutors. It was undeniable that our second building in the ghetto was deplorable compared to the first and was not even comparable to our home on Krochmalna Street. But we were there, and we were alive, which is saying quite a lot. There was a roof over our heads, and each person there mattered to the others. I would not have traded that cold, damp, run-down building for a palace of solitude and loneliness.

That afternoon I set out to see what I could find on the black market. There were fewer and fewer options even from smugglers. With aid from international communities shut down, especially from the United States, the ghetto had less food than ever.

I walked to the northern zone where I had heard that a woman sold pastries and cakes. It was so uncustomary for the ghetto, so out of reach, that I doubted the story. But I wanted something special for Christmas dinner. I knew it might be our last—or that a miracle might happen and the Nazis might lose the war.

I knocked, and a shockingly fat woman came out of the small house. The bodies of many people in the ghetto reacted to starvation with ironic swelling, but this woman was not swollen. She was truly obese.

"Are you Dr. Korczak?" she asked.

I was surprised to be recognized. Sometimes I could not recognize my own reflection in the mirror.

"Yes, indeed. I've heard that you sell pastries. I'd like some, as many as you've got. I want to give the children a Christmas party, and—"

"Come in, come in, please. Don't stand here in the door. It's freezing out there."

I followed her inside the house that had once been a cowshed to a small but comfortable parlor. We sat, and she picked up her knitting.

"It's really a pleasure to meet you," she said, working the wool across her needles. "I used to listen to you on the radio. I can't read, you see. My parents didn't think that girls needed to learn to read and write. They were old-fashioned like that, but at least they left me the dairy. We were here already, before they built the ghetto walls. The Germans took my dear cows right away. They each had a name, poor things. I miss them. Sometimes I wake up with a start, worried because I haven't fed them yet."

"Do you live here alone?" I asked.

Her face fell. The girlish smile was gone. "I was married, but my husband died on the front. He was in one of the last battles. It was just bad luck. So I'm alone in the world. We couldn't have children, you see; and, to tell the truth, now I'm glad. The world is too dangerous for children these days, isn't it?"

"It always has been a dangerous place for the young. Adults can't accept their innocence and try to force them to be adults far too quickly, as if childhood were a disease."

"You're absolutely right. Can I get you some milk?"

"Milk? But haven't you lost all your cows?"

"Yes, but I have a little ewe that gives me milk. It's not much, but it's enough for every day and to make my cakes."

"I can't refuse that offer. I can't even remember what it tastes like."

The woman went off and returned a minute later with a full glass.

"Thank you. How do you get flour for baking?" I asked.

"I still have a few friends on the outside. There's a little tunnel underneath the house. We used to use it to store hay, but now the millers use it to bring me flour."

I was shocked. Flour was practically nonexistent in the ghetto.

Suddenly she burst out, "I'm sick."

"Oh, I'm so sorry. These are very difficult times we're in."

"A few months ago I was able to see a doctor. I've got cancer. Ironic, isn't it? The Nazis kill us by starvation and privation, and my body is being eaten up by cancer. I feel like I'm disappearing little by little, as if I never existed."

"We all do return to dust after all."

"Sometimes I go to the cemetery to stand at my parents' grave, and my husband's grave is right next to them. Who will take them flowers when I'm gone? That's what makes me so sad. When I die, no one will remember them. Life is too hard."

"I'm so sorry about what's happening to you. Many people believe we don't die fully, that God keeps us in his memory to create us anew after death. After all, we are his creatures."

"Oh, I'm not religious," she tsked.

"Nor am I," I nodded. "But I believe we each have a spiritual side to us. Without it, the world would be pointless."

"And maybe it is pointless, don't you think?"

"The fact that we're thinking and talking about these things shows that there's got to be some level of meaning. We feel like we're eternal. Death seems to be a mere obstacle separating us from immortality."

The woman got up with an effort and went into the bakery part of her dwelling. She returned with two heavy bags and put them at my feet.

"I've made enough pastries for the holidays, but I'm not sure I'll even make it to New Year's. At least your children will enjoy one magical night."

"Oh, I can't accept all this!" I said, scooting back.

"But of course you can. The poor darlings have suffered enough already."

"Why don't you come join us? You don't have to spend Christmas alone."

She smiled, but it was more like a grimace. "Oh, I wish I could. I would be raging with pain, though. It's better if I just stay here and rest. I hope to get to sleep a bit; that would be a nice Christmas present. Sometimes I'm up all night."

I stood and placed my hand on her shoulder. "Thank you. No good deed goes unrewarded."

"I'm not looking for a reward. Just meeting you has been the best present I could have hoped for. If you've got time, come back by to visit me sometime. That would please me so much."

"Absolutely, I'll be back!"

I heaved the two bags over my shoulders with some difficulty, and she saw me to the door. Half an hour later I was at the orphanage, weary and out of breath. Two tutors helped me with the sacks and took them to the dining room.

"We were worried about you, Janusz," Stefa said. "The party is about to start."

"Well, I brought dessert!" I said with a wry smile.

One of the teachers had dressed up like Saint Nicholas and another as a clown. They played games with the children and then we ate supper by candlelight. Before we handed out gifts, the children begged for a story.

I stood and went up to the stage we had improvised. "We can respond to life in two ways. We can complain as if the universe owed us something, and doubtless we have the right to; or we can feel grateful. This building is much worse than our previous homes. But we have a roof over our heads, which is something millions of people throughout Germany, Russia, and Poland no longer can say. We're surrounded by friends who love us, and tonight we got to eat supper. Some of our companions have passed on to eternity. Don't worry, they've just gone a step further in the journey we'll all take one day."

Some of the children had teared up, and several tutors and teachers were dabbing at their eyes. I continued, "Life is about giving, which we symbolize through these gifts. In the face of the selfishness and disdain toward others that reign supreme in our day, we are called to love one another, even to love our enemies. It's said that when we can love like that, we turn our enemies into friends. I've taught you to forgive, and today is a good time to remember that. If you hold hatred and contempt in your heart, replace it with love. Leave bitterness behind, and together we can be happy. We like material things, that's true enough; but they distract us from the true essence, that secret something that true happiness is made of. The only thing that really matters is love, and tonight we celebrate the birth of love. What matters is giving one another our very selves with all our hearts."

I sighed heavily as I stepped down from the stage. I knew my words were true, and I had to keep sharing them, but they were harder and harder to believe. The worst year of our lives was coming to a close. I feared that what was to come would not be an improvement.

PART III
A PLACE NO MORE

CHAPTER 31

THIRTY MORE

I could remember looking forward to New Year's Day. People labored to prepare sumptuous feasts and kept an impatient vigil for the clock to strike the beginning of 365 good days. We had been told that the twentieth century was the time of progress and we would see things people had never dreamed of before. Now that almost half the century was gone, the only extraordinary marvels had been two cruel world wars, a terrible pandemic, and the greatest economic crisis in recorded history.

I had been slowly surrendering my inalterable faith in the world over the past few months. It was not that I had been an idealist. Working among the poor and the needy of this world does not allow idealism. But I trusted in the existence of a universal conscience and in the betterment of humans through culture and education. The arrival of the Germans had destroyed Poland. The saddest part was that the evil they were capable of producing sprung from the human heart. If humans were naturally good, they certainly did hide it well.

Now that the Americans were in the war, a ridiculous optimism spread throughout the ghetto, as if President Roosevelt could wipe the Nazis out with a magic wand. Meanwhile, news arrived of Allied losses in Asia, and the Japanese were pressing all the fronts. It was a global war at this point.

On the eastern front, the only seemingly good news was that the Russians had managed to stop the Nazis at Moscow, though it seemed like they would take Leningrad.

I looked across the street and across the wall to the Aryan zone where the Poles were suffering their own kind of hell. I thought I spied Irena walking back to her house, weary after another morning of helping the ghetto's increasingly miserable population. The figure ducked into an alley, and I lost her from view, but then I saw her stand upright again. I was shocked: she was tugging at a child emerging from a manhole. How had she found the girl? Was this her plan for getting them out? I had no answers to anything. The last report I'd had from her was that she needed more time for the rescue network to fully come together.

The blond child was very small. Even from this distance I could see she was dirty and frightened. Irena held her hand, and they walked quickly away. Had I dreamed what I'd just seen? I had just awoken from a restless nap. My stomach ached. We had to eat whatever came our way, and if that included meat or eggs, we ate it without asking questions. Today's portion was not sitting well with me. I lay back down on the bed.

Stefa knocked and came in, handing me a mug of some sort of tea. "How are you feeling?"

"A bit queasy. I haven't vomited, but my stomach isn't happy with me."

"This might help it settle." She set the infusion on the table beside

They acted like a group of children at a slumber party, piled together on mattresses, talking about their incredible adventure.

I walked Irena to the door, and she stared at me in admiration. "I'll never forget what you're doing for these boys. Tomorrow I'll bring food and vaccines, and I'm hoping to start getting the first few kids out very soon."

"Oh, well, my life has been one big swing of changes, usually for the worse. I'll do my best to keep them safe. The only thing I can promise is that as long as I'm alive, none of them will die, if I can help it."

Watching her walk off, I wondered if I could keep my word. It was true that I had somehow always miraculously kept going, pushed along as it were by some supernatural force. I hoped that force would help me keep all my children safe.

CHAPTER 32

THREE GOOD MEN

I was obsessively thinking about the things we could not or did not know to do in the early days of the monstrous Nazis' rule. Who finished off our democracy? Why did the world succumb so easily to fascism and Nazism? Many people argued that it was because of a fear of communism, which seemed absolutely unstoppable after the Great War. They said that the great magnates, relying on the small bourgeois that was losing its rights and jobs, together with workers with no particular ideology, had joined forces with the business class to conspire against the old, outdated world of parliamentary democracy.

I was thinking about my friends, both Jews and non-Jews, so many of whom had been murdered in some ditch or tortured in Gestapo prisons, whose only crimes were thinking for themselves and refusing to accept the rigid world of totalitarianisms. At that moment, I felt like there was no one left to resist. But when evil rages with all its force, there are always a few brave enough to stand up to it.

I was on my way to the Britannia Hotel to see Captain Neumann for the blank documents we could falsify, and I was unsettled. I jumped when I heard my name called.

"Dr. Korczak!" It was not uncommon for strangers to recognize me on the street, yet this voice sounded somewhat familiar. I turned and found the source: it was Marek Edelman, a leader in Tsukunfit. The youth organization of the Jewish labor union helped train teenagers in valuable skills and gave them a place to belong.

"Well, Marek, I can't say I'm pleased to see you here," I said by way of acknowledging our mutual misfortune at finding ourselves in one of the worst places in Europe.

"My sentiments exactly, though it's the hand we've been dealt. And, as my father always said, the important thing isn't the world around us but what we do with it."

"Your father was a great man, I've heard."

"He died defending his ideals against the Bolsheviks, and now it's my turn to do the same against the Nazis. Ironic, isn't it?"

"And what can be done against the Nazis?"

The thin young man twisted his black mustache and pulled me aside to a quiet corner. "That's in fact exactly what I want to talk to you about. The ghetto's youth refuse to die like sheep led to slaughter. We're slowly stockpiling weapons, and, when the time is right, we'll rise up."

"Oh, Marek, you might take down a few Germans, but Warsaw is packed with barracks, and others will take their place."

"No, a lot of Germans have left for the front. At least the Russians are doing something worthwhile. They're like a steamroller plastering entire German divisions."

"I've heard that, too, but I have my doubts. The Nazis whipped the French and the British and swallowed up the entire European continent. You really think the Russians are better than French soldiers? Allow me to question it. The more advanced countries have folded to the Germans. So I fear that the only thing that might save Russia is its size and the force of its winter."

"The war in the east is totally different than what happened in Europe. The Germans are wiping out whole populations. The Nazis want the land to completely repopulate it. But the survival instinct has always been one of the strongest forces of nature."

"So, what can this old man do to help you?" I asked, tiring of the theoretical banter.

"You should intercede for our cause. The Judenrat doesn't want an uprising, but they have contacts that could help us. We need a lot more weapons and the money to buy them."

"But think of the German tanks, the planes . . ."

"We've got courage on our side. Have you forgotten how Gideon conquered the Midianites with a tiny army?"

"Ha, since when do you appeal to biblical precedent? Anyhow, it was the Lord who fought for them back then."

Marek smiled, but his facial muscles were tense. I had the feeling that smiling no longer came naturally to the young man. "The same Lord of hosts will fight with us."

"I don't believe in violence. If we resist, we'll just give them an excuse to massacre us all."

"I understand you, Doctor. Like you, I'm dedicating my life to fighting for children and raising them up with values. But the only way to fight evil—at least, this kind of evil—is with violence."

"There's no victory to be had that way."

"We know we can't win, but sometimes the fight itself is the victory."

I rested my hand on his skinny shoulder. The skinniest German soldier was at least twice his girth. We Jews could only form an army of famished desperation.

"I'll speak with the Council, but they don't listen to me. The Germans have cast a spell on them, I believe. They seem to think all this will end and that at the end of the war, the Jews will be sent to Madagascar or Palestine—as if all the Nazis wanted was to not have to see our faces."

Marek thanked me, and I resumed walking to the hotel. The Gypsy at the door recognized me immediately and led me again through a side door to the room reserved for the captain.

"Good afternoon, Dr. Korczak," Neumann said amiably enough.

"Good afternoon, Captain, though I'm not sure what such a phrase means anymore."

He handed me a small satchel that held the precious papers.

"It was all I could get. It's all very tightly controlled, and blank documents rarely go missing."

"I understand. Thank you for everything."

"It's nothing, less than nothing. In a few days I'll be transferred to the Russian front."

"But why do they need military police in Russia?"

Neumann drained the glass he was holding. I could tell from his eyes and the smells in the room that he had been drinking more and more. He offered me a drink.

"Thank you, I think I will," I answered. My nerves were shot, and I often wondered how much longer I could hold it together before becoming completely derailed. Alcohol smoothed over that volatility.

A Jewish waitress brought me a vodka. Inside the club the workers did not have to wear their armbands, as only Jews from the ghetto could be employed there. I was dismayed to see that the young woman's uniform was lowcut up top and short on the bottom. The establishment knew how to keep the bored, drunk soldiers entertained.

I sipped the vodka slowly and tried to enjoy the music that wafted in. That place could make it feel like everything outside its walls was an illusion.

"It has been a pleasure knowing you, Doctor. I just wish it had been under other circumstances."

"I can't lie: I wish we had never met, by which I mean the Germans would not have invaded my country and this place"—I invoked the entire ghetto with a wave—"would not exist."

"You think so? We're not the first, and I fear we won't be the last to persecute you. I imagine this is simply the spirit of the times we've been given to live in."

"Is it that simple?" I asked, perplexed. His summary seemed to exonerate everyone from war, death, hunger, and everything that transpired in the ghetto.

"What else can it be? Do you really think we are this perverse?"

"I think the Nazis are simply human, too human in the worst sense of the word. Your people were scared and had an inferiority complex; you didn't know where to turn, and somebody rose up and told you what to do. By the time you thought about it, he had absolute control of your lives. Fear is the most dangerous weapon in the world."

"You may be right, you may be. But I was there when Hitler rose to power, and I was glad. My family had always been Christian Democrats, but we believed in the old ways that no longer worked. Later, a lot of us realized what was going on. In our own homes, a few of us were horrified over what was happening to our neighbors, to our Communist friends, to our Socialist colleagues, to our Jewish professors; but nobody dared speak against it in public. We should take responsibility and raise our voices, but we're too cowardly to do it. What will they do to my family in Germany if I refuse to follow orders? You know what happens to traitors."

"But if ten thousand like you rose up, Captain, who could stop you?"

There was deep sadness in the officer's eyes that afternoon. He seemed ready to give up and admit the futility of his final attempts to hold out against the barbarism surrounding us.

"A grave in Russia is probably what I deserve. Our whole generation is responsible for all of this, and dying in a foreign land would be an appropriate punishment for our sins."

"Death isn't the answer. You would be proving Hitler right. His power depends on other people not thinking or questioning it. Captain, you do think, and that's unfortunate for Hitler; it's also the way to redeem yourself. This"—I touched the satchel of papers—"is an act of rebellion."

I made to leave, and the captain stood at attention, a final act of honor at our parting. "I hope you get out of here before it's too late," he said.

"I won't leave without my children, and this may help." I nestled the satchel carefully under my arm and gave him a final nod.

Before returning home, I had one more stop to make. Father Godlewski was waiting for me in his church. There were fewer refugees milling about, and the chapel seemed sadder and melancholier than it had before.

"How are you this evening, Father?" I asked the priest.

"Weary. We've been smuggling people out for weeks, and a hundred more are waiting on me to help them get out of this hell. One never gets used to living in the midst of pure evil."

"The day we do will be the death of us, at least of our souls."

The priest nodded and got to his feet. I handed him the satchel. "We'll start making birth certificates and papers for your children. You know they're our priority."

"Thank you," I said.

"Sometimes I wonder, Janusz: What makes one man choose the light and another choose the dark?"

I often wondered the same. "Conscience, perhaps? That inner voice that tells a man what's good and what's bad?"

"I can tell you one thing: conscience can be manipulated. At one time, as you well know, I was anti-Semitic. I told myself that the Jews did not deserve my compassion. God put me in this ghetto to mend my ways and show me how to pay for my faults."

"Well, you're doing a bang-up job of it."

"Do you think so? In many ways I fed the hatred that many Poles are now showing the Jews. My dear doctor, evil is not from the outside; it nests deep in our hearts. The sooner we learn that truth, the easier it will be to put an end to it. Each of us has to be transformed into something better so the world can become a place worth living in."

"It certainly seems that good keeps quiet while evil is what makes history march along. But I am confident, Father, that in the end good will triumph."

The priest wrapped me in his arms. There we were, an old Jew and an old Catholic, embracing in the struggle against the devil who had locked both of us up in the ghetto walls.

The day's excursion had led me to cross paths with three very different, and yet ironically similar, men. Marek, Captain Neumann, and Father Godlewski were each trying to do good in their own way. One was a desperate freedom fighter; another clung to the last vestiges of his humanity; and the last was paying for the sins of his past. Godlewski's was a heavy burden, that of admitting he had been wrong while he had tried to do what was right.

I was no better than them. In fact, I was quite inferior. Young Marek was brave, something I never was; Neumann was sincere, while I had to trick my own self every morning just to get out of bed; and Godlewski had learned from his mistakes, yet mine kept me awake at night. I was proud and grateful that fate had surrounded me with men and women who were greater than me, and I was convinced that was the key to saving the world. The only way to save humanity is to shape one human at a time. The rest is just theology, and theology never saved anyone.

CHAPTER 33

MORE WEIGHT

Spring was on its way, but it did not bring better times. At least it had stopped snowing, and the streets were a bit more passable. After a few weeks, the snow ceased to be a beautiful, pristine movie set and instead became as dark and hard as mortar. None of us had enough warm clothing, and people stayed close together in groups for warmth. That morning I was headed into the Great Ghetto for a meeting of the orphans' care society known as CENTOS. I walked as briskly as I could, avoiding people and staying as far away as possible from the German guards who were always interested in ruining someone's day just for fun.

On one of the main roads, Henryk Szpilman, the brother of the famous pianist, was trying his best to sell off some books. I stopped and automatically began flipping through some. Reading was one of the few pleasures still allowed in the ghetto, though my sight was failing and it was hard for me to concentrate for extended periods of time.

"How's business?" I asked, smiling at him.

"Not good, but I can't complain. People spend the little they have on food and clothing, but books are still the only real way to escape the ghetto and the hunger."

"That's the truth. Reading is liberating. All throughout my youth, and the two times I've been in prison, I devoured books like the world was ending and each page turned would bring me closer to freedom."

"That's how it is with me. It's the only way I can deal with all this." He gestured to the downcast, ragged crowd walking by.

"My children and I are the lucky ones. The Small Ghetto looks almost like paradise compared to over here. Social differences are as pronounced in the ghetto as they are outside."

The young man set his book down on his makeshift stand and got to his feet. "Do you know what happened to poor Jehuda Zyskind?" he asked.

"Your brother's friend? No, I haven't heard." Sometimes I preferred not to hear. Not knowing about another's pain was a way of bearing less of it myself.

"The Jewish police went to his house to look for him, took his whole family away, and turned them over to the Germans. They accused them of publishing clandestine materials. They were shot yesterday."

"Oh, oh." I rocked back and forth with the sadness. "The whole family?" Zyskind had been a black-market smuggler and had often given us food and clothing for the children.

I noticed that Szpilman's face had frozen, and he was looking behind me. I turned and came face-to-face with a Jewish policeman who growled, "Why aren't you wearing your armband?"

"I do not care to do so. Is there a problem?" I replied curtly.

"Are you getting fresh with me, old man? You know all Jews are required to wear the armband. You think you're special?"

The bully was tall and imposing, but at my age I had long since stopped fearing death. Instead, I thought of death as a dear friend who would be dropping by soon for a visit.

"Are you not ashamed of yourself? You should be helping your people, not serving the Nazis as their hit man."

The brute raised his nightstick and walloped me. I held off a few blows with my arms, but he eventually got my forehead, and I started bleeding profusely.

"Stop!" Szpilman yelled, but the policeman grabbed me by the coat. I lost my balance, and he started dragging me off. In the disorientation, I did not know who I was or what was happening. My brain simply shut off.

I came to in a cell. It was dark, and the stench of damp filth was unbearable. I sat up and leaned against the wall, trying to recall what had happened. My knees, head, and shoulders were throbbing, but nothing was broken. The blood on my forehead had dried. My glasses were gone.

I heard footsteps, then a lock being opened, and a blinding light poured in.

"What are you doing here again?"

I was relieved to hear the voice of Captain Neumann.

"I thought you'd be in Russia by now," I croaked out.

"Me too, and to tell the truth, it's what I'd prefer. Everyone's afraid of getting sent east, but at least it would spare me from watching the ghetto become a cemetery or, even worse, a grotesque torture chamber." He helped me get to my feet. "A friend of yours filed a complaint about your detention. Apparently you weren't wearing your armband

and were rude to the policeman when inquiries were made. Will you never learn?"

"I'm not going to wear that symbol of ignominy. Let them shoot me if they want to, but I'm not backing down. The only thing that makes us men is our dignity, and there's not much of it left."

He led me out to the hallway, and I followed him clumsily to his office on the first floor, where he gave me my glasses. "They fell off at the door of your cell. I'll release you immediately."

"Thank you again. Why did they leave you here in Warsaw?"

"Apparently in about a month we're beginning a relocation operation, and they need staff for that. Bureaucratic nonsense, you know how it goes. The war is choking up the High Command, though they're still convinced they'll win. They need more free labor, and I presume that's what's behind the construction of all the work camps."

Walking me to the door of Pawiak, he asked in a low voice, "How are the children?"

"People keep dying of hunger and disease, which means there are more and more orphans. Would to God that some of them get out of here soon."

Out on the street, I took a long, deep breath. I was bruised, but it had never felt so good to feel ghetto ground beneath my feet. I knew that my time in the world had not yet come to a close. We are all here for a reason and cannot leave until we have fulfilled our purpose.

Amazingly, I was only fifteen minutes late to my CENTOS meeting. I labored up the three flights of stairs and found the office I had been summoned to. The head of that department was a young, handsome man with something of a movie-star air about him.

"Good God, what happened to you?" he exclaimed when he realized that the apparition standing before him was Janusz Korczak.

"Don't worry, I'm fine. Just a little mishap."

"You shouldn't go out on your own. The streets are more dangerous every day. People get mugged for a coat or a pair of shoes, and there's no respect for the elderly."

"Well, I'm afraid that what you see is the result of one of our Jewish policemen."

He shuddered. "They're a bunch of thugs with permission to steal and kill."

I slumped into a chair, and the man placed a heavy file on his desk. He cleared his throat. "Dr. Korczak, we'd like to ask you to do something very important. We recognize the great pains you take to care for your orphanage. There's another orphanage on Dzielna Street that is all but abandoned. It's in a deplorable state. The children have suffered greatly and need your help."

I was trying to make sense of his words. "Are you asking me to be the director of another orphanage?"

"There's no one more qualified than you to do it. There are six hundred poor children dying of hunger."

"Six hundred?!" I spluttered. "That's three times the number in Dom Sierot. Where would I find food, clothing, teachers, and coal?"

"We'll help all we can. Many of the children are very sick. The previous director died, and things have gotten very bad." He placed a ring of keys on the table. "You'll have to act as soon as possible. Without intervention, who knows how many will die by the week's end."

I struggled to stand, and not because of my fresh wounds. It was the weight of six hundred more lives that suddenly depended on me. I was in shock. How in the world could I help them? Some other time, some other place, this would have been an exciting new challenge. But right then, it was a deranged plan, a nightmare I needed to wake up from.

CHAPTER 34

DYING FOR NOTHING

That dark, cloudy afternoon we went to the Dzielna Street orphanage. Irena brought three of her workers to join Agnieszka, three of our tutors, and myself. Before I even opened the door, the nauseating stench smacked us in the face. The darkness over the entryway stairs seemed to welcome us into a cemetery. We entered, stepping with care. We could hardly see our feet, and it was eerily quiet. We threw back the dusty curtains and opened the windows to bring in fresh air. Two of the workers got busy cleaning the kitchen and common areas that were infested with bugs. The rest of us went up to the first floor. The creaking stairs seemed destined to cave in, like everything else in that building. We entered a large room that appeared empty, but coughing and whimpers drew our attention to skeletal shapes on the beds. Not until we opened the curtains and windows did we see the condition the poor creatures were in. It was unimaginable.

"Oh dear God." I sucked in my breath. After a moment's pause of incredulity, we ran to the beds and started assessing the children. They were all girls, and they were too sick and weak to get out of bed. It was horrible beyond the point of tears.

From there we went to the next room, where we were met by the same sight with young boys, though a few of them were strong enough to sit up.

On the next floor, Irena, Agnieszka, and I opened the door to an attic room with nearly two hundred very young children. The first two I touched were cold and unmoving under the blanket.

Agnieszka picked one child up. The small girl's skeletal body writhed, and Agnieszka held her tightly. Weeping, she whispered, "It's okay, sweetie. You're safe now."

I wondered if that could be true. Many of these children were beyond help, and I knew that scores of them would be dead before the day ended.

We spent hours cleaning the children, changing the bedsheets, and feeding the weakest. The poor things did not have the strength left to cry, but they stared at us with their huge, terrified eyes. A few smiled shyly, as if trying out those facial muscles for the first time in too long.

Two of our men brought the cadavers down and placed them at the door for the gravediggers to collect on their carts like household trash. That was all the funeral rites the dead received in the ghetto. A rabbi would say a few prayers over them as they were dumped into a mass grave in the cemetery.

Three of Dom Sierot's tutors stayed the night, including Agnieszka. At the door, I asked her, "Are you sure? Henryk will wonder where you are."

The tears that had been flowing down her face since we arrived continued. "God knows I can't leave them like this. More will die tonight. At least we can hold them as they go."

I gave her a hug. My heart, too, was torn open, yet I had to hold it together for all the ones who were still alive, for the ones we could still save. We retraced our steps to the Small Ghetto, and Irena held my hands and looked deeply into my eyes as we said goodbye.

"You know what makes me so mad?" she asked. "I spend all day here, among this horror that only gets worse, but then I leave the ghetto, and it feels like none of this is real—like everything that happens behind these walls is just a fantasy I made up. People outside the ghetto are suffering, they're starving and afraid, but they're still in charge of their own lives. Inside, people are slaves who are dying at any moment without understanding why they are so hated or what they've done to deserve this."

I sighed. "Get some rest. Tomorrow will be another day."

"Every time I lie down in bed I wonder if I'll be able to get up and come back. I hide under the covers like a scared little kid."

I nodded, then gently pressed her on her way. After parting ways with the social workers, the tutors and I returned to Dom Sierot. It felt like a welcoming paradise in comparison to 39 Dzielna Street.

Stefa asked how it had been. I, who always had a witty response, opened my mouth but nothing came out. There was no way to describe it. That home was not an orphanage; it was a pre-funeral home for children. So this is what we had come to: cadavers piled up on all sides and shadows stretching fully over us, a dark storm about to rain down in full fury and no way to stop it.

CHAPTER 35

THE MOVIE

There was no time for tears. My little chicks were dying. Some had been able to escape thanks to Irena and her network, but at the rate things were going, we would hardly get a dozen of them out before it was too late. To worsen the ghetto's typical woes, the Jewish police were now hunting people down in the streets and taking them away to be relocated—at least that was the official story. Working for two orphanages had me so busy that the days just sped by while outside chaos reigned.

That day Irena had asked me to bring her one of the younger girls who had the necessary features to pass unnoticed in an Aryan family. I held Anna's hand as we walked and wondered what would become of her. Perhaps a few years from now she would remember none of this. She would not even know that her rescuers were not her parents. Destiny might make her the daughter of wealthy lawyers or poor peasants. What is it exactly that makes us who we are? Our families? Our circumstances? Our genetic backgrounds?

"Where are we going, Teacher?" Anna asked me. She was wearing a clean dress, and Stefa had braided her blond hair into two smart plaits. She looked as much a princess as any I had seen.

"We're going to see Irena and then will hopefully go far away from here. How does that sound?"

"Will I see my friends again?"

"Oh, you never know. Life is full of twists and turns. We'll see what God has for you."

She scrunched up her face, unconvinced by my evasive reply.

"Why do I have to leave? What will everybody else do?"

Her questions surprised me, but the ghetto had made even young children grow up too fast.

"I'm not really sure. We don't always have all the answers, Anna. I hope that one day all of our children at the orphanage will be happy, that you'll find one another again later in life, and that you'll look back on these difficult times as maybe even exciting."

We got to Irena's office, and I was relieved to find it empty. It was better to avoid notice.

"Hello, Anna, I'm so glad you're here," Irena said, kneeling down to stroke the girl's face.

"Hello, Miss Irena."

"We've found a family for you. You're going to spend the night at Father Boduen's home, and then a pretty lady named Władysława is going to take you to your new home. Does that make you happy?"

"Is it supposed to?" Anna asked in all seriousness.

ink so. There are lots of children who don't get to have a
're very lucky."

all right, Anna," I said, my hand on her small head. "You'll get
u᷉ to it and will enjoy your new home." Change was never easy, and
so many of the children who had left Dom Sierot in the past had told us
how they always missed their friends and their life with us.

"These are your papers, and here's your new name."

"Why do I have to change my name? Don't you like it?"

"Anna is a wonderful name, but now that you're going to start a
new life, you need a new name. Really it's like a game. Nobody can
know that you're Anna. If the Nazis learn your real name, they might
hurt your new family, your old friends, and everybody. Does that make
sense?"

"Oh, don't worry. I'm good at games, and I'm as silent as the grave
when it comes to keeping secrets."

"How are you going to take her out, Irena?" I asked.

"Fortunately, she's very small. There's a compartment in the munic-
ipal ambulance we can use. Anna, you're going to need to be very quiet.
Can you do that?" Irena asked, smiling into Anna's sweet face.

"I'll be the quietest girl you never heard of!" she giggled.

The ambulance and driver were already waiting behind the welfare
office. The driver wore a long white jacket that did not manage to hide
his sizable belly. "Dr. Korczak, it's an honor to meet you. I'm Aniol. May
God bless you for all that you're doing for these children."

"Oh, they're my sons and daughters. Thank you for putting your life
at risk for them."

He took off his cap and scratched his curly blond hair. "We've got to
do something," he said.

Irena folded Anna into the little space and kissed her forehead. "All right, stay calm. We'll be on the other side soon. You can breathe; there's plenty of air." Anna smiled back and closed her little eyes. Irena closed the compartment and the back door of the ambulance, and Aniol got behind the wheel.

"Don't worry, Janusz," Irena said. She could tell I was nervous. Actually, I felt near hysteria. I gripped my hat in my hand and forced a smile. "We've done this many times before."

"Wait just a moment," I blurted out.

I opened the door and then the compartment where Anna was curled up. I kissed her warm cheeks and said, "Anna, sweetie, I love you, and I'll never forget you."

"I'll remember you, too, Teacher. Thank you for being so good."

We closed everything up again, and the ambulance pulled away. I followed from a distance until it got to the gate. I did not breathe until they were beyond the checkpoint. I raised my arm in triumph. So at least one life, little Anna, was safe from the Nazis. At least they could not destroy her. I said it over and over as I walked back to Dom Sierot. I had not gone far when I noticed some Germans with a camera. I had seen soldiers taking pictures every now and then, but this was a professional team taking video.

I did not feel like going straight home. It had been a while since I had been out stretching my legs and feeling the air on my face. I redirected my course to the office of Adam Czerniaków, the chair of the Judenrat. Czerniaków was not busy at the moment, so the secretary waved me through. Where he sat, he looked more upbeat than usual. If I felt overwhelmed trying to run two orphanages, I could not even imagine what that man must have been feeling, charged as he was with the care of several hundred thousand people.

"Dr. Korczak, always a pleasure. What brings you here now? You never drop by without cause. Are the supplies not arriving?"

"Well, it's never enough, but you already know that. And the situation on Dzielna Street is not quite as absolutely horrendous as at first."

"You know I'm doing all I can."

"Sure, sure, but just now I'm curious about the German camera team out there."

He raised his hands and with an annoyed gesture said, "You know how dramatic our occupiers are. Now they want to film a documentary about life in the ghetto. Their propaganda machine is as active as ever."

"But what are they after?"

"All I can think is that they want to make the Jews look bad and at the same time show how humanely they're dealing with us. Though it would take about thirty seconds of real footage to show what they're really doing here, killing us with cold and hunger."

What bizarrely macabre notions the Nazis had. Now we were their zoo animals on exhibition.

"They'd better not try to get into my orphanage. I'm telling you right now that I won't stand for it. Not a single photo."

"I understand, and I don't think they're after you. They've already announced their locations. They want to film a meeting in my office, some of the ritual washings, some of the streets, and the cabarets and other places like that."

"It would be best to steer clear of their games."

"I've no choice. Too many lives are at stake."

"I tell you, Czerniaków, I don't know how you do it. How can you speak and deal with these beasts? I actually admire you, you know."

"Sometimes we have to deal with the devil himself to save a few. Some of the reports we get say that Britain's RAF bombings over

Germany are really picking up. They've destroyed countless factories, trains, and supply networks. So the Nazis are getting a taste of their own medicine. In Yugoslavia the Communists have rebelled against the Germans, who've had to send in lots of troops to chase them down. An even bigger deal is the assassination of Heydrich in Prague. He was the right-hand man of Himmler, who dreamed up this whole scheme. Not to mention that the Russians are pushing the Germans back on all sides."

"That's all good news. I can only hope that the war will end soon, though I fear Hitler and his henchmen will get what they're after."

"How do you mean, Dr. Korczak?" Czerniaków asked.

"The world has gone stark raving mad, and nobody respects human life anymore. Do you think the Allies aren't fully aware of what the Germans are doing to us? Even Pius XII knows it. But no one cares about the Jews. The Allied countries closed their doors to thousands of refugees before the war. Anti-Semitism is well entrenched all the world over." I was getting riled up by my own words.

Czerniaków bobbed his head noncommittally. "The Nazis are barbarians, no doubt about that, but they belong to a very rich culture. I trust that in the end they'll realize that we're worth more to them alive than dead. Their men are all at the front, and we can continue producing the thousands of supplies they need to win their war."

His optimism peeved me, but I understood that Czerniaków was doing the best he could and that he needed something to grab onto to keep from falling into a pit of despair.

"Well, the ghetto youth are organizing armed resistance. They asked me to talk to you about it."

"Oh, Korczak, more madness! They'll get us all killed!" he exclaimed, his face contorted by indignation.

"They tell me it's better to die standing than live on their knees. They may be right. Collaborating with the Nazis hasn't gotten us far."

"We're still alive, aren't we?" Czerniaków insisted. "Your children are eating and breathing. That's what negotiation with the Germans has gotten us. If we give them one single excuse, they'll wipe the whole ghetto out with all of us inside."

"Well, my job was just to let you know. If the Judenrat helped them, they could get more weapons and put up a stronger resistance."

"As long as I'm in this office, we will not use violence. I find it unthinkable that you, a declared pacifist, would suggest this."

"Even pacifism has its limits. When it comes to saving the elderly, the women, and the innocent children, we ought to be able to defend ourselves." I stood. God knows I had not meant to argue with the poor Judenrat chairman. He did not need an old man adding more pain and trouble to his already complicated life. "I'm not defending violence, Czerniaków; you know me. But the young men have a right to die with dignity. It's all they've got left."

"I gave it up long ago in the attempt to save at least some part of my people."

"I admire your efforts. And I hope that one day people appreciate what you're doing," I said, bidding him farewell.

Back out on the streets, I watched the camera crew, who were recording a woman moaning in anguish over the dead baby in her arms. It was inhumane and cruel to be robbing her of that intimate act of pain, and I was tempted to go after them and bash their cameras. Yet just as horrifying was the indifference of the people all around. The Nazis had dehumanized us to such a degree that I felt they had already won their war. If our bodies were ever free of the ghetto hell, our souls just might remain trapped in it forever.

CHAPTER 36

LOVE IN THE GHETTO

For a long time I had known that I was not protecting my own life and work but was defending the lives of all the children in my care. They had lost everything: first their parents, siblings, and whole families; and now the hope of a future. They did not realize the tragic fate that awaited them; childhood innocence would not allow them to look reality in the face. It was entirely plausible that what they perceived was the actual truth and we, puffed up and aged by years, could not see that there were things more important than life or death, health or illness.

Some of the poor dears had suffered so much trauma that I knew we teachers could never overcome it. I had seen mothers take their own lives in front of their children and fathers shot dead while walking hand in hand with their young boys or girls. Sometimes we rescued children out of rubble and pried their hands free from the dead parents who had already started to decompose. Though this was not my first war or revolution, I had never seen so much pain unleashed over any people group, especially my own.

Every day I went by the Dzielna Street orphanage. The situation had improved drastically thanks to Irena's help and, above all, the determination of Agnieszka and some of our other educators who had given their hearts and souls to those neglected children. The poor orphans needed much more than food and clothes. Their souls were so withered and numb that a simple smile or a story read aloud softly lit up their faces and improved their health as much as ghetto existence allowed.

"Thank you for coming even though you're so busy," Agnieszka greeted me that day.

"There's nothing more important than spending a few minutes with a child," I said.

We went to the room of the youngest children. Some of them had cheeks that were almost chubby again. Others, while still sick, were at least clean and loved. Seeing their faces, I thought of the hundreds of children I had tried to save over the years. Many of them were now dying because of the ghetto's harsh conditions, but the work had still been worth the effort. After all, what is existence? Hardly a minute of infinity; we are like shadows God has entrusted with a flame that will never go out.

I made the rounds and greeted each child, stroking their shaved heads, kissing their injuries, pulling off a clumsy magic trick, or simply giving them a smile.

"Dr. Korczak is going to tell you a story," Agnieszka announced.

The children who could walk sat in a semicircle around me on the floor. The rest stayed on their beds or in the arms of their caretakers.

"Allow me to tell you the story about a pussy cat—not just any cat, but a very peculiar pussy. Everyone called him Puss in Boots, and I'll explain why."

Their eyes widened with the effort of drinking in all my words. As I narrated, they laughed and clapped and gave such lively responses that it pained me even more to know that their hopes were dissipating little by little each day. Every time I thought like that, I would tell myself, *One more day.* I did not need to wear myself out; each day had enough trouble of its own. Today was unique and would never happen again.

I started to wrap up. "We don't need much for things to go our way. A simple pussy cat with a pair of boots used his intelligence to transform his young master from being the penniless son of a miller to a rich marquis who married the king's daughter. If people outside the ghetto could see us, they'd think we're the unluckiest people in the world. They may be right, but what matters is how we see ourselves. The way we see ourselves is the way everyone else will end up seeing us."

The children all cheered and clapped.

"Please, my dear children, never give up."

I stood, and Agnieszka came up to me.

"Oh, thank you, Janusz. Every time you come, you breathe life and hope into them. Look at their faces."

"It might be cruel to give them hope. We're at the end of May now, but we won't make it through another winter."

"The war might end first."

"Not soon enough for us. The Russian front has stabilized. The Japanese are giving the Americans a run for their money in the Pacific, and resistance in Poland is nearly nonexistent. Who's going to come to our aid? The only solution is to get as many children as possible far away from here, but it's like draining a pool with a dropper." My sagging face matched my disconsolate tone.

"Well," Agnieszka said, "we'll just hope that by winter we've been able to get most of the children out."

I stroked her hair and smiled. "I wish you and Henryk would get out while you can. You've already risked too much."

Agnieszka shook her head. "And what would happen with these children? I can't leave them alone."

"They won't be alone. I'm in charge of them, and they'll have the care they need as long as I'm breathing."

She hugged me, and I could feel her tears on my neck.

"Janusz, you're a wonderful man."

"No, just an old kook trying to die with a measure of dignity."

She walked me to the door and before I left asked if I would be going to the wedding of our friends Poldek and Bela.

"I'm not much one for weddings," I answered, dubious.

"Oh, come, at least it'll take our minds off things for a little."

Stefa also insisted I go to the wedding. A few caretakers stayed back with the children, and the rest of us dressed the best we could. The celebration was in the Great Synagogue, an awe-inspiring building with Greek columns and a classical portico with a dome that looked like a royal crown. It was one of the few gems that remained from the glorious past of Warsaw's Jews. Perhaps it was actually a sign of the problem: our people had prospered too much, inspiring the jealousy of those around us.

The group of us went up the synagogue's stairs. The bride and groom were teachers at another orphanage and were good friends to Dom Sierot.

I had expected the wedding to be a rather small affair, but inside the synagogue we were shocked to find that a large crowd had gathered for the celebration. Perhaps the festivities were a way to forget what we were going through.

We sat at the front near the family and could see everything unobstructed. Stefa was on my right and Agnieszka on my left. Both had dressed up, though Stefa's version of fancy was rather austere compared to the young widow's.

From underneath the chuppah, the rabbi called the bridegroom and his family and then the bride, who was escorted by her uncle. Her father had died some months prior.

The rabbi began the seven blessings, the *Sheva Brachot*. Then he passed the cup of ceremonial wine to the couple. They drank, and a child handed rings to the bride and groom.

Placing the ring on his betrothed's finger, Poldek said, "You are consecrated by this ring according to the law of Moses and of Israel." Then Bela repeated the words of the vow. Both were dressed in simple black clothes, as there was no money for extravagance in the ghetto, but their faces shone with joy.

I wondered how it was possible for two people to want to get married in our present circumstances, but that is, after all, what life is about. We must keep believing, fighting, and celebrating. The day we stop, we are as good as dead. Love is the strongest antidote to despair.

The rabbi read out the marital obligations included in the ketubah. First Poldek and Bela and then the witnesses signed the document. The couple was wrapped in a long veil while ritual prayers and blessings were spoken over them. Poldek threw the glass of wine on the floor and crushed it, destroying all over again the temple in Jerusalem. Even that happy ceremony was marked by the memory of life's tragedies.

Stefa gave my hand a tight squeeze. I knew what she was saying. Many times I had thought about asking her to marry me, but our lives were challenging enough as it was. Nor did I want to bind her to a man who did not want to have children and who might go insane like his father. I kissed her hand and whispered into her ear,

> You have stolen my heart, my sister, my bride;
>> you have stolen my heart
> with one glance of your eyes,
>> with one jewel of your necklace.
> How delightful is your love, my sister, my bride!
>> How much more pleasing is your love than wine,
> and the fragrance of your perfume
>> more than any spice!
> Your lips drop sweetness as the honeycomb, my bride;
>> milk and honey are under your tongue.
> The fragrance of your garments
>> is like the fragrance of Lebanon.

Stefa smiled. She knew the verses from Solomon's great love song came from the depths of my heart. We were not husband and wife, but we had shared a life together. We were one in joy and grief, in sickness and in health, knowing that we needed each other to bear up under the immense loneliness that was part and parcel of an ever-changing world.

The gathered crowd cheered and clapped. In the hubbub, the strength of love—more powerful than any force on earth—coursed through my body. Evil was driven back for those moments, and we brushed against something like happiness.

CHAPTER 37

CEREMONIAL
PREPARATIONS

I had searched so long for death, and now it was coming out to meet me. I was so weak. My legs trembled, and getting dressed every morning had become a tortuous challenge. My fingers refused to cooperate, and I could not button my own shirts. My chipped tooth lacerated my tongue, breathing was difficult, and my eyes stung. Despite all this, every morning I got up and tried to keep our ship from sinking for just one more day.

June had started out badly. More and more people were being rounded up, never to be seen again. The overcrowded ghetto started to feel a little less packed. The Judenrat estimated that nearly one hundred thousand people had died since the ghetto had been established, most of starvation and disease. Those of us who were left knew that most would not make it through another winter. We were too weak to survive the cold again. The Germans also kept shrinking the limits of the ghetto to expand the section of Warsaw available to non-Jews. In every possible way, the Nazis crushed us like rats in a cage.

I dragged myself out of bed and headed to Dzielna Street. As I passed by Serbia, the women's prison, I caught a glimpse of Nosjztar, the American worker for the JDC. She was propped with her head looking from behind a barred window.

I waved and shouted, "How are you today?"

She snapped out of her reverie to answer. "Terrible, and worse every day. They've promised many times to release me, but I'm still a prisoner in an enemy nation. I had been warned that war was imminent and that I should get out, but how could I leave my Jewish brothers and sisters in this mess? The people in my country have no idea what's going on here in the ghetto or anywhere in Poland and Germany. There are dozens of places like this all over. The Nazis are wiping out Europe's Jewish population."

Her words cut to the quick and were hard for me to comprehend. How could the world stand by and let this happen? Anti-Semitic laws, abuses, and outrages in Germany itself for almost a decade—those were one thing. But a carefully calculated, continent-wide plan was something else altogether.

Nosjztar drove her point home to make sure I was left with no doubt. "They're murdering thousands of Jews along the eastern front. They'll end up wiping us all out."

From the window beside her, the actress Klara Segałowicz glanced over with scorn. They had cells right next to each other but could not have been more different. She called out, "I don't believe a word of that. I've seen what the Nazis do with us, but they're incapable of such an organized plan. We're useful to them, and the brutes should be taking care of us. When the war is over, they'll send us somewhere or other."

"Klara, your optimism is absurd," Nosjztar snapped. "You're from Ukraine, and they've denied your right to leave a Polish ghetto. You're a famous actress, a shining symbol of the theater and film. So just think about what they'll do to common Jews that no one in Kiev or Minsk would recognize walking down the street."

"I'm watching you!" someone yelled in German. That was a serious warning. Guards would shoot passersby without warning, almost as a pastime.

I continued my walk. That day we were bringing the healthiest children from Dzielna to Dom Sierot to participate in a solemn ceremony.

An hour later all of Dom Sierot's children sat together with the stronger Dzielna Street children in the dining room on Sienna Street. I was glad to see all the children together. We had not had special ceremonies or speeches at Dom Sierot since Christmas. The children were sitting quietly, too quietly. They lacked the strength for their typical boisterous hullabaloo.

"My dear children!" I began. "Your beloved teachers are giving their lives for your present and future because children are not just a future. At the end of the day, what is the future? It doesn't exist yet. It's an uncertain tomorrow, and we never know if it will come to pass. Today we are here. Our legs are supporting us, and our heads are held high. Today some children from another orphanage are joining our wonderful Dom Sierot. We all belong to the children's republic. We're gathered here today to declare our independence and proclaim the values of our republic."

I motioned for one of the boys to approach, and he read out the laws of our new republic:

"We the children commit ourselves to creating a better, more just world where we all have the same rights and nobody is treated badly because of the color of their skin, their nationality, or their religion.

"We the children commit ourselves to creating a just society where all workers receive fair wages that let them live well and take care of their families.

"We the children commit ourselves to spreading love for all people so that hate doesn't rule the hearts of any human beings.

"We the children long for peace and a world without war or violence.

"We the children love our enemies because the only way to turn an enemy into a friend is through love.

"We the children, with God's help, want to be happy, and we know that the only way to be happy is to also secure the happiness of those around us."

The boy stopped reading and stood firm at attention. I brought the flag out. All of Dom Sierot's children recited our pledge: "Our flag is green for hope because we all want a better future."

I felt weak, but I mustered the strength to continue the ceremony and said, "Our work as educators is to cultivate love for human beings, for justice, truth, and hard work. Love is the foundation of everything we are. We are born in love, our mothers and fathers raise us by love, we learn how to love, and this shapes us into true human beings. Justice is what allows us to live together. Justice is our defense against the evil actions of others. Truth is like a torch that guides us through dark nights and one day will defeat all the shadows. We work together as one for food, but above all for unity. The forces of hatred will never break our spirits. May God keep us all."

After another round of applause, we held the flag aloft and marched outside around the perimeter of our building. People stopped to watch us, puzzled at the sight of our spontaneous parade. We were the tiny army of the republic of love, and we were not afraid of anything.

After the ceremony, the children returned to their rooms. They were tired even from the minor exertion. With our allowable calorie count reduced to subhuman levels, the children moved around like weak, depressed elderly people. I did not feel good either, but I went with the group that took the Dzielna Street children back to their home.

As we walked, Agnieszka put her arm through mine and said, "That was a wonderful speech, Janusz. The old lion still has his teeth."

"They're kitty teeth, my dear. I'm in a lot of pain. All I can think about is getting to bed and having a swig of the brew I keep under my mattress."

"You're a good man," she said, stroking the crevices of wrinkles across my brow.

"You know I'm immune to flattery."

"That's true enough except for when it comes to your children. You've founded a nation of free men and women and that, in the times we're living, turns you into a true hero. We're all slaves to our conventions and have become scared, selfish things; but these children are truly free."

We walked beneath the warm June sun that was about to set. For so long the arrival of summer had presaged a full, happy life. Summer was packed with camp, visits to the country, and fresh river water. I missed trees, with squirrels scampering up and down their trunks and birds continuing the celestial concert they had been chirping for eons. In contrast to that perfection stood our world, this little inferno called civilization made by humans. How I longed to return to Eden, to be free again, to be free at last.

CHAPTER 38

ABRAHAM

We had set aside one room for prayer. Some of our teachers found this odd, since they knew I had always claimed to be agnostic and had even flirted with atheism in some periods of my life. Our orphanage was secular. We had never taught the Torah or the Bible, though we always assiduously respected the beliefs of our little ones and their families, if they had them. Yet all the same I had found myself praying of late. I had not learned Yiddish until I was older, and even then, never completely. I was unfamiliar with large parts of the Scriptures and would be at a loss to define my beliefs. Perhaps a good way to sum it up would have been to say I was "seeking."

I had once heard a wise rabbi say that prayer is not heaven bending toward you but the wings on which you reach up to it.

That morning a small group of children and adults was praying in the little room when I looked up and asked, "Why do you all pray?"

The first boy who looked up came from an Orthodox family and was wearing a yarmulke. "Why wouldn't I pray? I'm Jewish."

Another boy, who was generally a bit of a rabble-rouser, said, "I'm up early and don't have anything to do before breakfast. It's comfortable in here, and I like how the light comes through the windows."

"I'm trying to collect all two hundred prayer cards, and I've only got forty left to go," said a third boy.

And another said, "Somebody told me that if I don't pray, a ghost will get me at night." At that, everyone laughed.

"My mom always told me to pray," a young girl said.

The oldest boy in the group straightened up. His eyes looked like they could cry at any moment. He said, "My dad always wanted me to go with him to the synagogue, but I was sleepy and never wanted to get up in time. One day he died, and I felt terrible. Not long after that, I saw him in a dream, and he told me, 'While I was alive, I looked after you and fed you, and you never lacked for anything. I got up early every morning to take care of you, in winter and summer, in the cold and the heat. I got up in the middle of the night and even when I was sick to make sure you were okay. And you're too lazy to wake up and pray a Kaddish for me?' Since then I pray every day."

One girl said very seriously, "My grandparents taught me that our people have suffered a lot, that we've been attacked and killed and even burned in our synagogues. So it would be a shame for me not to pray just because I was lazy."

And another girl added, "A lot of people don't like it when girls pray, but we're equal to boys, and God listens to us just as much as to them."

The comment that most moved me came from young Abraham: "I

don't understand what prayer is, but I'm an orphan. I don't have my mom or my dad anymore. So it's really comforting to me that God is my father and that he cares about me. He's the father of everyone, so he's my father too. Prayer is something I feel in my heart."

"Children, thank you so much for your answers. I've loved them. You're such wise little ones. Prayer is more than talking with God. Above all, it's a way to involve him in what's going on in our lives. Many people accuse God of allowing the Nazis to hurt us. They may be right, but he's actually suffering right alongside us and comforting us. Let's not allow fear, sadness, or weakness to keep us from praying. It's one of the only things we have, the hope that still lives in our hearts."

CHAPTER 39

THE PLAY

I thought about my sister, Anka, quite a bit. I wrote her a last letter, though I had no guarantee that she would receive it. None of the services we had in the ghetto were working anymore. Chaos—and soon enough something worse, I feared—had taken hold of us. I left the house much less in those days, and my fundraising visits were barely more than downright begging. I was forever groveling before those who might give us something, masking my pain and my rage. All of it was for the children. I could no longer pay attention when I read, and writing in my diary was a chore. I did not know if I could continue; it seemed pointless.

It was very hot on July 18, too hot for Warsaw, quite unusual for Poland. But nothing was like it used to be, at least as far as I could recall. The world had changed too much. A few days before I had heard that the Germans had taken Sebastopol. They were inhumanly unstoppable. The Americans had accomplished little for Europe, though they had their hands full defending their territories in the Pacific and propping Australia up.

Stefa came into my room. I was still in my pajamas and had not shaved.

"Oh, Janusz, please! This isn't like you; you always take care of yourself. Do you remember when you told me that the man who shaves every morning keeps the depression at bay?"

"My pulse is unsteady, Stefa. I can hardly stand upright. I think it might be the end."

"Excuses! Since when has that kept you from fighting?" She went to the bowl, beat up some foam, and spread it across my chin.

"Now I'm scared," I said. "You're reminding me too much of Judith decapitating Holofernes."

"You've always liked that story, haven't you? Deep down you've got a touch of misogyny."

"No, it's just a casual similarity. You say I drink too much, just like the Assyrian general."

"But you don't want to destroy the Jewish people."

"No indeed."

Stefa kept giggling as she shaved me. Apparently my biblical joke had hit the spot.

"Do you think many people will come to the play?" she asked.

I had no idea. Three days ago I had invited the ghetto authorities, as well as friends and donors. There had been very few shows and events within the walls since the beginning of summer. Being out on the street was dangerous, and starvation was rampant. Yet people needed entertainment more than ever.

"The truth is, I don't care who comes. You know why we're putting on the play."

Her face clouded over. Of course she knew.

"*The Post Office*, a sad story by Rabindranath Tagore."

"Yes, one of my favorite authors. I always dreamed of being like him: a poet, a reformer, and a musician. What more could you want? It's a story about learning how to die. Typically we don't get taught how to walk that road that each of us must go down sooner or later."

Stefa nodded but hastily changed the subject. "Plus, he was the first non-European to be awarded a Nobel Prize." His was, of course, in literature.

"Yes, he was a genius. But geniuses die too."

She finished shaving me and wiped my face off with a towel. "Okay, there are two hours before the play. I want to see you well dressed and radiant, as if this were your last production."

"You're absolutely right, my dear. Life is a comedy, and we've all been cast in a role. I remember when I was angry at God after my mother died. I ranted against him about the very same thing, that I knew that all of this was just a rehearsal and didn't really matter."

"Janusz, why did you pick *The Post Office*? Tagore wrote so many things to choose from."

"Don't you get what's happening? It's all over."

Stefa frowned while helping me into my shirt. "You're talking like this because you'll be sixty-four—or is it sixty-three?—in just a few days. You've never taken kindly to aging."

Her comment aggravated me because the fact of being older did not bother me one bit. In fact, I was pleasantly surprised. I had never expected to live this long. What bothered me was the weakness that came with it. Inside, I still felt like a child full of curiosity or the fearless young man I had been.

"Stefa, the Nazis are preparing something big. I've heard it from several members of the Judenrat."

"What more can they do?" Her question was full of innocent sincerity.

"Well, it's simple: they can kill us. They're not going to waste any more time. They're so sure they're going to win the war that they're going to make crystal clear exactly what they've been trying to do since 1940: wipe us all out."

Fear and confusion filled Stefa's eyes. "I just can't believe that. I'm pretty sure it's another one of your crazy ideas. Lately you're not all here."

"No, my friend. We have to prepare the children for their—"

"Their death? Janusz, that's horrible, even for a mind like yours."

"But it's reality."

"They won't do anything to the children."

"What makes you think not? They've been killing innocent children for years, even directly and in cold blood. I know they've exterminated thousands in the east, and how many more murdered through starvation and exposure to the elements? Does the precise method actually matter?" Stefa started crying softly and covered her face with her hands to block out the clarity of my explanation. I made my tone gentler. "So that's why I chose this play, the story of an orphan with a terminal disease, just like us."

"And what is our disease?"

"The disease of being yanked out of the family tree of humanity by the Nazis, who think we're beasts and treat us like that."

The mood had changed, and now Stefa was the deflated one, crushed by harsh reality. I held her and let her cry.

"Then we have to do something," she said, muffled against my shoulder.

"That's precisely what we're doing. We're preparing them. This play is their dress rehearsal for death."

We walked together to the dining room where everything was ready: chairs arranged in rows, a curtain strung up, the children nervous but ready behind it in their costumes.

Henryk came up and hugged me. I loved all of our orphans, but Agnieszka's son was special and had burrowed himself particularly deep into my heart.

"How are you?" I asked, ruffling his hair. "Nervous?"

"Yes, this is my first time to play a lead role. I've never had lines or anything before." His eyes were bright with excitement.

"You have wonderful intonation. I'm old, and many of the things I do, I know it'll be my last time to do them. But you're just starting out . . ." I swallowed the rest of the words I found myself saying before thinking. I did not actually know if the child had a future ahead of him or just a few days.

One of the teachers came backstage and exclaimed, "The hall is full! Everybody has come!"

I peeked through a tear in the curtain: the ghetto's elite filled the rows of seats. Almost everyone I had invited was there, plus some.

Before the production began, I came onstage and stood before the audience. "Thank you all so much for coming out on this hot afternoon! The children have worked very hard on this play. To prepare a piece like this with everything that's going on around us is nearly epic, but the little ones have poured their hearts and souls into it. As you're already aware, our students will now perform Tagore's immortal work, *The Post Office*. We hope you enjoy it."

I climbed down from the stage and sat in the audience. The lights were dimmed the best we could manage, and the stage lit up.

MADHAV: What a state I am in! Before he came, nothing mattered; I felt so free. But now that he has come, goodness knows from where, my heart is filled with his dear self, and my home will be no home to me when he leaves. Doctor, do you think he—

PHYSICIAN: If there's life in his fate, then he will live long. But what the medical scriptures say, it seems—

MADHAV: Great heavens, what?

PHYSICIAN: The scriptures have it: "Bile or palsy, cold or gout spring all alike."

MADHAV: Oh, get along, don't fling your scriptures at me; you only make me more anxious; tell me what I can do.

PHYSICIAN [*Taking snuff*]: The patient needs the most scrupulous care.

MADHAV: That's true; but tell me how.

PHYSICIAN: I have already mentioned, on no account must he be let out of doors.

MADHAV: Poor child, it is very hard to keep him indoors all day long.

As I listened to the actors, I thought about the sad story of Amal. His adopted father was a wreck about the boy's illness, especially about the fact that Amal could not leave his dark room ever again. No other work could better symbolize the story of my poor children, locked up in the walls of the ghetto, dying a slow and agonizing death, losing their strength until they would fully succumb sooner or later. Henryk was the lead role of Amal, and I got choked up listening to him. Yet the last scene was the most poignant:

SUDHA: Amal!

PHYSICIAN: He's asleep.

SUDHA: I have some flowers for him. Mayn't I give them into his own hand?

PHYSICIAN: Yes, you may.

SUDHA: When will he be awake?

PHYSICIAN: Directly the King comes and calls him.

SUDHA: Will you whisper a word for me in his ear?

PHYSICIAN: What shall I say?

SUDHA: Tell him Sudha has not forgotten him.

The audience was immediately on their feet and clapping. Henryk still lay in his bed, presaging the deaths of us all. I thought of my parents, of my sister, and of happier years when everything felt possible and life was one big expectation.

All the guests came up to me and gushed with congratulations. Irena was one of the last and among the few who seemed to understand the play's message. The rest were too blind to intuit their own impending demise.

She shook her head and said between tears, "I'm so sorry I haven't been able to do more."

"You pulled off more than I had thought possible," I said, hugging her.

The poet Władysław Szlengel came up and spoke with exuberance. "This is the first truly artistic performance since 1939! The children created true atmosphere. It was more than exciting; it was an experience. Congratulations, Doctor!"

The room started to empty, and Henryk came up to me. I could not hide my grief.

"Why are you crying, Teacher?" he asked.

"Oh, because life is so short, and you my children are just now start-ing to really know what life means."

"There's plenty of time for us to learn."

"Well, that's one of the things the Nazis have stolen from us."

I could not sleep that night. The scenes from the performance played before me over and over. The poor child Amal was so hopeful about getting a letter from the king—and I, so hopeful for a word that would free us all from our terrible horror, from the interminable nightmare. I thought about the cemetery where my parents lay. They, too, had flowers over their chests for when they awoke. One day the King would come to see them. He would raise us all up out of our beds, and we would cele-brate together with the biggest party in the world. I longed for that with all my heart. It was the only thing left to hope for.

CHAPTER 40

TREBLINKA

Once I grew older, I came to understand that I was my grandfather, my father, and all my Jewish ancestors. I was part of a long chain that was about to be forever broken. My fear of insanity and the insane place that the world had become would successfully wipe out my lineage. Nothing would change. When the sun set, it would still rise the next day. The seasons would continue to change one after another, the birds would keep building nests, and only perhaps a dozen people left alive would be impacted by the life of the man who had been Janusz Korczak. Yet a dozen was likely an exaggeration. Most of my friends and the people who loved me were in the ghetto. And those of us who had two working eyes knew pretty well what our final destiny would be. Life would continue, and, even if it made no sense to us, no one would remember us.

As the biblical preacher said, "Vanity of vanities; all is vanity." How true! We were anxious and worn out for nothing.

It all started when we learned that the devious ghetto entrepreneurs Kon and Heller and their business associates had allegedly been transferred to a suburb of Warsaw. Even the Nazi newspaper *Warschauer Zeitung* published an article reporting that the Jews would be transported to a new ghetto with businesses and factories, but it was all a sham.

I shook off my weariness, dressed, and went to see Adam Czerniaków.

"Dr. Korczak, you'll need to wait here. The chairman is in a meeting," the secretary told me.

Through the frosted glass doors I could see two men on their feet in heated argument. Their words came out all too clearly.

"Mr. Auerswald, you cannot empty the ghetto. There are hundreds of thousands of people here, and many of them are weak and sick."

"You need not worry about that. Everything will be done with the utmost care. We will be relocating the entire population. It's too crowded here, and not even the most basic sanitary conditions are met. We have spent months building factories and adequate housing. Czerniaków, your people's situation is about to improve greatly, I can assure you."

"It's not that I don't trust you, but we've received horrifying reports about what's occurring in other ghettos. We've heard about the concentration camps all over Poland and that most people die soon after arrival. I cannot allow something like that to happen to my people."

"That's absurd, absolutely absurd. We need the Warsaw Jews. You're our manual labor. How could we afford to lose you? That would make no sense!"

Czerniaków snorted. "Much of what you do makes no sense! Why hunt us down and kill us? What have we ever done to the Germans?"

Auerswald's tone remained patient. "It's nothing personal. You know that I respect you, Czerniaków, but the Germans are responsible for purifying the races, and yours has always been detrimental to the world's peoples. The Jews are behind communism and the most savage capitalism. Your degenerate artists have contaminated the arts, literature, and theater. You multiply like rats and refuse to adapt to society. You'll never truly stop being Jews. What else can we do to control your propagation? But murder you—absurdity!"

Czerniaków threw his hands up. "I don't know what to think."

"There's no need to think. You have your orders. Over the coming weeks we will deport all the Jews who are not working in the factories, all the sick, the children, and their mothers. For now the only ones who will remain in the ghetto are the Jewish police, those with essential positions, and you and your Judenrat leaders."

"If you're resettling us to work, why are you taking the weakest ones first?"

"To tend to them and protect them. Then the rest will follow, don't worry."

"Not worry? All of these people are under my watch."

"The first trains will come tomorrow. The police should bring six thousand people daily to the plaza, no more and no less. I'm telling you for your own good."

The German nodded and excused himself from the office with excruciating confidence. The chill of his haughty look fell ever so briefly on me as he proceeded to the stairs where his escorts waited.

"So that's Auerswald?" I whispered to the secretary as the sound of their boots faded.

"Yes, Heinz Auerswald, the German commissioner of the ghetto."

I went cautiously into Czerniaków's office. The weary man was massaging his forehead with his hands, his glasses on his desk. I took a seat across from him.

"How are you, Czerniaków?"

"Not well. These German pigs want to liquidate the ghetto. All the years we've been trying to make it livable—for nothing."

"The Nazi might be telling the truth."

He slid his glasses into place and tapped a file folder on his desk. "Have you ever heard of Treblinka?"

"The name's familiar. Isn't it a woody region northeast of us?"

"Just about sixty-five miles from here. There's been a work camp there since 1941, according to reports I've received from members of the Resistance. The reports document that there are political prisoners there from many different countries. They do forced labor and hardly anyone gets out. The living conditions are terrible, and most don't survive long."

I nodded. "I've heard about camps like that in Germany. But how could they take us all there? There are hundreds of thousands of us. They'd have to build an entire new city to accommodate us." My imagination was formulating a reply, but my confused brain refused to accept it.

"The Nazis have recently expanded the camp. Jewish workers on the inside have told us they've built wood and brick barracks, but those would only house a few thousand of us at best. What will become of the rest?"

My heart was racing and my breath was short. "I really couldn't say."

"There are two other places like it in Belzec and Sobibor. Thousands of prisoners are taken in every day, and they don't come out again."

My legs had sagged useless beneath the chair. "But what will happen to my children?" The question came out as a rasping whisper.

Czerniaków did not answer at first, but his face said it all: reddened eyes surrounded by dark circles and indescribable sadness. Then, "It's over, my friend. It's the end of the game."

I shook my head. "I never thought it would end like this. I thought we might die in some epic way, like in a Greek tragedy, in bed with the sleep of hunger and cold. Maybe it would be better to rise up and sell our lives at a high price."

"Dr. Korczak, it would do no good. It would lead to terrible massacres and unnecessary pain."

"And yet the other option is to be led like cattle to the butcher. We can't do that either. The world has to know what's happening in Warsaw."

"The world hasn't cared about us for a very long time. The countries are wrapped up in their own wars. We thought it was our war, but no, it's theirs. The British are fighting for their survival, the Americans for hegemony in the Pacific, the Soviets against their former allies. We've always been on our own. I had hoped—hoped, ha!—that as long as we were useful to them, they would leave us alone. But not even that matters to them anymore."

I trudged out of the Judenrat's building disoriented with grief. How could I go home and speak to the children? What would I tell my workers? We had managed to save so few of them, and the rest would face a pointless, absurd, cruel, heartless death.

I went to Irena's office first. People were packed at the door, but the doorman let me through. Irena was in the stockroom.

"Irena, have you heard the news?" I asked. She nodded. "What are we going to do?"

"All those people out there are requesting work permits. They want to delay their resettlement, but it would just drag out the agony. I understand them. We all want to live, even if it's just one more day."

"Did you know about Treblinka?"

"Yes. The Resistance has been watching it for a while. But it's not the only one. There are camps like it in several places."

I shook my head in disbelief. "But, it's just . . ." What could I say? Words like *terrible* and *unbelievable* were too soft.

"I know, Janusz. It's indescribable. It kills me that we haven't gotten more children out of your orphanage. Right now there's a woman named Henia waiting outside to give me her baby to take away from the ghetto. We take a few children out each day, but there just aren't enough families to receive them. And if we don't act with the most extreme caution, the Gestapo will be on to our network, and thousands more people will be killed."

"I need you to help me with just a few people. Stefania has to get out, and so do Agnieszka and young Henryk. I'll bring you a list. It's a terrible thing to decide who lives and who dies."

Irena put her hand on my shoulder. "I know. Some get to survive just because they have blond hair and light eyes. I make those decisions every day, and I have no idea how I'll live with myself once all this is over, if I make it."

"You've done marvelous work."

She shook her head as tears fell softly. None of us was prepared for the pressure we were living under and the terrible dilemmas of our work.

"Well, I'll go home, and I'll make my children's last days the best they can possibly be. Please, try to get the people on my list out."

"I'll try, Janusz; that much I can say. I'll try."

I left the storeroom and looked at the long, long line of people. Most would be forced to leave the ghetto on the trains, and those who stayed a little longer would only be postponing the inevitable. It is hard to be born and learn how to die. We are never prepared to abandon this world. My priorities had shifted to hoping I would die conscious and lucid. Others tried to keep fooling themselves with the hope of a last-minute escape. I preferred to look at what was going on through the eyes of a man with a death sentence. I would enjoy each moment until the lights went out and the curtain dropped for the last time.

When I arrived back at Dom Sierot, the children were seated at their activities, reading and studying and playing. The tutors tended to them with such care and attention that it brought me to tears again.

"Janusz, what is it?" Stefa asked.

I did not want to go into it right then. I needed time to digest it all and figure out a way to soften the reality and make her see what needed to be done.

"Oh, it's been a marvelous day. I'm just stupendous."

"It's almost your birthday."

"Old men don't have birthdays," I huffed in mock offense.

"Oh yes they do, and we should be grateful."

"Well, all right. Let's have a drink and talk about old times, what do you say?"

We went to my room, and I pulled out my last bottle. I filled two glasses, and we toasted. The sun poured in through the windows, testimony that the planet spun on, indifferent to our fate. Autumn would come, and the leaves would blanket our graves to protect us from the world's harsh winter.

CHAPTER 41

RESISTING

The noise of the army trucks entering the ghetto and roaring by Dom Sierot woke me and the other caretakers with a start. I got out of bed and looked out the window. I hoped the children were still asleep. Their weakness had lengthened their response time to stimuli, and they spent much of the day resting. The line of trucks with their lights on stopped its advance. Soldiers' boots slapped against the cobblestones as they jumped down and formed a long line. Then they broke up and started beating on doors. Fortunately, Dom Sierot's was not one of them. The lights in houses that had electricity flicked on. The night was filled with the sounds of doors being kicked or pounded on and the cries of those inside. There was a brief pause as the world held its breath, and then families were dragged out of the houses or tossed like sacks down the front stairs. The youngest were forced onto the trucks, and those twelve and older were lined up. The soldiers opened fire. A man I knew, a famous antiques dealer, tried to run, and two soldiers took him down. Then the soldiers jumped back into the trucks and drove away with the children. The sidewalk was littered with cadavers, and the dark street ran black with blood.

"What . . . ?" Stefa ran in and asked in terror.

"They've killed some of our neighbors."

She was horrified. "But why?"

"I imagine they caught wind that Mr. Braun was printing pamphlets warning the ghetto about the deportations, so they decided to take out two entire blocks. I know they're also murdering high-profile ghetto leaders to keep us from organizing any resistance."

Stefa pulled her shawl tighter around her nightgown. Her eyes looked more sunken than usual. "At least they're taking us away from this terrible place."

"No, friend, don't deceive yourself. They're emptying the ghetto by killing us all. I didn't want to tell you yesterday, but Czerniaków explained it all. I've talked with Irena. We're getting false papers to get you out of here."

"Have you lost the little bit of mind you had left? I'm not going any-where without you and the children."

I had known she would say that, but I had to convince her. The deportations would begin soon, and there was no time to lose.

"Stefa, you're much more useful alive than dead. I'm sick and don't have much time left regardless. And someone has to stay with the chil-dren. They've already lost their parents, their siblings, and their friends. At least I can be a friendly face before they disappear too." She was crying uncontrollably now and clinging to me. "I've always thought I'd have a short life. God has given me many good moments. I've been happy. You've made me happy. Now it's time to make the final journey to eternity."

"But I need you," she mumbled into my shoulder.

"Really all we need is time. You'll get used to it."

"No, I won't. We dreamed about living in Palestine and giving our lives to the children there. I'm staying with you, and that is final. You're not going to change my mind."

I felt unbelievably honored. To be loved like that was the best thing life could give me.

"You've got to go."

"I won't do it. I'm staying by your side, and together we'll go with the children to the end."

I left the house a few hours later, in spite of many warnings to the contrary. It seemed that the Small Ghetto was being emptied, and they might sweep me up with the unfortunate passengers on the first few trains. But I arrived without incident at Irena's office. There was no longer a line stretching to the street. Everyone was hiding out in fear of both the Jewish police and the Nazis.

"Irena, it's me, Janusz," I said, knocking lightly. "What happened?" I asked when she opened. She looked more distressed than I had yet seen her. Her white coat sagged carelessly, and her eyes were red with recent crying.

"They just took one of the girls helping me, Sara. She was pregnant, and even though I told the police she was essential, that I absolutely needed her, they took her because she's pregnant."

Just then a thin young man rushed in. "Where is she, where's Sara?"

"I'm so sorry, Josel. They're on their way to the Umschlagplatz, where everyone's being boarded onto trains," Irena explained. As he turned and dashed away, Irena called out, "There's nothing you can do for her!"

We went after him as best we could and glimpsed him catch up to the long line of people. He found the woman and held her hand tightly.

"He got to her," I said, wheezing at our pace.

Josel veered away from the human column and pulled Sara toward an alley, but the Estonian guards were after them immediately. A guard aimed right at Sara's belly, but Josel jumped in front. The guard smacked him away and fired. Josel saw the remains of his unborn child and rose to attack but fell back dead with a gunshot to the head. The column of Jews kept marching by while the lovers' bodies bloodied the street.

Irena buried her face into my shoulder. "Oh God, oh God, oh God," she moaned.

"We have to stay strong, for the children. Don't give up," I begged her.

"I can't, I can't do it anymore. Sara . . . her baby . . ." Then she tossed her head and, with a crazed look, took off for the plaza. Fearing for her life, I followed.

The Umschlagplatz was packed with people, and many more were approaching from side streets. It smelled of cauliflower and cabbage, the goods that had been emptied from the trains. The engine was puffing white smoke. Everything was chaos in the plaza, but the Germans knew what they were doing. The Jews were all gathered in the center, and Ukrainian soldiers stationed all around kept their guns aimed to discourage any attempt at escape.

Some of the prisoners had been standing there for hours. The children were slumped to the ground, and many of the elderly had passed out with the oppressive heat.

"Halt!" a soldier barked at Irena. Just then I caught up to her and grabbed her arm.

"Excuse us, we're leaving now."

The German guard eyed me with suspicion but let us go, as neither Irena nor I had an armband. We had not gone far when we heard shots. Soldiers were firing at people looking into the plaza from nearby windows. A man fell from a building and crashed onto the ground. The terrified crowd drew back and closer together, seeking any sort of protection.

"We're going, Irena," I insisted, and she finally gave in.

"This is the worst thing I've ever seen in my life. I can't believe that even the Nazis are capable of this."

We walked away from the crowd. The streets were absolutely deserted, as if the ghetto's population had instantly disappeared. The buildings loomed like a grotesque, cruel stage. Perhaps the gods were watching our painful performance from Olympus and enjoying it or, worse, not even caring.

CHAPTER 42

SUICIDE

My birthday had happened. I had never really liked birthdays, and there was absolutely nothing to celebrate in the ghetto right then. The children seemed to sense that something big was happening even though we kept them occupied all day and they slept long and deep every night. I wrote a few pages, which I presumed would be among the last entries in my ridiculous diary. All it really did was keep my head clear amid the ghetto's chaos. That morning, July 23, I decided to visit Czerniaków again. The children were not ready to go to the trains, and I hoped to convince him to delay us just a while longer.

I got to the Judenrat offices so early that he was alone. His untouched breakfast lay before him: coffee and toast with a very light film of butter. The rest of the desk was covered with resettlement orders and passes for those who would be allowed to stay.

"Ah, Korczak, I didn't hear you come in."

I studied the man. Though I was the one who had had a birthday, he seemed much older than two days ago. His shoulders sagged with the ghetto's plight.

"I've come to—"

"I know, but I can't do anything. They've asked me to decide who goes first on the transports. It's been complete chaos."

"That's exactly why I've come, to beg you to delay our evacuation. That's all I'm asking."

"The Nazis have made it very clear: the orphanages will be emptied today. You'll be among the first on the trains."

For once, I had no suggestions, no alternatives, no solutions to offer.

"I'm so sorry, Janusz. I can assure you that I've fought for your children, but it's been in vain." The Judenrat chairman broke down in tears. I had never seen him in this state. The man, one of Poland's great intellects, could bear it no longer. I tried to cheer him, but he waved me off. "It's over, and perhaps it's better this way. We've all been through a nightmare. I don't know what's on the other side of death, but it can't be worse than this. The Nazis have no hearts—I mean, no souls, like we do. You were right. No regime has ever persecuted any people group so cruelly, not even the worst Russian pogroms were this bad."

"Thank you, Czerniaków, for all you've done for your people."

We heard footsteps in the hallway. Czerniaków looked around frantically and hissed, "Get out of here! Quick, hide in the closet!"

I slipped inside and closed the door just as an officer preceded by a band of soldiers burst into the office.

"Herr Czerniaków, you're out of time. Have you signed the orders? We'll begin rounding up the orphanages in an hour."

A chair creaked, and then the chairman spoke. "I can't let you take my people. I will not collaborate in the murder of innocent children."

The officer's voice was gruff and devoid of emotion. "You understand you are thus signing your own death sentence and that of your family."

"God help me, I cannot be party to this massacre."

There was a loud *crack*, then the scuffle of boots and angry voices. They were beating the poor man. When the room had been silent for some time, I cracked the door open and peered out. Czerniaków was alone, on the floor bleeding. I helped him get up. His eyes were swollen nearly shut, and his face looked very bad.

"I'm so sorry," I said.

"Go on, Janusz," he urged me. "They're coming for your children."

"What are you going to do?" I asked.

"Have my last breakfast," he said. Slumping into his chair, he carefully laid a capsule of cyanide beside his cold toast.

I wept as I descended the stairs. On the walk back, snapshots from my entire life rose up before me. There were my grandparents, the house where I grew up, my parents, the school of medicine, all the different places and times I had enjoyed. I was almost at the end and had to make one final surge. I did not want my children to suffer. That was all that mattered right then.

CHAPTER 43

THE PARADE

Even prayers can be terrible, harmful things if they are spoken to hurt or destroy a neighbor. It is too easy to slip, to let hatred find harbor in our hearts. I got to Dom Sierot as the troops were surrounding the area where several orphanages were located. A German officer was knocking at our door. I stepped up, and he looked at me in surprise.

"Who are you?" he asked.

"I'm the director of this orphanage. Please, let me get the children ready."

"We're in a hurry. There's a lot to do today."

"Just a few moments, please. They are very young."

His gray eyes stared at me. Did I see a spark of compassion? If so, it dissipated instantly.

"Fifteen minutes. If you're not out by then, we'll force you out. Don't try anything. We shoot to kill."

I slipped inside and shut the door quickly. The tutors and teachers were all gathered at the door holding their breaths.

"Well, the time has come. If any of you want to try to escape, I understand perfectly. You have to save yourselves if you can. I will go with the children; don't worry about them."

Several of the tutors nodded and split, running for the windows that opened onto the back alley. To the rest, I said, "Please get the children ready. Stefa and Agnieszka, please come with me to my room."

The tutors got busy helping the children finish getting dressed and handing them their small suitcases. Upstairs, I turned to my two friends and said, "I thought that you two would get out of the ghetto, but Stefa has decided to stay."

"I'm staying too," Agnieszka declared. Her hands were worrying with her dress, her hair, my desk. She was beside herself.

"No, you have a child to look after and your whole life ahead of you. I want you to go. Do it for me." She was crying but trying not to. "I'm going to write a few more lines, and then I want you to take my diary. Promise me you'll take care of it and finish it. People have to know what has happened here."

"Okay, Janusz, I will. I promise."

"I'm going to leave it behind this portrait. There's a hole in the wall. We're going to leave, and you're going to come get it later."

Agnieszka clung to me in an embrace, then left the room.

"Oh, Stefa," I turned to my longest friend. "Thank you for being so faithful to your children and to your principles."

"I know no other way to be."

I sat at my desk and wrote for just a few moments. They were my last words. What else could be said? The children were waiting. Perhaps Jesus's words about becoming like a child were the secret for saving a world that had gone up in flames.

• • •

Additions by Mrs. Agnieszka Ignaciuk:

That day is forever burned into my memory. After saying goodbye to Janusz, a very small group of the tutors and children hid in the coal cellar. We heard the students lining up at the door and filing out orderly to the street. The Germans were waiting impatiently. I slipped out of a window and spied from a distance.

"Dr. Korczak, the children must continue on alone."

Janusz looked at the officer and, without the slightest waver in his voice, said, "They will not go alone. I will be with them. I will not leave even one child alone in the dark. We do not abandon our children in times like this."

The officer stepped back, and the children passed down the street escorted by Nazis. Janusz asked young Marcus to play his violin as they walked, and one of the older boys held our green flag aloft. Janusz held two children by the hand as the group advanced.

The heat was unbearable. The sun was high overhead, and the children were fatigued. The march went slowly and with plenty of pauses. The Germans were clearly impatient, but they did not intervene. The few passersby on both sides of the street stopped to stare in horror and wonder at the parade of children but quickly looked away, not wanting to attract attention. The Old Doctor, meanwhile, walked upright and with a firm step, his chin held high.

I broke down. *What have these poor children done to deserve this?*

I thought, and then a chill ran up my spine. Henryk could have been among them. I stared at the girls, most of them holding tightly to the dolls that old Professor Witwicki had made for them. They were my darlings. I had spent almost three years of my life watching over them at night and encouraging them not to give up in spite of everything.

Janusz began singing, and the children joined in. They were a chorus of angels in the bowels of hell.

It was so chaotic when they got to the Umschlagplatz. The place was crawling with children, probably ten thousand of them, all the ghetto's orphans in one place. Janusz tried to keep all of Dom Sierot's children together, and they made a space for themselves beside a train car. I stared at the teeming mass of little lives. Their innocent eyes held no understanding of what was happening. I did not understand either. Even the Germans and Ukrainians looked on in disbelief, though this did not keep them from being cruel and heartless to their prisoners.

A friend called to me, and I ducked into an alley. It was Chaim, Janusz's former student who had helped us so much.

"Agnieszka, are you crazy? What are you doing here? The guards are catching anyone who's lurking about the plaza."

"Dr. Korczak and the children are there," I said. "It's just horrible." I was weeping.

"Are you serious? We have to tell someone. We've got to get him away from the Umschlagplatz as soon as possible. There's hardly any time left."

Chaim's words perked me up. We headed for another street, and, as we ran, the fleeting hope of saving Janusz and our children revived me.

CHAPTER 44

THE FINAL INVITATION

Chaim took me to a hole in the wall where Resistance leaders were gathered, including Marek Edelman.

"Marek," Chaim said, recovering his breath, "they've taken Korczak to the Umschlagplatz."

"Oh, no. We have to get him out immediately."

Marek joined us, and we snuck our way back toward the plaza. There was a first aid station on one side with a hidden door that led into the Umschlagplatz.

"I'll go in and get him," Marek said.

"You're too valuable. We can't lose you," Chaim protested.

"There's no other way. Some of the guards know me, and they won't hurt me."

He walked into the building where half a dozen nurses and doctors were looking after a few patients. Before we knew it, he was back, dressed in a white coat with a stethoscope around his neck. We went to a second-floor window in a building where Jewish Resistance members holed up and watched.

Marek entered the plaza unhindered and made his way to Janusz. We could not hear their exchange, but we could see the real doctor shaking his head firmly. The plaza was a beehive of screaming, crying children. The only ones who seemed to be calm were Dom Sierot's orphans, who continued singing.

Marek threw his hands up in frustration but stepped back when a German officer started to approach. He kept his distance and then returned to the first aid station.

He came up to where we were and tossed the white coat into a corner. "He won't leave them," he huffed. "He won't leave the children. He told me it's his duty and that he's too old to keep fighting. We're losing one of the brightest minds in Poland. Good God, what lunacy!"

I started crying again. I just could not believe it was happening. All of those children were about to disappear forever, and no one could stop it. "He's not just one of the brightest minds in Poland. He's the man with the biggest heart in all of Warsaw. The world has just gone completely mad," I moaned.

"What was that German officer doing?" Chaim asked.

"I stepped back when I saw him, but I could still hear. It was a German captain. He said he could get Korczak out of there, but of course the Old Doctor told him no. When the captain insisted, Korczak snapped at him, 'Leave me be! I will go with my children and will not leave them alone!'"

Soldiers had opened the train cars, and the children started to file in. Most were too small to climb up on their own. Janusz helped the weaker ones on board, and then one of the older students held out his hand to help him get up. From inside the car he turned and looked up. He helped Stefa inside, and they embraced quietly for a moment. Before the doors shut, Janusz glanced our way. For the briefest of seconds his smile flashed, and his hand waved—saying goodbye before a long holiday. The children's singing rose above the screams and cries of the crowd, to me the sound of an angel chorus come down from heaven to bless the Teacher.

As the train lurched forward, my heart broke irreparably. I thought back to when we had first met, when Janusz gave me and my son a place to live and a chance at a new life. Janusz Korczak had lit up a country swathed in darkness. All of Poland had to know his story and admire his example. I vowed to make that happen. I felt proud then to be a Pole and swore that one day we would break the yoke of the Nazis forever.

As the hours dragged on, the Umschlagplatz slowly cleared of the thousands of children carted off to their deaths under the indifferent gaze of the world. Theirs were lives that would forever disappear, erased as if they had never existed, mere shadows of a culture going extinct. Silence replaced the unbearable shrieks. The last violin notes rang in my mind's ears. I closed my eyes and beheld the face of the Teacher, the Old Doctor, my friend. I vowed to keep his memory alive and share the treasure of his wisdom so that everyone could know that good does triumph over evil.

CHAPTER 45

ESCAPE

We waited for Michal Wroblewski and three students who had gone out to work that morning at their jobs outside the ghetto. Then we went to Irena's office. She gave us our forged documents.

"I'm splitting you into two groups. You," she looked directly at me, "need to go see Igor Newerly. He'll tell you what to do. Be very, very careful." Henryk was by my side, and Irena ruffled his hair. "Take care of your mom."

"I will, Miss Irena."

"Be wary everywhere you go. The Gestapo, the SS, and the police are all watching the city. They don't want anyone getting out. We're so worried. We managed to save a few children, but time has run out." Irena looked more flustered and weary than I had ever seen her before. Etched onto her face were all the sleepless nights and the ever-increasing worry.

"Irena, take care of yourself. What you're doing with the other social workers is so dangerous," I said, hugging her. She made the effort to smile. We both knew it was likely the last time we would see each other. The future was so uncertain; the best we could hope for was to live for one more day.

We separated and crouched into the false bottoms of two supply trucks. Irena had raced to get everything together. The Germans planned to empty the ghetto within a month's time, and raids were constant.

The first truck stopped at the checkpoint, and we held our breaths.

We heard the voice of the guard. "Where are you coming from and where are you going?"

"I've just delivered a load to the welfare office," the driver said with shocking ease. These people were risking their very lives for us.

"Open the back doors!"

We heard footsteps, the lock, things being rummaged through. "Fine, move along, but you'll want to stay away from now on. Things are about to get ugly."

"I hope you're clearing all these Jews out," the driver spat.

"Don't worry, soon enough they'll all go up in smoke." The guard cackled too loudly.

The truck drove on through and away from the ghetto. Listening to the motor and the wheels turning over the bumpy streets, I thought about our many months inside those walls. We had paid too high a price for survival. Korczak, Stefa, and so many others were gone forever. And tens of thousands, no, hundreds of thousands would soon be joining them. Their one crime was being Jewish, bearing the blood deemed accursed by the Nazis. I did not know what kind of country I would find outside the ghetto. Would fear and indifference have shredded our beloved Poland so thoroughly as to be unrecognizable? I hoped that over the rubble of war, beyond all the pain and suffering, our country would rise again. The truck slowed to enter a garage and then stopped. We all held our breaths again. The driver let us out of our saving captivity and explained how to get to Igor Newerly's house.

Henryk and I were trembling as we stepped onto the street. It was my first time to be outside the ghetto in over eighteen months. I felt like everyone was staring at us, but that was not true. Everyone else looked as frightened and worried as we were. Their clothing was as pitiful as ours inside the ghetto, and their sunken cheeks reflected the starvation that had spread throughout Poland for the greater glory of the Third Reich. We made it to Igor's house.

Seeing us at the door, his face was worried, but his words were kind. "Come in, come in; don't stand there waiting."

His small home had little furniture and was very hot.

"So you made it out," he said, nodding. "You're the lucky ones. They're carting the Jews by the thousands on the trains to Treblinka." He shuddered.

We sat, and I pulled out Janusz's manuscript and placed it on the small kitchen table. He started flipping through it.

"Incredible. The Old Doctor wrote until right before deportation. The world has to read this. I know the right publisher, but we have to keep it hidden for now. I've got a spot for it here in my house. I don't know how much longer I'll be free. The Nazis are arresting everybody. Here, take a key. Will you promise to come back for the diary if the Gestapo gets me?"

"Yes, yes, I promised Janusz I would get his diary to safety." I was willing to go to great lengths to keep my word.

Igor served us some coffee. The bread was delicious and spread with butter that tasted divine to Henryk and me. We had not eaten in at least forty-eight hours. We rested then, and a few hours later a car came, and we were taken outside of Warsaw. The feeling of danger persisted as we drove away from the capital, but something like freedom started wiggling its way up in our hearts as we saw forests and lakes.

"Mom, is that like where we used to live?" Henryk asked when we passed a farm. He had been locked up among concrete, wire, and gray buildings for so long he could hardly recall life on the outside.

"Yes, it's a farm, where they raise animals."

He smiled. Three years of stockpiled sadness started—ever so slightly—to dissipate. We would live. We would be happy. That would be our revenge on the Nazis and their diabolical system. Janusz always said that living one day more was the most virulent act of rebellion against evil.

EPILOGUE

After reading the entire manuscript through, I was so perturbed I sat back in my desk chair and wept. I had thought the war—and all the despair—had sufficiently hardened my heart against caring for anyone or anything, but literature came to revive it. The words of the Old Doctor, Poland's greatest teacher, took my breath away. Yet at the same time, they smoothed over my soul's deepest wounds with healing balm.

After a few minutes of weeping, I gathered the loose sheets, pock-marked with coffee, corrections, and smudges. This treasure trove had to be published. I stood and looked out the window and vowed to do it. There were the ruins of my city, the dying skeletons of what had been a beautiful metropolis. Yet buildings were nothing compared to the inhabitants who had suffered so much behind the ruined facades.

The ghetto rebellion in 1943, the Warsaw uprising of 1944, and now the proclamation of the Polish Provisional Government of National Unity—they had pushed us to the breaking point. How long can a people endure? The only thing that gives me hope is to think that one day, over the ashes of this terrible war, we will build a better country together. There, the memory of Janusz Korczak will inspire us to fight to the end for the cause of freedom. But meanwhile, this ghetto diary must be safely kept under wraps until the world is free again and we are once more the masters of our destiny.

ACKNOWLEDGMENTS

A book is always a joint effort of all who believe in it and wager on it until it sees the light of day. Thus, I would like to thank the following individuals for their contributions to the publication of *The Teacher of Warsaw.*

Edward Benitez, my editor at HarperCollins Español, for his wholehearted love of my stories.

My agent, Alicia González Sterling, for putting up with my idiosyncrasies, for believing in my books, and for passionately dedicating herself to the cause of literature.

My dear friends at Harper Muse, for their support and passion for my novels, especially Jocelyn Bailey, editor, and Gretchen Abernathy, translator. Gretchen always improves my books, and Jocelyn dresses them up to the nines with her careful edits.

ACKNOWLEDGMENTS

My Polish editors Lukasz Kierus, Agnieszka Stankiewicz-Kierus, and their team, for making me fall in love with Poland and its people.

And finally, my readers in Spanish, English, Portuguese, Polish, and many other languages, for loving the truth and dreaming of a better world.

REFERENCES

Epicurus, *Letter to Menoeceus*, trans. Robert Drew Hicks (Cambridge, MA: Internet Classics Archive), http://classics.mit .edu/Epicurus/menoec.html.

Janusz Korczak, *Ghetto Diary* (1978; repr. New Haven, CT: Yale University Press, 2003).

Kahlil Gibran, *The Prophet* (New York: Alfred A. Knopf, 1923; Project Gutenberg, 2019), https://www.gutenberg.org/cache /epub/58585/pg58585-images.html.

Rabindranath Tagore, *The Post Office* (New York: Macmillan, 1914; Project Gutenberg, 2014), act 1, https://www.gutenberg.org /files/6523/6523-h/6523-h.htm.

Stefan Zweig, *The World of Yesterday*, trans. Benjamin W. Huebsch and Helmut Ripperger (1934; repr. New York: Viking, 2011).

CLARIFICATIONS
FROM HISTORY

Janusz Korczak was a real person (his name at birth was Henryk Goldszmit), and the basic facts of this book are also real, with the exception of dramatized conversations and dialogues. Korczak's pedagogical work has been recognized for decades and inspired the Declaration of the Rights of the Child, adopted unanimously by the seventy-eight member states of the United Nations General Assembly on November 20, 1959, as Resolution 1386 (XIV).

The information described about Dom Sierot (the Orphans' Home)—and the pedagogical methods and organizational systems—is real. The information described about the Dzielna Street orphanage is also real, although in reality, Korczak himself applied to be the director of the mismanaged home in order to save the children from their deplorable living conditions.

Stefania Wilczyńska was a real person as well, and she was an intimate associate and collaborator of Korczak's. She was with him until the end and, like him, sacrificed herself for the ghetto's orphans.

Agnieszka Ignaciuk is not a real person, nor is her son, Henryk, though the chief actions in their story arc are based on historical fact.

Maryna Falska and Igor Newerly were close friends of Korczak and attempted many times to convince him to leave the ghetto. Their last attempt was right before he was deported.

The chairman of the Judenrat, Adam Czerniaków, was in leadership over the ghetto until his suicide on July 23, 1942. He killed himself rather than authorize the Nazi orders to send the ghetto's children to be exterminated.

Irena Sendler was also a real person. The heroic social worker saved countless children, some say up to two thousand, from certain death. The collaborators and helpers mentioned herein were also real people, including Helena Radlinksa, Ala Gołąb-Grynberg, and Jan Dobraczyński.

The Catholic priest Marceli Godlewski and other parishioners helped hundreds of people escape through a network of monasteries and orphanages. Many of them paid with their lives.

Captain Neumann is a character invented for the purposes of this book, but it is true that various German officials inexplicably tolerated Korczak's refusal to wear an armband. Among the legends that have surfaced regarding Korczak's last parade, one claims that at the last moment, a German official offered to save Korczak from being transported to Treblinka, but the Teacher refused.

The majority of the scenes described in the ghetto are real and are based on the testimony and stories of numerous witnesses and diaries from the ghetto that survived.

The ghetto's orphans were deported on August 5 and 6, 1942,

although for dramatic reasons these events have been compressed in the novel to occur on July 23, the day that Czerniaków took his life.

Additionally, Janusz was in jail for several months (instead of one night), from the end of November 1940 through the winter of 1941, and Stefa ran the orphanage in its first months at the ghetto.

A group of three Dom Sierot orphans and one teacher—Michal Wroblewski (Misha Vruvlevski)—managed to escape deportation. The rest perished on August 6 or soon thereafter at Treblinka.

It is believed that Korczak's diary was rescued from the ghetto by Michal Wroblewski and taken by a redheaded boy to Igor Newerly, who kept it in hiding. A short time later, Igor was detained and sent to Auschwitz. He managed to survive. After the war, he retrieved the diary and handed it over to an editor, but it could not be printed immediately due to Communist control throughout Poland.

Korczak's actual diary is short and encompasses only a few months of 1942. While several passages from it served as inspiration, *The Teacher of Warsaw* is a work of fiction. It is based on the direct or indirect testimony of Korczak himself and people who knew him.

TIMELINE OF THE
WARSAW GHETTO

SEPTEMBER 1, 1939

World War II begins.

OCTOBER 16, 1940

The Warsaw ghetto is established and 140,000 Poles are ordered to leave their homes. Jews are ordered to move into the ghetto. Food and medical supplies are rationed at a level below basic subsistence. Many die of illness and hunger.

NOVEMBER 15, 1940

The walls that have been built around the ghetto are officially closed. The walls are ten to twelve feet high and run for a length of eleven miles. As the population inside the ghetto increases, more people die of hunger and illness.

NOVEMBER 30, 1940

Janusz Korczak and the inhabitants of Dom Sierot are forced to
move into the ghetto.

DECEMBER 11, 1941

The United States of America declares war on Germany.

JANUARY 1942

A man named Ya'akov Grojanowski escapes from Chelmno
killing center and tells the leaders of the Warsaw ghetto what is
happening. The people of the ghetto do not believe him at first,
but Resistance leaders begin to distribute propaganda encouraging
people to resist.

JULY 22, 1942

The Nazis begin deporting Jews from the Warsaw ghetto to the
Treblinka killing center. The ghetto's inhabitants are forced by
the Jewish Council, the Judenrat, to go to the Umschlagplatz, the
deportation area.

LATE JULY 1942

As news of the mass killings at Treblinka reaches the Warsaw
ghetto, the ZOB, the Jewish Fighting Organization, is formed. It
grows to some five hundred people.

AUGUST 5–6, 1942

Orphanages and children's shelters, including that of Janusz
Korczak, are deported by train to Treblinka.

MID-SEPTEMBER 1942

Mass deportations from the Warsaw ghetto to Treblinka cease. Only some sixty to seventy thousand Jews are left in the ghetto, some as essential workers and others illegally in hiding.

JANUARY 1943

The Nazis enter the ghetto to deport the remaining Jews. Most are young people who remained as factory workers. The Jews resist for four days of combat. News of the uprising spreads, and many more join the act of rebellion.

APRIL 19, 1943

SS Chief Heinrich Himmler orders the final deportations of the Jews remaining in the Warsaw ghetto, but his SS forces are met with armed resistance. The Warsaw ghetto uprising lasts nearly a month. German tactics change to burning down the ghetto.

MAY 16, 1943

The Nazis blow up the Great Synagogue and finalize the destruction of the Warsaw ghetto. All members of the Jewish Resistance are killed, deported, or flee and go into hiding.

A NOVEL BASED ON
A TRUE STORY

Henryk Goldszmit, more commonly known as Janusz Korczak, was born on July 22, 1878 or 1879. His family was Jewish, and his father was a respected lawyer. When Janusz was young, his father battled mental illness, and Janusz determined never to have children of his own.

Janusz was well known for his pedagogical and educational contributions. He founded an orphanage and worked with several others, and for years he had a popular radio program. For his orphanage, Dom Sierot, he and the children adopted a set of laws that acknowledged the rights of children. Korczak's work would later inspire the United Nations.

Though Jewish by birth, Janusz did not practice his ancestral faith until the end of his life. It is believed that he did so to encourage and comfort the children in his care.

In 1898 he began studying medicine at the Imperial University of

Warsaw. He was accused of being anti-Russian on the basis of several comments and his activities. At that time, Russia controlled most of Poland.

In 1905, after graduating with a medical degree, he began working as a pediatrician in the Bersohns and Baumans Children's Hospital in Warsaw. He traveled throughout Europe and spent a year studying in Berlin. He joined the Pomoc dla Sierot (Aid for Orphans) Society and, with their help, founded the orphanage Dom Sierot.

During World War I, Korczak served as a military doctor in the Imperial Russian Army and was stationed in children's shelters on the outskirts of Kiev. He met Maryna Falska in Kiev, and they worked together in defense of children the greater part of the rest of their lives.

During World War II, Korczak refused to wear the armband with the Star of David. On August 5 and 6, the children and adult staff of Korczak's orphanage were taken to the Umschlagplatz, from which trains carried prisoners to killing centers. His dear friend and coworker Stefania Wilczyńska was among them. Janusz Korczak was murdered together with his orphans at the Treblinka killing center.

DISCUSSION
QUESTIONS

1. Would you consider Janusz Korczak a hero, or would you—like
   he does—consider him ordinary? How might his actions and
   his demeanor defy the typical definitions of what it means to be
   heroic?
2. What is the purpose of hope in this story? How does someone
   like Janusz maintain hope when all seems lost, when no day
   seems better than the one before?
3. Many of the women in *The Teacher of Warsaw* (Stefania,
   Irena, Agnieszka) do everything they can to care for and
   love the orphans—often at great sacrifice to their own safety
   and comfort. How does this change or enhance your view of
   motherhood?
4. Describe how Warsaw changes throughout the story and how

the residents respond differently to their home's occupation. Do the changes happen quickly or slowly? Do you imagine yourself resisting the occupation or simply doing whatever it would take to survive it?

5. Consider how Janusz and Maryna Falska see the world differently. Do you relate to one more than the other? If so, how and why?

6. When we are introduced to Adam Czerniaków, he believes in the process of leadership and trusts that compliance with the Nazis is the best way to survive. By the end of the story, he has died by suicide after refusing to authorize Nazi orders to send the ghetto's children to Treblinka. Describe his evolution and discuss whether or not you would have been able to trust such a man.

7. What does this story tell you about the power of love? About the power of mercy and sacrifice?

8. Of all his many losses, what do you consider Janusz's greatest loss in this story?

9. Which character did you connect with the most? And which do you admire the most?

10. The novel ends with Agnieszka taking Janusz's diary to a book publisher in an effort to make sure his story is told. Do you think there are instances of everyday heroism that have been lost to time and circumstances? How does that affect how you view history and your own story?

Through letters with a famous author, one French librarian tells her love story and describes the brutal Nazi occupation of her small coastal village.

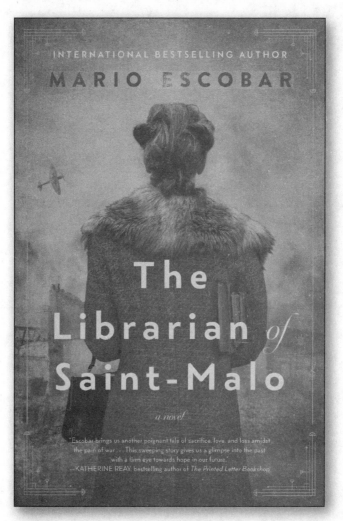

Available in print, e-book, and downloadable audio

THOMAS NELSON
Since 1798

From international bestselling author Mario Escobar
comes a story of escape, sacrifice, and hope amid
the perils of the Second World War.

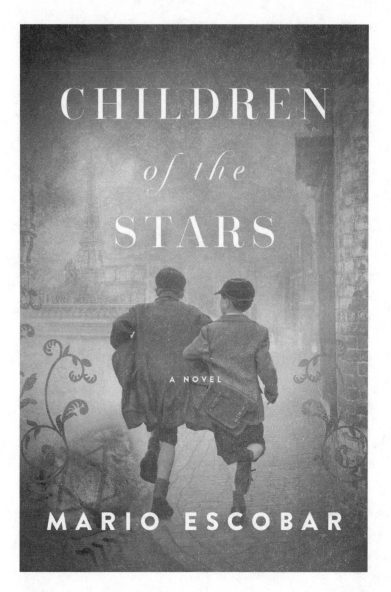

ABOUT THE AUTHOR

Photo by Elisabeth Monje

Mario Escobar, a *USA TODAY* and international bestselling author, has a master's degree in modern history and has written numerous books and articles that delve into the depths of church history, the struggle of sectarian groups, and the discovery and colonization of the Americas. Escobar, who makes his home in Madrid, Spain, is passionate about history and its mysteries.

Visit him online at marioescobar.es
Twitter: @EscobarGolderos
Instagram: @marioescobar.oficial
Facebook: @MarioEscobar

ABOUT THE TRANSLATOR

Photo by Sally Chambers

Gretchen Abernathy worked full-time in the Spanish Christian publishing world for several years until her oldest son was born. Since then, she has worked as a freelance editor and translator. Her main focus includes translating/editing for the *Journal of Latin American Theology* and supporting the production of Bible products with the Nueva Versión Internacional. Chilean ecological poetry, the occasional thriller novel, and audio proofs spice up her work routines. She and her husband make their home in Nashville, Tennessee, with their two sons.